Silverwood

Book Two in the

House Next Door

Trilogy

By

Jule Owen

JULE OWEN

SILVERWOOD

First published in 2015 by Mean Time Books

ISBN: 0993409733
ISBN 978-0-9934097-3-8

www.juleowen.com

www.meatimebooks.co.uk

Cover illustration by Jule Owen

JULE OWEN

For my mother Patricia Anne Owen,
31 August 1934 to 21 October 2008
who taught me the value of words, stories and
kindness and left a huge hole in my heart.

1 THE BEST AND BRIGHTEST SCIENTISTS

DAY TEN: Wednesday, 1 December 2055, London, England

"Eva Aslanova!" he shouts. "Eva, if you can hear me, I badly need a door!"

A roaring column of furnace-hot flame blasts the tree for five, ten, fifteen, twenty seconds – leaves, bark, branches, and trunk all igniting and burning ferociously. Mathew, scrabbling and clinging precariously to the higher branches, feels the heat blast towards him, toasting the soles of his dangling feet. The tree slumps and gives beneath him. He's falling. Then somehow he's on his feet. Yet another in a series of near-death experiences survived, he knows, only due to the fact that in this world his body is an avatar. Presumably, Eva doesn't see the need to program into him the means to die a hundred horrible different ways, mostly by fire. She thinks his project childish. She wouldn't have put that much effort into it.

Or so he hopes.

He gets up from the scorched and smouldering earth

beside the tree and gives himself a moment to glance back.

Two dragons, as tall as London double-decker buses, shift on their feet, flex their claws, and flick their long, serpent-like tails ridged with spikes and plates. The power of a tail-swipe brings another tree crashing to the ground. It gets skewered by a cluster of spines, and the dragon thrashes its tail around until the tree, now uprooted and spraying earth and rocks and birds' nests, is pulled loose.

They are trashing Eva's world.

The larger dragon belches, and smoke billows out of her enormous nostrils. The male yawns, displaying a mouth full of splinter-sharp white teeth the size of large bottles and the blue tongue Mathew had been particularly proud of when he'd designed them.

They have grown enormously. They are huge. And now, completely oblivious to the fact that he created them in the first place, they think he is dinner, and they are very hungry.

He is fairly sure that he can't die in Eva's world, but just in case, he runs.

He is dodging trees as he goes, stumbling over tree roots. A hot blast of air funnels past him with such force that it blows him sideways. He dares not stop to look, but as he steadies himself, the rough bark of a redwood scraping the skin on the palm of his hand, out of his peripheral vision he catches the image of a red glowing cindered tree crumbling into a pile of charcoal and ash.

Up ahead, on the crest of a small bank, is an unusually large trunk, the width of several men standing shoulder to shoulder. In front of the tree he sees a young woman with very straight, thin, white-blonde hair and paper-white skin. She's small anyway, but she seems tiny, dwarfed by the giant conifer. Behind her is a door.

"Eva!" he gasps, lurching forward.

He scrambles up the bank, yanking at saplings to pull himself up, his feet slipping on the loose earth and stones. His leg muscles are burning.

"Thank god!" he wheezes, bent over double before her, grasping his knees.

She grabs him, pulls him inside the tree, and shuts the door.

He's back in his Darkroom. The blackened bare walls and floor seem less real than the forest. He sits down heavily in the chair behind him, still catching his breath. In a large armchair in front of him, Eva is curled up in her pyjamas.

"You do realise it's four hours ahead here?" she says. "Bedtime. You were lucky you caught me. I was just brushing my teeth. Fifteen minutes later, I'd have been asleep."

"I hope I didn't get you into trouble with your dad?"

"No, no, don't worry. He's not here. Off again on his travels, immortalising the story of our great and glorious army to anyone who will listen."

"St Petersburg again?"

"St Petersburg is done and dusted. Not sure where this time. He wouldn't say. No doubt, we'll see it all on the news soon enough."

"You're sure you're safe talking to me like this?"

"As safe as anyone is these days."

"That's not very reassuring."

"Best I can do. Look, Mathew, I think we need to talk about these dragons."

"It's not turning out quite as I'd planned."

"Yes, well, that's what's confusing me. How did you plan it, exactly?"

"I'm not sure I did that much, to be honest. Beyond getting them into a world where they could evolve."

"But in your programming, what did evolution consist of exactly? Growing endlessly larger?"

"They are quite big, aren't they? They should stop, though. I made them what I thought was dragon size."

"Which is? Forgive me, I've never seen a dragon."

"Oh, you must have, in films."

"I don't watch those kinds of films."

"About twice the size of a large dinosaur."

"Right. Why did you do that?"

"Because I could?"

"What I mean is, what are you trying to achieve with this project?"

"I was just trying to make dragons, using the new genetic coding program I had. And I wanted them to be able to interact with their environment and evolve their behaviour over time."

"You succeeded. Congratulations. So we can close the server down, then?"

"No. They were meant to breed."

"They can breed?"

"Yes."

"You want more of those things crawling about in that virtual earth of yours?"

"Obviously, I don't now, but when I coded them, I did."

"Wow. I don't wish to put a downer on things, but a few more of them and you won't have much virtual earth left."

"Yes, I know."

"It seems a bit . . ."

"What?"

"Pointless . . ."

"I know."

"You can still code them, can't you?"

"I'm not sure. I packaged them. Doesn't that seal off the creation?"

"Just go back to the source code, amend, repackage, and then redeploy."

"Won't that overwrite them?"

"Yes."

"It will kill them."

"They're not alive, Mathew. Besides, they are fairly

unpleasant, destructive creatures the way they are."

"I suppose."

"Why don't you have a think about how you might make their behaviour a bit more interesting, rather than just predatory and destructive?"

"Such as?"

"For instance, if I was interested in creating fauna-type programs rather than creating worlds, I wouldn't be interested in making stupid animals. I would see if I could make a mind more interesting and better than a human mind."

"But the best and cleverest scientists alive aren't able to do that."

"So?"

"So how on earth am I meant to do it?"

"Mathew, I thought you and I were training to be the next generation of the best and cleverest scientists."

"Uh-huh."

"Shouldn't we be cleverer than the last generation? Shouldn't we be able to do things they can't? Shouldn't we at least be trying?"

"I'd never thought of it like that."

"My father is always saying that the West is degenerate, and your schools and universities aren't a patch on ours. I'm always arguing with him that he doesn't know what he's talking about. Please don't let him be right. Look, why don't you at least try and concentrate on improving the dragons' minds and behaviour? Give them some higher reasoning, a personality, even? You must have done some personality-typing courses?"

"Yes, but I hated them."

"There's a surprise. Anyway, what do I know? They're your dragons, and it's your world, for however long it takes them to burn everything to a cinder. Next time you decide to go in there, can you make sure you check the time difference, though?" Eva yawns. "You wouldn't want to be toasted while I'm asleep. It could be an uncomfortable eight hours. I'm off to bed. Night, Mathew."

"Night, Eva. And thanks," he says, but the armchair has gone.

2 HAUNTED BY DREAMS

Mathew stares at the empty space in front of his chair for several minutes. He is exhausted and his body is battered and bruised. His nervous system is still trying to reconcile the physical punishment of the virtual forest with the banal reality of sitting too still in a Darkroom chair for an hour and a half.

He considers deleting the dragons in Eva's world, but he wants to have time to think it through properly, to work out if it's worth saving anything from the work he's done.

Besides, it is dinnertime and he is starving.

Before he leaves the Darkroom, with Eva's advice still ringing in his ears, he makes a voice note to investigate synthetic biology and the human brain project. Perhaps he'll learn something to encourage him to make the intelligent AIs Eva thinks he should.

In the kitchen he summons the news on the Canvas while he hunts around in the cupboard and the fridge for something to eat.

Leibniz hovers above him and says, "Can I help you Mathew? It is dinnertime. Would you like me to cook you dinner?"

"I'm finding out what there is," Mathew says.

"We have the ingredients to make fifty-six different meals, if you include the use of the SuperChef replicator. However, the information streamed to me from your medibot processed through my nutritional planning program tells me there are only ten meals to aid your health at this moment. Do you want me to list them?"

"No. I know what your lists are like and I don't want to eat any of those meals. I want to eat something I like."

"If you tell me what you would like to eat, then I'll make something both nutritional and tasty."

"I don't know what I want, which is why I'm searching in the cupboard. I'm hoping I will get inspiration."

"I don't understand 'inspiration'," Leibniz says.

Mathew sighs. "Can you make me a burger and chips?"

Leibniz's blue light flickers for a moment. "We have the ingredients. We had a delivery of fresh cultured beef yesterday, but Hoshi Mori instructed me to make sure you eat a balanced diet and your instruction would not comply with her request."

"Did she program you to treat her instructions with greater priority than mine?"

"No, Mathew."

"Can I have a burger and chips?"

"Yes, Mathew."

In the fridge, there are six cold cokes, the ones that claim to actively aid digestion, which his mother had agreed to add to Leibniz's weekly TechnoFoods shopping list, after much badgering. He takes one, opens it, sits at the kitchen table, sips his drink from the can and watches the Canvas while Leibniz prepares his food.

The newsreader says, "Today Turkey announced it has joined the US and their allies in the war against Russia and China. This follows the news that Russia invaded Turkish-controlled Georgia."

The image switches from the newsroom to shaky

footage of Turkish foot soldiers retreating under a hail of bullets from the advance of a mass of eight-foot-tall Russians in exoskeletons.

Leibniz sets the table, putting a placemat and a knife and fork in front of Mathew. It pours Mathew's drink into a glass, removing the can.

"Ketchup please," Mathew says.

"Yes, Mathew," Leibniz responds immediately and goes to the fridge.

The newsreader continues, "Yesterday the Ukraine capitulated to Russian forces and hypersonic air attacks were reported in Romania, Serbia, Bosnia and the Croatian plains, as well as Hungary and Slovakia. Military commentators predict this is to prepare the way for a land invasion.

"Meanwhile, Poland has massively increased security along its borders and has sent troops to support its allies in Eastern Europe. They have formally requested on-the-ground assistance from the US and NATO."

"Your dinner is ready," Leibniz says, putting down a plate.

"Thank you, Leibniz." Mathew takes off the top of the bun, liberally spreads it with ketchup, reassembles it and then greedily tucks in. Ketchup squeezes through his fingers as he bites.

"Earlier this morning, the President of the United States issued a statement to say everything must be done to protect and secure Europe from invasion."

The burger and chips are gone too soon and Mathew is licking his fingers when a call request comes in from the Blackweb. It is Clara on the beebot, the tiny flying machine he made so they could communicate in secret. Mathew issues a voice command to dim the sound on the Canvas and accepts the call.

An image of Clara in murky light flickers in front of him.

"Hey," she says.

"Hey. Where are you? I can't see you very well."

"I'm in my bedroom." She moves slightly into the light. "Better?"

"Yes."

"Do you want a tour?" She stands and turns around slowly.

At Mathew's command, the beebot takes off from the palm of her hand and hovers by her shoulder.

"My own personal domain," she says, revealing a room, twelve foot square, with drawn curtains of indeterminate colour, a wardrobe, a bed with a duvet and a crumpled pillow. There's a desk like his own, with a Swiss ball-type seat. On the desk there's a rolled Paper scroll. The walls are decorated in the latest morphing wallpaper. As he watches, the view switches from a bird's-eye view of a mountain range to a projection of a famous Hubble photo of a storm of turbulent gases.

"That's the Omega/Swan nebula," Mathew says.

"Is it? I've no idea, to be honest. It's the latest free image pack shipped with the program. I did have holiday photos but I got sick of them. The defaults are cooler. What are you up to?"

"Dinner."

"I should have thought. We don't eat until half-seven. I'll call back."

"No, no. I've finished."

"What did you have?"

"Burger and chips."

"I thought you had that yesterday?"

"Yes. I did. I love burgers. Could eat them each day."

"Clearly. Didn't your mum program Leibniz to feed you properly?" Clara goes back to her bed, props her pillow and settles with her back against the wall, her knees drawn to her chest. The beebot flies, following her, and then lands on one of her knees, giving him a headshot.

"Yes she did, but she didn't set her instructions as

priority. She probably doesn't know she should do this."

"When was the last time your mum made it home for dinner?"

"She has dinner at home every night."

"With you?"

"Well, no. She comes in too late. But I often sit with her while she has her dinner."

"So you eat dinner alone?"

"Not every night. We had dinner together last Saturday."

"Don't you get lonely?"

"I don't have time to be lonely. I have Leibniz and O'Malley. Besides, there's always someone to chat to. You, my grandmother, my school supervisor and Eva."

Leibniz appears and starts clearing away Mathew's dishes. "That's the HomeAngel making such a racket, by the way," Mathew says.

Clara says, "I can't hear a thing." Then, "Who's Eva?"

"Just this Russian girl I know."

"A Russian girl?"

"Yes. She lives in Moscow."

"Isn't it illegal or something, talking to a Russian?"

"Probably. But then it's not exactly acceptable to use the Blackweb either."

There is silence at the other end of the line. "So she's a friend?"

"Yes, I suppose she is. But not *that* kind of friend."

"What kind of friend?"

"You know."

"No, I don't."

"A girlfriend."

"Oh. Right."

There is an embarrassed pause.

"My supervisor introduced us. We're working together on a virtual reality project."

"And you're allowed to, in spite of the war?"

"No. Not exactly."

"You know what you're doing."

Mathew wonders at her confidence.

"I met with her in her virtual world. It was a relief to speak to her. It made me realise where some of my weird dream came from."

"What dream?"

"I was going to tell you."

"That's why I called. You said something strange had happened."

"I got trapped in Mr. Lestrange's house."

"Oh my God! How?"

"I fell through his conservatory."

"You what?"

"My cat, O'Malley, escaped again when the locksmiths came to change the locks. He caught a blackbird and jumped onto Mr. Lestrange's conservatory. I was worried he would kill the bird. I climbed after it. I managed to catch O'Malley and free the bird but the glass panels on the roof of the conservatory collapsed under me. I totally destroyed it."

"Has he come round to complain?"

"No. This is messed up. I was only trapped in the house for half an hour but it seemed like days. When I got home, I was incredibly tired and I went to bed early. The next morning, when I went to check out the conservatory, it was absolutely fine, like nothing had ever happened to it."

"He can't have fixed it overnight."

"Of course he can't. Yesterday, I had this crushing headache. In the afternoon I went to bed and fell asleep and had these vivid dreams."

"You think you dreamt it?"

"Some of it. It's all mixed up with things I know really happened yesterday, like I made the beebot for you, the locks were fitted and O'Malley escaped. But the other parts, which I know can't be true, seem so real, like me being in his house. You know Gen said he has a library?"

"Yes, she said she saw it."

"I saw it too."

"In your dream?"

"I don't know. In my dream. In reality. I saw it. There's a book on each of my parents and my grandmother. There's a book on you, Clara."

"On me?"

"Yes."

"What did it say?"

"I don't know. I didn't read it."

"There were lots of other books too. History books."

"Gen said she thinks he's a historian."

"I'm not sure what the hell he is. I read some of his book about me. It describes my death."

"What?! What did it say?"

"It wouldn't let me read it. It flung itself away from me."

"Mathew, you know this bit *must* have been a dream, right?"

"It was so real."

"It's just a disturbing dream."

"It doesn't feel like a dream."

"So what happened after you read the book?"

"I was pretty spooked. I tried to escape from the house, but the front door was locked. The network connection was jammed. I couldn't call for help. I went into his Darkroom, thinking I might be able to get a connection via his skullcap."

"And did you?"

"No. I got sucked into a game. It was like a kind of puzzle at first. But it wasn't an ordinary game. Firstly, I was stuck there once I was in. There was no way to end the game. Secondly, it was the most amazing, real, terrifying game I've ever played. It went on for days."

"You haven't been gone for days. You must have been dreaming."

"It felt like I was gone for days."

"How did you escape then, in the end?"

"I was rescued."

"By who?"

"One of the characters in the game."

"Please tell me you know you were dreaming."

"Of course it must have been a dream. But that's why I'm glad I spoke to Eva. I realised the Russian parts must have come from her. There were Russian soldiers... Her dad's a journalist who reports on military parades in Moscow and St Petersburg. Her project is to create virtual worlds to model various climate change impact scenarios, in particular places warming to an extreme degree. She mentioned a place in her virtual world called Chukotka. There was a Chukotka in my dream and a tropical rain forest. But this bothers me because I'm sure she only told me what the place was called after I had the dream."

"You must have forgotten."

"Yes, I must." He is silent for a moment. "It just won't go away, you know, losing O'Malley, falling through the conservatory. This huge cat chased and attacked me. I even have a scratch."

"O'Malley must have scratched you."

"Yes, it must have been O'Malley. But there are other strange things..." He remembers the beebot he flew down Mr. Lestrange's chimney and the books that re-wrote themselves right in front of him. The ones that wrote about him Although he has no video evidence, he is sure it happened, and *before* his dream. He *saw* those books.

Or did he?

He starts to doubt himself.

"What things?"

Mathew knows from Clara's voice he is stretching credulity. He says, "Never mind."

"I don't think being on your own is good for you. Why don't you come round to Gen's tomorrow afternoon? I'll get my car to take me back later. Perhaps we could all have dinner together? Gen's mentioned a few times she'd like to have you round. I'll ask her. I'm sure she'd be up for it."

"Sure."

"You don't sound enthused."

"Yes, I am. Sorry. It's this dream…"

"You should have a night off. Watch the holovision or something. Distract yourself."

"Yes, you're right. I will."

Mathew goes to the Darkroom with the intention of playing a holofilm, but as he scrolls through the options via his Lenz, the robotics project pops into his head.

Earlier, he received a message from his professor, Nan Absolem, to tell him the school project will reconvene via the holophone conference centre next Monday. Mindful of his recent humiliation at the hands of his antagonistic classmate, Theo Arkam, Mathew is determined to have a working version of a drone with arms by the start of the session. He goes back to his bedroom and starts to draft ideas.

The first beebot is on his desk on its back, its tiny carbon feet poking in the air. Bees fly and have legs to carry pollen, but Arkam had already taken the bee idea to pieces. Dragonflies have arms, fly and carry prey. He searches on the Nexus and finds 3-D blueprints for one that might work. Using a virtual robotics program, he experiments with wings of various sizes and flexibility and with retractable arms, resizing the blades to counterbalance the weight of the arms, even when moving, even when the arms are lifting something heavy.

By eleven pm, his mother hasn't come home and he is tired, so he turns in and is dreamlessly asleep within minutes.

3 BROKEN GLASS

DAY ELEVEN: Thursday, 2 December 2055, London, England

In the morning, he finds a note on the kitchen table.

```
Mat,
I am sorry I was late home last night and left
early this morning. I know it must be lousy for you,
stuck in the house alone. There's a lot going on at
work. I wish I could talk about it. I am trying to
find a solution so we spend some more time together.
Please know I love you and am doing my best, in
spite of everything.
Mum
```

Mathew crumples the note in his hand and puts it in the kitchen bin. Leibniz immediately opens the bin lid again and moves the scrap to the paper recycling. "Unbelievable," Mathew says, shaking his head, and he is suddenly angry. Glaring at the bin, he considers kicking it, but instead, he stands for a minute, until his heartbeat stops raging fast, then turns and goes to his room.

When he logs on to the school register, he receives

another reminder about the group robotics session on Monday, as if he could forget. He also collects the voice notes sent to himself the day before about researching synthetic biology and the human brain project. The latter was a project begun more than forty years earlier to build a simulation of the brain and to create neuromorphic computing and neurorobotic systems, the basis of much of the artificial intelligence used in contemporary technology.

In his study plan, he establishes a new line of investigation and makes a mental note to discuss it with Nan Absolem. The education system encourages lateral thinking and exploration, but Mathew suspects his recent learning choices may be perceived as random. Nevertheless, he spends the next three hours doing a course on neurorobots.

When he breaks for lunch, he sends the dragonfly to the 3-D printer and, after he has eaten, he spends some time watching the nano-assembler put together the various parts on the kitchen table. The workings of the assembler are almost invisible to the human eye and the dragonfly appears to be assembled by a ghost.

The flying robot is three inches long, nose to tail. It has two sets of wings or mini-blades. It is iridescent, like it has been dipped in oil. He hasn't bothered to finesse it with any design. That can be done later. He wants to test it will actually fly.

Mathew finishes the assembly and reluctantly goes upstairs to log back on to the school system. He starts to work, but his mind wanders. He wants to fly the machine.

It takes him an hour to connect the dragonfly to the control software. He downloads an application he hasn't tried before that projects an insect-eye view of the world via his Lenz.

As he puts the assembler away, he receives a text message from Clara. It reads:

        Gen would love it if you came round tonight.
Arrive at four and you can watch me play, then we'll

have an early dinner together. Let me know if you
get this. C x.

He contemplates the kiss for a moment then send a
message back,

Sounds great. Looking forward to later. M x.

At first he flies the dragonfly around the kitchen. He
manages to grab a fork and lift it a few feet and carefully
lower it. *It should be able to carry heavier loads.* He tries to grip
a banana. This is trickier mainly because of the awkward
shape, but the design of the little machine manages the
weight. It is disproportionately strong for its size. The
simulations in the virtual robotics environment predicted
this, but he is nevertheless delighted it actually works. He
flies around the kitchen searching for something heavier,
but the kitchen is minimalist. Leibniz keeps the whole
house laboratory-clean. There is hardly anything on the
kitchen surfaces.

He walks behind his creation and goes upstairs. The
machine hovers while he opens the door to his bedroom
and then flies in. The Chinese art book, the paper one his
grandmother gave him, is on the floor. The dragonfly's
robotic arms extend and grip one of the book's covers.
Once they have locked on, Mathew tries to get the
dragonfly to gently pull upwards. The front of the robot
tilts forward as it takes the weight of the book and the
wings pivot as he has designed them to do, remaining
parallel to the ground. The main body of the book flips
open page after page, slowly at first and then faster and
faster. The book upturns with a loud thump and the
machine-insect loses its balance and is yanked towards the
floor suddenly, before the safety mechanism fires and the
arm releases its grip.

"Close!" Mathew says aloud. His voice sounds strange
in the empty house and for the first time since he has been
grounded by the Curfew, he feels alone.

He follows the dragonfly and goes to his mother's room at the back of the house, where he stands by Hoshi's window and scrutinises the garden. The leaves from the trees at the back are fallen and piled against the wooden fence. The ivy cloaking the little tool-shed that runs along the red brick wall boundary adjoining Mr. Lestrange's house is the only thing still vibrantly green. He decides to test the dragonfly outside.

The air has a winter bite. Although the sky is a clear blue, the sun is cold, too far away to warm anything crawling on the earth.

Mathew decides to test how easy it is to control the dragonfly when it is beyond sight. He flies it into Gen's garden and patrols the perimeter, snooping for an object to pick up. There's an old broom propped against an empty greenhouse. *Too heavy.* Inside the greenhouse there are things the dragonfly might potentially lift – shrilk pots, garden canes, a small ball of string – but the greenhouse door is firmly shut. He flies back into his own garden and hunts like a real dragonfly in straight lines, angles and sudden changes of direction and height. As he climbs higher, he has a good view across the three gardens. The little machine turns and pans from Gen's garden all the way across to the back of Mr. Lestrange's house. It brushes the ivy as it wings over the fence and skims the roof of the conservatory, its tiny rainbow body cast back on itself, submerged in a blue pool of reflected sky in the mirror-like glass.

At the back of the conservatory there is an area of greenery, untended shrubs and brambles, stripped to leafless winter brown. Mean spikes pierce the cold air. A glinting object catches his eye and he turns slowly and hovers.

There's something lodged in amongst the thorns. He takes the flying machine in to get a closer view. He instructs one of the arms to reach out and it takes hold of an object with slick smooth and jagged edges.

Shakily, it pulls back away from the foliage but he has a good grip on it. Carefully, the dragonfly retreats with its prize and comes back to him. It lands on the paving slab next to his feet, and he bends and picks it up. The shining thing in the hand of the robotic insect is a piece of glass, the sort of thick glass with a slight tint that Mr. Lestrange has in his conservatory. Seeing the fragment stirs a vivid memory of him kneeling, gazing at the floor with shattered glass all around him. A crystal clear mental image of a piece of glass like this one stuck to the skin of his palm.

He goes to the garden bench, stands on it and pokes his head above the top of the wall to take a closer look at the conservatory roof.

With a shock he realises Mr. Lestrange is there.

The peculiar man stands with a watering can poised above the pot of an orange tree. There are other plants too, plants that give every impression that they have been growing for a long time, undisturbed. Mr. Lestrange regards Mathew with his hollow, dark eyes. He doesn't smile. There is no sign of recognition but Mathew *feels* him, watching. It is like the man is inside his brain.

Mathew drops from the bench onto the ground, hurriedly retrieves his dragonfly, goes into the house and shuts the door.

It seemed real, he thinks, for the first time in days sure of himself, *because it was real.*

4 HOSHI MORI COMES HOME EARLY

It is five to four. Mathew sits in his front room, his right leg dancing, his fists clenching and unclenching on his knees.

He is wearing dark blue jeans, a t-shirt and jacket. To the untrained eye they are indistinguishable from the clothes he wears every day, but they are his favourites. His t-shirt is made from sustainable bamboo. It is jet black and snugly fitted across his chest. The jacket is his best winter one, made from fine merino wool with deep pockets and wide lapels, as is the fashion. His jeans are tight-fitting and snug at the ankles; Leibniz washed them that morning.

It took him forty minutes to choose the outfit and a further fifteen to style his hair in the bathroom mirror, after taking a shower, something he never normally does during the day. The cloud of aftershave surrounding him is still quite overpowering. For once, he is grateful for the absence of his mother. She would tease him mercilessly.

He doesn't really understand why he is nervous at the thought of meeting Clara.

In his pocket is the piece of glass the dragonfly retrieved from Mr. Lestrange's garden. He pulls it out now. His fingers roll it around and hold it to the light.

Through the window he watches a black car pull up. He takes a deep breath, stands and goes to the front garden. Clara smiles at him as she exits the car.

"You look nice," she says and he immediately regrets dressing up.

"Just my normal clothes," he mumbles awkwardly and senses himself flushing.

She smiles a small, mischievous smile and her eyes shine.

"What?" he says.

She shakes her head, walks to Gen's front door and rings the bell.

Gen opens the door. Mathew has already tensed up. He expects her to comment on his clothes and tease him, but she isn't focused on him at all. She stares over his head. He turns around. Another car has parked behind Clara's and the back door opens.

It is his mother.

"Hi, Hoshi!" Gen shouts.

Disorientated, Hoshi gazes at their little group gathered on Gen's doorstep and vaguely registers Mathew's presence. He expects her to ask what he's doing leaving the house, but she doesn't.

Gen says, "We're having a little gathering, an early dinner at mine after Clara's lesson. There's plenty of food, enough for a fourth if you want to join us?"

"Another time," Hoshi says.

"It would be no bother."

"Not tonight," she says brusquely and then immediately realises how rude she sounds. She says, "Sorry. Long hours at work."

"Are you alright? You seem…"

"Yes," Hoshi says. "Thanks. Just tired." Her face is pale and grey and her movements cramped. She forges a determined path to the porch and slumps against the front door, waiting for the lock to sense her bioID and open.

Mathew glances at Gen. "I'd better go."

"Yes… of course," Gen says.

Mathew hurries after his mother, who has gone into the house.

"Mum?" he says, not sure at first if she has gone upstairs. A chair scrapes on the floor in the kitchen and he goes after the sound.

"Mum? Are you alright?"

Hoshi is slumped in a kitchen chair. "I felt dizzy at work. I couldn't concentrate. I thought it might be what you had the other day; remember, your headache? Perhaps you had a virus and passed it to me."

"What does your medibot say?"

"It didn't find anything."

"Did Dr Girsh call?"

"No."

"That's strange. You would think he would have immediately called you. Do you want me to call him? You don't look well at all, you know."

"I'll be fine. I just need to lie down." She stands shakily, her legs barely strong enough to hold her. Her eyes find his and she sees his fear. She says, not very convincingly, "Don't worry. It's just lack of sleep. A migraine probably. A few hours' rest and I will be much better."

"Let me help you," he says, rushing to her and taking her arm. She leans against him heavily. He has to almost carry her as they climb the stairs, one by one.

"Nearly there," he says.

Somehow they make it to her bedroom door; he pushes it open and helps her to the bed. He lifts her feet onto the mattress and takes off her shoes.

"Can I get you anything? A drink?" *Where is that fricking robot when it is actually needed?* "Leibniz!" he calls.

"No. No. I'm fine. I just need to sleep."

"I'm calling Dr Girsh." Mathew starts a Nexus call.

Leibniz comes into the room, "You called, Mathew.

How may I help?"

"Get a glass of water for Hoshi. Quickly."

"Yes, Mathew."

The call to Dr Girsh takes a long time to connect. Finally, he gets a message that reads, "Unable to connect to contact at this time. Please leave a message." Exasperated, he sends a message, requesting the Doctor call as soon as possible.

Leibniz returns with the water. Mathew takes the glass from the robot and passes it to his mother, "Here," he says. She struggles to sit and he has to help her hold the glass. "Mum, what has happened? This isn't just tiredness. Something serious is wrong."

"Did you get the Doctor?"

"No. I couldn't get through."

"That's odd." She is staring at him. His face is close to hers as he bends and holds the glass. Then he watches a thought occur to her. Her face whitens further. An expression of horror spreads.

"What?" he says. "What is it?"

"Get away from me!"

Mathew is startled. She pushes him away, upsetting the glass. Water spills and the glass falls onto the bed and then smashes on the floor as she continues to push at him.

"Go! Leave the room! Please!"

"No. I won't go. What on earth's the matter?"

Pain passes through her and she closes her eyes and gasps.

"Mum…"

"Please. You must leave!" She speaks through gritted teeth.

"Are you in pain?"

"Get out of here," she says.

"Mum…"

"Get out!"

"You're scaring me!"

Pain convulses her. She grips the bedclothes, then falls

sideways onto the bed and is still.

"Mum… Mum, for God's sake!"

Her medibot attempts to connect to the Nexus to dial an emergency ambulance. The connection spools, redialling again and again and failing. He tries Dr Girsh again to no avail and then tries emergency services. Finally, desperate, he tries the beebot and sends a voice-to-text message to Clara. He says, "Help, please! Pick up!"

Clara calls immediately. An image of her sat at Gen's piano materialises in his Lenz. "Hi, Mathew! Are you ok?" She turns, frowning at Gen, "It's Mathew."

"What are you…? What is that?" Gen begins.

Mathew says, "Please. I don't have time to chat. We need an ambulance. Mum is sick and our network isn't working. I can't get through to our medical services."

"I will get right on it," Clara says. "I'll call you back."

"Thanks."

Mathew turns to Hoshi. She is quiet.

"Mum?" he says.

Then a call notification comes through to him. The words float above Hoshi's head. The message includes the Panacea logo. The 'From' tag says Pan Special Medical. He answers, frowning.

A voice says, "You are listed as Hoshi Mori's emergency contact. Can you confirm?"

Mathew says. "I'm her son."

"Are you with her now?"

"Yes. She is sick. I can't get a line out to our doctor."

"Your name is Mathew, isn't it?"

"Yes."

"Mathew, we are going to help you. Okay?"

"Who are you? You're not our usual medical service."

"We're a division of it."

"Why couldn't I get through to Dr Girsh?"

"Don't worry now. Let's help your Mum, shall we?"

"Okay."

"Her medibots show some pretty serious indicators.

She isn't responding to my calls. Is she conscious?"

"She was a minute ago." Mathew leans above Hoshi's prone body. "Mum," he says, gently shaking her. "Mum!" Her eyes are closed. She is motionless. She doesn't even groan. "I'm not sure now. She's not speaking."

"She has a pulse. And I am getting data that says she is breathing. Can you confirm?"

"Yes. She is breathing."

"We have an ambulance on the way."

"Thank you," Mathew says. "Please hurry. Does the data tell you what it is?"

The woman on the end of the connection says, "No. But don't worry. She needs you to stay calm. We will be there in four minutes. You need to put her in the recovery position. Do you know how to do this?"

"I do. I used to. I… Tell me. Please." Mathew feels like his brain has frozen.

"Okay. Kneel to one side of her."

"Is she on her back?"

"Sort of."

"Can you activate video on the call?"

"Yes. Yes. Sorry!" Mathew says. He mentally fumbles his Lenz controls.

"Okay. Good. I can see you. Put her left leg flat." She waits. "Yes, good. Put her arms to the side." Another pause. "Good. Put her left arm at a right angle with her hand pointing upwards." Again she waits for Mathew to respond to the instruction. "Pull her other hand across her body and tuck her hand under the side of her head with the palm touching her cheek. Bit more. Yes. That's it. Bend her right knee. Pull it a bit further. Pull on her knee so she's on her side. Lift her chin and push her head back. That's good. Well done. She is breathing steadily and I have her pulse. Are you ok, Mathew?"

"Yeah."

"We're in your road. The ambulance is here now." A short pause. "They are outside. You'll need to let them in."

There is a loud knock on the door. Mathew scrambles, runs down the stairs and opens the door to a man and a woman in crinkly white boiler suits. Their faces are covered in masks. They are carrying a gurney.

"Are you Mathew?" asks a man's voice, muffled by the mask.

"Yes."

"I'm Alice, that's Mike," the woman says, nodding to her partner.

"Hi," Mathew says numbly.

"Where's Mum?" Mike asks.

"In her bedroom."

"Show us the way."

Mathew leads them up the stairs. They immediately get to work beside Hoshi. Mike speaks to the Nexus connection linked to the ambulance.

Alice considers Mathew sympathetically. "Great work on the recovery position." She smiles and Mathew manages a small smile back.

Gen and Clara appear and hover in the doorway.

"The door was open. Are you alright?" Gen says. She comes across the room towards him. "I tried to call an ambulance but when I got through they told me one was already on its way. Looks like they are here already."

Mathew shakes his head. "I didn't know they were coming. Thanks, Gen."

"Don't worry, she's probably just exhausted. She has worked herself into the ground," Gen says.

"I don't think it is exhaustion," Mathew says. He catches Clara's eyes.

The medics gape at them. "What are they doing here?" Mike asks.

"It's okay," Mathew says. "They're friends."

Mike says, "It's not okay, actually." He turns to Gen. "Didn't anyone try to stop you?"

Gen shakes her head, "No. We walked straight in."

"Those security cretins are useless!"

Alice says, "Okay. Not now. Let's get her on the stretcher. We need to go."

Mike stands to one side and says, "This is Pan IDC3. We're coming down with the mother and the boy. Plus we have two other guests. Please confirm."

"Who are the guests?"

"Neighbours. There was no one at the door to stop them. PanSec is fricking useless. They were meant to be right behind us. What are we meant to do, hang around on the doorstep and wait for them while our patient dies? I'll have McMurphy roasted."

"Okay, confirm. Security is there now. I am looking right at them. You are okay to come now. Bring the neighbours."

"What is going on?" Mathew asks.

The man turns to Gen and Clara. "You need to come with us to the hospital."

"I'll happily accompany Mathew, but Clara needs to get home."

"You'll all have to come. Did Ms Mori enter your house before she came home?"

"No," Gen says. "She came straight here from her car. Why does Clara need to come to the hospital?"

"It's a precaution…"

"Against what?"

"We don't know what is wrong with her yet, but she may be contagious."

"But we only just walked through the door."

"As I said, it is a precaution."

"We need to go, Mike," the woman says.

The medics work together to get Hoshi onto the stretcher and then lift her and start to carry her from the room. The man speaks to his Nexus communication connection again. He says, "We're on our way."

The back doors of the ambulance are open. Two armed, uniformed men stand in the middle of the road. Mike says to one of them, "Where the hell were you?"

They start to explain. The medic interrupts. "Never mind. We don't have time. Don't let anyone in the house until the investigation team gets here."

They get the stretcher into the ambulance and put it on a trolley and locks the wheels. "You as well, please," he says to Gen, Clara and Mathew.

There's a bench attached to the side of the ambulance, facing the stretcher. Alice follows them and pulls the door shut. She helps them find seat belts and checks Hoshi and the stretcher are secure.

"When will you tell us what is going on?" Gen asks. "Why is this ambulance unmarked?" When the medic doesn't offer any response, Gen says, "We have a right to know where you are taking us."

"We're going to a medical centre to help Hoshi. I know you're worried," she says, "but the best thing you can do for her right now is stay calm."

"Will she be alright?" he asks.

"Honestly, I don't know."

Mathew pins his elbows to his knees and leans forwards, resting his chin on his clasped hands and stares at his mother, unconscious on the gurney. She has to be okay. She just has to be. He can't lose another parent.

5 COLD WAR AND MISSILE CRISIS

They enter the building at speed from the back of the ambulance, through battered blue-painted double doors. The stainless steel plates at the bottom take the impact from the stretcher trolley.

Mathew only gets a glimpse of his surroundings as he is led inside an old brick pre-21st century building with black drainpipes and bars on the windows. There is no signage above or on the doors. Whoever owns this place wants it to be anonymous.

Three other medical staff meet them, all in protective clothing. Hoshi's trolley is wheeled away. Mathew moves to follow after it, but Mike holds him back.

"I want to go with her," Mathew says.

Alice says, "I know you do, but the doctors need to be given room to do their work. You'll be in the way. We also need to run some tests on you." She puts a gloved hand on his shoulder. "Come on. The sooner we get these tests done, the sooner you'll see your mum. Okay?"

Mathew nods but he is sick to his stomach as they walk away.

They are led along a wide corridor with strip florescent lighting flickering, lightening and darkening a section of their route. The walls are a dull, sickly orange. There's a scruffy grey panel that runs at waist height with a hand rail and scuffed stainless steel plates instead of skirting boards.

They pass through three sets of hospital doors, turn, turn again and stop in front of two sets of scrubbed steel door lifts. The medic presses a button on a panel. They watch the floor indicator illuminate and the numbers count down as the lift comes to them. Mike stares ahead, stony-faced. Alice studies Mathew's face and tries a smile. She pities him. The man does too, but he is angry as well.

The doors open. They get in. There's an old faded poster on the wall of the lift with health warnings about TB. The place mustn't have been used properly for years.

They ping through floors and then the doors open again.

They are disgorged into another corridor, much like the others they have travelled through. The lights comes on as they walk.

"What *is* this place?" Gen asks.

"It's a special facility for infectious diseases."

"There's no one here," Clara says.

"This is a quarantined section."

"Why do you need all this space? It looks abandoned."

"Panacea likes to plan ahead."

They enter a long corridor that splits two rows of hospital rooms. They all have floor-to-ceiling plate glass windows and are furnished identically with metal-framed hospital beds on wheels, white mattresses, clinical tables and mobile screens.

"Here we are," the nurse says, as she comes to a halt, "We have to keep you apart for now, I'm afraid. One of you may have been infected and not yet passed it on. Gen, if you could come with me. Mathew, go with Mike. Clara, I'll be back to deal with you, if you could wait here."

Mike leads Mathew through a door into a small anteroom, lined with cupboards and shelves full of medical kit. Directly ahead there is another door, which leads into the main room that will be Mathew's. It unlocks automatically as Mike stands before it. It is bioID-controlled, Mathew thinks.

"You'll need to change into this," Mike says, holding a pale green hospital gown, taken from the anteroom. "Behind there," he indicates to the corner of the room and a screen on wheels. "We'll need all your clothes. You'll get them back when they've been cleaned. Oh and remove your e-Pinz, please."

When Mathew reappears, Mike puts his clothes into a white shrilk bag and ties the top. Mathew places his e-Pinz in Mike's outstretched palm.

"I should take your Lenz as well, but I don't have a box for them. I'm trusting you. Don't use them here, okay?"

Mathew nods.

"There's water there," he points to a jug and a glass on a table. "And a toilet." Mathew watches as Mike opens a door, revealing a toilet and washbasin.

"I'll leave you to it. Someone will come to do the tests shortly."

Mike retreats to the antechamber, taking the bag containing Mathew's clothes. It takes a few minutes for him to pass back into the corridor. When he emerges he is no longer wearing the boiler suit.

The room is fifteen foot square. A series of small Canvases hanging on the far wall display an array of constantly changing data and graphs. Mathew goes to examine them but each data label is an abbreviation or a specialised term. They make no sense to him. Instinctively, he tries to search for them on the Nexus but fails to get a connection. He realises that wherever they are, it is sealed like a military bunker.

He perches on a hospital bed on a crinkly blue paper sheet, wearing the thin backless hospital gown Mike gave him. Clara is across on the other side of the corridor, facing him. Long panes of glass run floor to ceiling, separating them. They stare at one another. He feels calmer looking at Clara.

Someone new comes along the corridor dressed in a white protective suit, pushing a stainless steel container on wheels. The stranger goes into Clara's room. Mathew stands and walks to the window. Clara talks to the suit. She waves and smiles slightly at Mathew as if to say, "It's alright."

Another Panacea staff member comes into Mathew's room and the door shuts securely behind.

"Hello Mathew," says a male voice behind the mask. "I'm Dr. Wilson. I'm here to do some tests. How are you feeling?"

"Where is my mother?"

"She's upstairs in intensive care."

"What are they doing to her?"

"Running tests."

"What kind of tests?"

"We're trying to find out what is wrong with her."

"But you suspect it's a virus of some kind. Otherwise you wouldn't have us here."

"Correct."

"I want to be with her."

"That's not possible right now. We need to complete the tests on your mother and run tests on you and your friend."

"How long will it take?"

"Not long."

"Then can I see her?"

"Probably, yes. When we know more."

"Have you told Clara's mum and dad where she is?"

"Yes, we have let them know she is safe and that we will take her home as soon as possible. Now, it is important I do these tests. We want to get them to lab as soon as possible."

"What tests are you running?"

"We already have your medical data from your biobot.

That gives us all the information we need about your blood, urine, faecal, the functioning of your organs and a host of other data. I'm going to inject another kind of biobot. Don't worry, it's not permanent. It's actually made from a synthetic material, which will dissolve naturally and totally disappear in a few weeks. It's a little machine specifically designed to hunt viruses."

"Doesn't my biobot already do that?"

"Yes. It's programmed to find all known viruses. The virus your mother has isn't on the biobot's central database. The one I'm injecting is more intelligent, and can detect the signs and shapes of viruses not yet catalogued."

The doctor opens a flap on the top of his shining silver trolley to reveal a needle attached to a tube, in turn attached to a machine hidden in the metal box. Mathew remembers the time he had his own medibot fitted by his mother's health insurance company. The machine was similar. The doctor finds one of Mathew's veins. There is a sharp punch.

"Right, you're done," the doctor says. "We should have the results soon. A few hours, max."

"I have to stay in here for *hours*?"

He contemplates Mathew and says, "It's pretty boring isn't it? Especially without the Nexus." He goes to the wall of Canvases, opens a control panel and fiddles with the interface of buttons that appears on the screen. The channel flickers and then switches to the TV.

"Any better? You adjust the channel using these buttons here. They respond to voice command. Okay? The access code is PanMenu. Designed to be top secret, obviously."

Mathew nods. "Thanks," he says.

"You're welcome. There's a button above the bed. Press it if you feel unwell, but we'll monitor your biobot and will know before you if there are any bad signs."

Mathew wonders if he's meant to be comforted.

The doctor leaves and Mathew gets off the bed and

pads to the window to stare at Clara.

"Are you alright?" she mouths.

He nods and mimes back, "Are you?" He puts his hand against the glass. Clara does the same.

Later, Mathew is on his bed, watching the news. Russia has pushed back the allies to the Polish border. A US military spokesman explains that although the situation may seem bad, the Russian supply line is dangerously stretched. Another news story covers the floods. Someone points to a watermark on the side of a building and says the water level has dropped.

Mathew wishes he could find out what is actually going on via the Blackweb.

The Blackweb! Mathew thinks. *I haven't tried the Blackweb!*

The medic took his e-Pinz but he still has his Lenzes. He opens Charybdis by voice and initiates a connection.

This will never work, he thinks, waiting.

But it does. He is in.

If Clara had her beebot they'd be able to speak, but the hospital staff have taken it away with all her other things. He hopes they don't examine it too carefully. He is grateful now that he went to the effort of making it appear like a brooch.

Who should he call? His grandmother? He doesn't want to worry her.

I need to be careful.

Mathew does a quick search for Panacea on MUUT. He gets hundreds of results, the most recent a list of articles about a new anti-stress drug called the Pacifier. But his mother's name is missing.

What *is* his mother working on? *Why did I never ask her?*

He stares at his hands.

An ad appears, floating above his thumbs. It reads, "

Unbelievable value! Outsourced technical support. Absolutely free for a period. Say 'Yes' to connect for more information.

Mathew smiles and says, "Yes."

"You are Missile Crisis. I am Cold War."

"Hello Cold War."

"Didn't we discuss wild, unmasked searches on the Blackweb and decide they're a bad idea?"

"Extenuating circumstances."

"They'd better be good."

"I'm locked in a secret virus hospital owned by biotech company Panacea being tested for an unknown, probably highly contagious virus. My mother is unconscious in a quarantined room somewhere else in the hospital and they, whoever *they* are, won't let me see her."

"Holy shit! That is extenuating. And seriously screwed up."

"They have blocked our access to the Nexus, but for some reason they haven't blocked the Blackweb."

"Ha! All those corporate guys are idiots."

"Lucky for me."

"Lucky for you."

"I need to know if there are any recent rumours about Panacea and viruses."

"Those guys are evil. I wouldn't expect it to be anything good."

"There's something else. I need you to do a search on someone. Her name is Hoshi Mori. She works at Panacea."

"I know the name from somewhere. Is she the one you think is working on this virus?"

"I don't know. That's what I'd like to find out," Mathew says. For some reason he doesn't want to tell Cold War she is his mother. "Can you help?"

"You bet."

"Thanks, Cold War."

"Don't mention it, Missile Crisis. Keep strong."

"I don't think I have a choice."

6 MATHEW ERLANG'S WORLD FALLS APART

Mathew watches a woman in a white nurse's uniform approach. It is the first time he has seen the face of a member of the hospital staff. She stops by the outer door to Clara's room and takes a parcel from the trolley, pauses to check the label on the top, then goes in. The door remains open as she walks into the decontamination chamber so he can see in. There is a small metal table, large semi-opaque shrilk bottles full of blue and green liquid, a small stainless steel sink and a number of shrilk bins. It is like the antechamber he passed through when he came into his room.

The nurse goes to Clara and hands her the parcel. Clara gets off the bed. She mouths something through the window at Mathew, but he doesn't get it. Then she disappears behind the white screen on wheels. Her bare feet move at the bottom.

She's getting dressed.

The same nurse comes from Clara's room, walks the length of Mathew's window and passes through decontamination room. The door opens. She comes to

Mathew and hands him a parcel - his clothes. They are washed, ironed and shrilk-wrapped, and his name is printed on a label on the top.

"Get dressed now, please," she says.

Once they are all assembled in the corridor, the nurse leads the way back to the lift, past other rooms, identical to the ones they have been in, all empty.

"It's like a ghost hospital," Clara says.

The nurse is silent as she opens the door for them at the end of the corridor. On their immediate left, there is a large room with chairs, a couple of sofas, a Canvas showing the news and a basic kitchen. A HomeAngel is docked against one wall, charging, its blue heart light slowly pulsing. It wakes as they enter and beeps, signalling its initiation routine has started.

"Please make yourselves comfortable," the nurse says. "There is a food replicator and a variety of drinks, if you are hungry. The HomeAngel is called Nash. He will help you get anything you need. The bathroom is over there. We have ordered you all cars. They will be here in forty minutes. I'm sorry for the delay, but since the floods, it is hard to get authorised private cars at short notice."

"Where are they taking us?" Mathew asks.

"Home, of course."

"That's it?" Gen says.

"Yes. You can go home."

"I meant, you are not going to explain what is going on?"

"Didn't the medics and the doctors explain to you? I'm not sure I…"

"Yes. They said Hoshi is ill, they think she has a virus and they were testing us in case we have it too."

"Oh, I see; no one gave you the results. You are all totally clear. You are fine."

"Haven't we got the right to know what you tested us for? What did you inject us with?"

"You shouldn't notice any side effects but we will send you the details of the person you should contact if you do."

"Will the details of what you tested for be passed to our doctors? Will we get a copy of the medical records for our visit?"

"I don't have access to that information, I'm afraid."

"Then send someone to talk to us who does know," Gen says.

"That won't be possible."

Gen breathes deeply, trying to manage her exasperation. She asks, "How is this legal?"

"I assure you it is. We operate completely within the law here at Panacea."

"I bet you do," Gen says.

The nurse is irritated. "If there's nothing more, I will leave you. Someone will come to collect you when the cars arrive."

"I don't want a car," Mathew says abruptly. He is slumped on one of the low armchairs nearest the door. He gazes up at the nurse and says, "I want to stay here."

"I'm afraid we don't have the facilities."

"You have an entire empty hospital! It's not like people are fighting for beds," Gen says.

"It's against hospital policy for non-patients to stay overnight and you are being discharged," the nurse says brusquely.

"I want to see my mother."

"You should ring the hospital tomorrow morning and ask if it is possible for you to visit during the day."

"I want to stay," Mathew speaks quietly enough, but it is clear he has no intention of going anywhere.

The nurse says, "You will have to stay here if you do." She glances around at the banks of chairs. "There's nowhere to sleep, other than the sofas. I suppose I could bring you a blanket."

"I won't be sleeping," Mathew says.

"I will stay as well," Gen says.

Mathew stares at her, surprised but grateful.

"I don't…" the nurse begins.

"He needs someone with him," Gen says, cutting her off.

The nurse considers this. "Are you a relative?"

"I live next door to him. I've known him all his life."

The nurse is still frowning sceptically.

"I'm his godmother."

The nurse raises a sceptical eyebrow. "Well I suppose, if you *are* his godmother…"

"I am."

The nurse turns to Mathew, "But you will be confined to this room unless someone comes to escort you to your mother. Understood?"

Mathew nods.

"Then I will cancel your cars, but Ms Barculo is going home."

Clara opens her mouth to argue but Gen shakes her head and Clara stops, staring at Mathew.

He says, "You should go home. Your parents will be worried."

"Will you call me as soon as you know anything?" she says.

"Of course."

Clara's car arrives within the promised forty minutes and Mathew and Gen are left alone.

Nash is a revelation to Gen, who has seen HomeAngels on TV but never had one herself. Mathew calls the robot, orders his own food and invites Gen to select her choice from the options Nash projects before them.

"I suppose fresh food is too much to ask?" Gen says.

"I'm sorry. We don't stock perishable food. We don't have enough visitors," Nash says.

"What is your healthiest option?"

"I'll try to match what we have on our menu to your current nutritional needs. Permission to read your bioID?"

"I'll have the pizza," Gen says quickly. She's had enough of strangers poking at her personal data.

"Coming up," Nash says. It walks towards the kitchenette, activates the replicator and returns minutes later with the food. "Where would you like it?"

"Over here, please," Gen says. She points to a low table by the two armchairs they are seated on.

Nash puts their food down. "Would you like something to drink?"

"Water," Gen says.

"Coke," Mathew says.

"Just a minute, Sir," Nash says. It turns back to the kitchen.

"So this is what I'm missing," Gen says, trying to raise a smile from Mathew, but she stops herself when she sees his face. He is close to tears. "You should eat."

Mathew nods but he doesn't touch the food.

Gen eats silently. The news churns on a carousel on the big Canvas on the wall, the same stories Mathew has already watched - Russian troops at the border and the retreat of the London floodwater.

"Gets a bit old, doesn't it?" Gen says. She starts to take her plate back to the kitchen, but when Nash sweeps towards her, she hands it to the robot instead, bemused. "Do you want me to change the channel?" she asks.

"Doesn't matter," Mathew says.

Gen turns down the volume with a voice command.

There are a number of basic Papers lying around the room, preloaded with books and magazines. Gen takes one as she returns to her seat.

"Are you really my godmother?" Mathew asks.

"No," Gen says. "I said that because the nurse wasn't going to let us stay. You weren't christened. But I have known you all your life and I was good friends with your mum and dad."

"When Dad was alive. Mum said."

"Yes."

"Thanks for staying with me, Gen," he says after a while.

"Of course. There's no need to thank me."

A few hours later, Gen is asleep on one of the couches and Mathew has nodded off over his Paper, when the door to the waiting room opens. A lab-coated woman and a grey-suited man enter the room and perch on seats next to Mathew. Gen wakes and rises groggily.

"I'm Dr. Assaf," the woman says. "This is my colleague, Mr. Truville."

Truville leans across to shake Mathew's hand. Mathew takes his hand but doesn't return the man's smile.

"Mathew, I know you are worried. I am sorry no one has been able to tell you anything but we have been pulling out all the stops to help your mum."

"Can I see her?"

"Yes. I'm here to take you. You'll be able to talk to her through the window of her room. She is conscious but I have to warn you, we have her on drugs to help with the pain."

"Pain?"

"I'm afraid so. But the drugs are working, so don't worry, she's not in any pain now. She may be confused, though, delirious. She doesn't always know where she is and who she is speaking to. If she says strange things, remember it is the drugs talking and not her."

"Why can't I go in?"

"We think she is contagious."

"The nurses go in."

"They're nurses."

"Do you know what virus it is yet?"

"We still don't know for sure."

"But you think you know…"

Something nearly imperceptible passes between Assaf

and Truville. Then the woman says emphatically, "We don't know."

"Would you tell me if you knew?"

"Mathew, your mother is a valued employee of Panacea and a colleague and friend to many of us."

Mathew doesn't remember his mother ever mentioning a Dr. Assaf before.

"We are all upset about what has happened. We are doing our best to save her," Truville says.

"Save her?"

Dr. Assaf glances at Truville and frowns. "The prognosis is not good. Whatever is making her ill is virulent."

"You mean she may die?"

"We are doing everything we can for her. We haven't abandoned hope yet. But the situation is serious."

"Isn't there an antidote? I thought medibots could cure ninety per cent of known illnesses."

"This is one of those illnesses in the ten per cent medibots can't cure."

Mathew searches Dr. Assaf's face. *She is lying*, he thinks. He says, "Then how did she catch whatever it is she has?"

"We don't know that either."

"It's something she was working on, isn't it?"

Dr. Assaf hesitates; Truville cuts across her, saying, "No, no, of course not! The thing we need to do now, all of us, is concentrate on getting her better. Dr. Assaf will take you to your mother now. We've updated security for your bioID to let you come and go as you please to the corridor outside your mother's room. Gen, you will need this."

The suited man hands a blank shrilk card to Gen, who doesn't yet have a bioID. "Let's go up, shall we?"

They use a lift to go up a floor together in silence.

They walk along a corridor, similar to the one they had spent the last few hours in.

Gen says, "This place is empty and huge. You must be preparing for an epidemic."

"Yes, it's precisely what we are preparing for," Truville says. "Our purpose is to be ready to respond to biological warfare."

They approach the one occupied room on the floor. Dr. Assaf says, "She's in here."

Hoshi lies on a bed, dressed in a hospital gown, covered to the chest in a light sheet. She is surrounded by medical equipment, monitors, data, and lights. A nurse tends her.

Assaf hands Mathew and Gen their e-Pinz. She says, "You will need these. We've arranged it so you can talk."

Mathew re-fits his e-Pin. Dr. Assaf says to the nurse caring for Hoshi, "Rhea, do you hear us?"

"Loud and clear, Dr. Assaf."

The nurse raises the head of the bed until Hoshi is upright and carefully rearranges the equipment to make space near the window. Then she moves Hoshi's bed closer to the glass. Hoshi's eyes are open but unfocused. Her head falls to the left, the side nearest to Mathew. Her mouth is slack. The nurse gently lifts her head; her eyes stare right at Mathew. Her face is drawn, aged, her skin ashen. She has huge black rings under her eyes, like she has been punched.

How did this happen in just a few hours?

Mathew's is overwhelmed, angry, powerless. His eyes fill with tears. He slumps against the window and puts his face and hands against the glass, getting as close as possible.

"Mum!" he says. "Mum! It's me. I'm here," his chest heaves.

Her eyes continue to stare off vaguely into space.

"This is no good. She doesn't know I'm here," he says. "I want to go in."

"That's not possible," Truville says.

"The nurse is in there. Can't you get me one of those

suits?"

Dr. Assaf half turns to the man beside her, while still looking at Mathew. Before Truville responds, she says, "Yes, okay. Come with me, Mathew. Let's get you suited up."

The suit is light and quite mobile, much more so than he imagined. The mask has an air filter built in. It fits snugly to his face. A band secures it tightly around his head. Dr. Assaf activates the door. He passes into the decontamination chamber and waits. The door behind him closes. He takes in the equipment. There is a container the same colour and shape as the ones pushed along the corridor downstairs. It has a label on the top that reads 'biohazard'. As he stares at it, the door opens. The nurse indicates that he should move forward and he follows her to Hoshi's bedside. The bed has been pushed back. The nurse brings a chair to the headboard. Mathew sinks down, reaches across the sheets and takes his mother's hand.

"Mum. It's Mathew." This time his voice isn't being filtered through an e-Pin and a speaker system.

His mother turns her head slightly, focuses her eyes. It takes a lot of effort.

"Can you hear me?" he says.

"Yes," she says, her voice laboured. "I'm sorry."

"There's nothing to be sorry for."

"Yes. There is."

"What?"

"This."

"Getting sick? That's not your fault."

"It is," she says. "I should have been more careful. I should have never agreed."

"Agreed to what?"

"You must go to your grandmother, Mathew."

"I don't need to go to Grandma, I'm with you."

"You have to go. It will be all right, if you go. Promise me."

"Mum, I'm not going anywhere."

"Hmmmm," she says as she gets a new dose of morphine.

"Mum. Stay with me. Talk to me. Don't go to sleep."

But she is snoring slightly already.

He holds her hand for a long time, losing track of time. The whole world has contracted to this one room. He wishes time would stop, because horrific as this is, for this moment he still has her, and he knows he is losing her and he will never get over it. He gazes at her face, her eyelashes, her hair, her bare arms, her hands, imprinting it all on his memory. He does not want to forget.

Between his tears he says, "Don't leave me. Please don't leave me alone." But she doesn't respond.

Aeons or a moment later, someone enters the room. It is Dr. Assaf. She puts a hand on his shoulder. "Mathew. It's six am."

He gazes at her, confused.

She says, "Why don't you let Gen take you home with her for a bit? Get some sleep, something to eat and come back later."

"I can come back?"

"Whenever you like. We'll put a car at your disposal. But it won't do her any good if you get sick as well."

Mathew nods his assent. He still has his gloved hand firmly in Hoshi's. She grips it as she sleeps. He has to gently prize it open. He stands up, leans across the bed, touches her face and kisses her awkwardly through the shrilk. "I won't be long," he says.

7 GREEN FAIRY

DAY TWELVE: Friday, 3 December 2055, London, England

Gen's dinner party seems a lifetime away.

As they pass through the house, Mathew spots the laid dining room table, the cutlery, the glasses, the good table cloth, place settings and candles. It is like one of those museum rooms for the famous dead, frozen for posterity, or the scene of a crime, taped off to preserve the evidence.

Mathew follows Gen through to the kitchen and takes a seat at the scrubbed wooden table at her request. She clears away the meal she had prepared the night before.

"What would you like for breakfast? Eggs? Cereal? Toast?"

"Maybe some toast," Mathew says. "We should have had breakfast at my house. Leibniz would have fed us."

"I needed to clean this away anyway," Gen says.

"I'm sorry about your dinner, Gen."

"Oh, for goodness' sake. That's the last thing that should be on your mind."

Gen makes hot tea and toast and Mathew eats mechanically. "Another piece?"

"No, thanks."

"Not hungry?"

He shakes his head. The toast tastes like cardboard.

Gen says, "You should get some rest. I have a spare bed."

He shakes his head. "No, don't worry. I'd like to go home and sleep. And there's O'Malley. He's been alone all night."

"Of course."

"The car will come for me at one," he checks his Lenz for the time. Gen doesn't have a Canvas in her kitchen. It is nine am.

"I'll come back to the hospital with you," Gen says.

"Don't you need to work?"

"I'm due some leave."

"You need to be here at four for Clara's lesson."

"Mathew, I'm coming with you. Clara will manage without me for a few days."

"Thanks, Gen." He is incredibly grateful. He remembers what his mother said about Gen. That she is kind.

Back at number nineteen, O'Malley greets him at the door, vocal and upset at being left alone all night. Mathew gathers him in his arms and perches on the bottom of the stairs for a few minutes, stroking him, but really he is comforting himself. Upstairs, he showers, goes directly to his bedroom and logs on to the Blackweb as he walks. There is a tech support advert waiting for him. He accepts.

"Greetings. You are Burning Crusade. I am the Lich King." Lich King's voice is strange, like it's run through a bad simultaneous translation filter.

"Hi, Lich King."

"How goes it?"

"Not great, as it happens."

"Are you still at Panacea?"

"No, they let me go. I'm at home."

"Did their tests find anything? Are you sick?"

"No, I'm clear."

"Whoa. Close shave, man."

"And your mum?"

"Not so good."

"I'm sorry to hear."

"Yeah. Did you manage to find anything?"

"Affirmative. Hoshi Mori's thick on the Blackweb but mainly in relation to her husband, Soren Erlang. You didn't tell me who she was. I mean, to you."

"No, I didn't."

"You know about the Helios Energy trial, then?"

"Yes, of course. What about Hoshi Mori and Panacea?"

"Not a thing."

Mathew doesn't know whether to be pleased or disappointed.

"Which is surprising. Usually the Blackweb publishes stories before the roaches know it themselves."

"Roaches?"

"You know, the men in suits? Cockroaches. Highly adaptable, indestructible, low-level intelligence, no imagination, no souls, live parasitically off humans. Will be there at the end of the world."

"I didn't know."

"One for your personal dictionary. Anyhow, there's not a sniff of suspicion around Hoshi on the Blackweb, other than this trial and she's the wife of... well."

"Yes, I know."

"You got my blood up. So I decided to play a little."

"Play?"

"You know, tinker. See if their servers have any soft spots. It was ridiculously easy. If I didn't hate them with every living molecule of my body, I would contact their security team. They clearly need help. Anyway, I waltz in, like the door has been left wide open for me personally. Once you get through the doors they have a few quite nasty guard dogs, but before one of those got hold of my ankle, I managed to swipe Hoshi's files. There's a whole bunch of correspondence about a project called Project Green Fairy. I downloaded them. I'm sending them to you now."

"Did you look at them?"

"Yeah, some. It's pretty heavy shit. Biological weapons, I think."

Mathew's heart freezes.

"You should post this stuff on MUUT you know. It would cause a shitstorm. Psychopomp would kill for it."

"No. This must stay between us for now. Promise?"

"Okay. But it's burning a hole in my virtual drive."

"Delete it, then."

"Look, I gotta go. I'm way behind on my support calls. Let me know if you need anything else. And take care of yourself. Keep away from the viruses."

Mathew gets into bed, sick with tiredness. He doesn't have the energy to study the files.

It'll wait until tomorrow.

O'Malley is curled on the duvet. Mathew has to shift him across. He mews loudly in protest, pads around and settles on Mathew's chest, purring like a tractor.

A call comes through from Clara. He answers.

"Hi."

"Hey," she says, "Where are you?"

"In bed."

"Oh jeeze, I'm sorry. I'll hang up."

"No, don't. It's good to speak to you."

"Did you get to see her?"

"Yes. They let me sit with her."

"Is that safe?"

"They gave me one of those suits and a mask."

"Oh. How was she?"

"Barely conscious. Completely drugged up. They said they are *trying* to save her, meaning she's dying."

"Oh Mathew. I'm so, so sorry."

Mathew is silent. She hears him swallow.

"I wish I was there with you," she says.

"Me too," he says.

"It's unreal. Do they know what it is?"

"Some kind of rare virus. An incurable one. Probably the sort of virus that will be automatically neutralised by a medibot five years from now."

"Perhaps they will still find a way to help her. It is Panacea, after all. They must have all the latest experimental drugs at their disposal."

"Yeah," Mathew says. "They do."

"And she's one of their own."

"That's what Dr. Assaf said."

"Who is Dr. Assaf?"

"The doctor who is treating her." He yawns. "Sorry," he says.

"You should get some sleep."

"Yeah. I'm shattered."

"I'll hang up."

"Stay with me a little bit, will you?"

"Sure."

"You know, I can't shake my dream, the one where Mr. Lestrange's house is a sort of time machine. You take a history book off the shelf and you put it on the table. You turn to the page you want, open it and leave it there. Then you go to his Darkroom and join the game. There is this incredibly long corridor with lots of doors. One of the doors is unlocked. If you open it and step through, you will step into another time."

"It's a very elaborate dream."

"I wish it was true because if it was, I would use Mr. Lestrange's house to travel into my own future and ask myself how to cure my mother. You know, Clara, if anything happens to my mum, I will spend the rest of my life finding a cure for this virus."

"You didn't mention the book being a kind of key

before. I mean, you told me about the books; you dreamt you fell through some kind of door, but you didn't say the book controls where you travel to in time."

"That's because the book part wasn't a dream. I saw it." Clara's silence is loud across the connection. He knows he sounds crazy. "Oh, never mind. My mind is scrambled. I can't think straight."

"Yes, you should sleep now. I'm hanging up. I will be thinking of you. Call me if you need me, whatever time it is."

"Thanks, Clara."

"No need to thank me. Now I am actually going."

And she hangs up.

In the afternoon, back at the hospital, Mathew is alone with Hoshi. She hasn't spoken since he arrived and is asleep now, still gripping his hand. Mathew is exhausted and his mind is a mess, turning over and over. He doesn't dare move, worried he will wake her, and he does not want to doze off - he is terrified she might die while he sleeps.

Whispering, he issues the voice commands to open the files Lich King had found for him. He browses through them and searches for Green Fairy. They are mainly technical, internally focused documents he doesn't understand but he recognises some words and phrases: *entomological warfare*, *mycoherbicides* and *anti-crop capability*. As far as he can make out, Green Fairy is a military project to use insects to deliver fungus-based herbicides to kill crops. There had been a report on the news. An email catches his eye from James Truville. He scans it and reads,

```
You will be aware of the escalation of tension
between the US and Russia. In the event of war, we
would have no choice but to shift our focus to
human-grade infectious agents and pull more
resources from other projects, including Green
Fairy. In other words, you should be prepared to
move projects at short notice. I know your feelings
on the matter and I truly hope it will not come to
that.
```

He stares at his mother in horror. She was working on a biological weapon. *That* is why she is dying.

8 DRAGONFLY

DAY THIRTEEN: Saturday 4 December, 2055

The Aegis car snakes through deserted streets as Mathew makes his early morning journey home. A winter mist hangs over London. He's left Gen at the hospital. They are working shifts, taking it in turns to watch over Hoshi. Mathew took the night shift; Gen is sitting with her during the day.

Hoshi has been asleep or delirious since she last spoke to Mathew. Dr. Assaf says it's partly the morphine and partly the virus. Mathew hasn't told Gen what he has found out about his mother. He hasn't told anyone.

Bone-tired, he exits the car. The door of his house unlocks and swings slightly ajar as he walks towards it. O'Malley jogs down the stairs, mewing in a complaining way. Mathew smiles sadly and picks him up; he contemplates breakfast, decides he can't face it and makes his heavy legs climb the stairs, still holding the cat. He puts O'Malley on his bedroom floor and throws himself onto the bed fully clothed. He falls asleep wearing his boots.

He wakes at noon, his mind thick and disorientated, and lies staring at the ceiling. He closes his eyes again, trying to sleep, willing it, knowing he hasn't had enough, but the light streams through his curtains and messages scroll across his Lenz, including several missed calls from his grandmother who had tried to reach him at various points during the previous afternoon and evening. He feels guilty not calling her, but he is overwhelmed by the thought of facing her grief and the interrogation he is likely to get. He tells himself he will call her once he has showered and eaten and is stronger.

There are messages from Clara too.

In the shower he starts to worry about school, whether he would be expected to continue his studies, but he doesn't think he can. With a sinking feeling, he remembers the collaborative robotics project session due to take place on Monday, and he also remembers his dragonfly.

Downstairs, dressed and waiting for his food, he writes to Professor Absolem. He explains what has happened and tells her he doesn't think he will be able to log on to school the next day. He writes up his notes to explain the prep work he has done, gathers the blueprints for the robot to send and then decides he should also provide video evidence. The dragonfly is on his desk upstairs. He boots up the program that allows him to control it and flies it into the kitchen, filming a few flypasts and then a 360° close-up with a voice-over of his design decisions. Then he packages all the material up, attaches it to a message and hits send.

Now, the dragonfly is settled before him on the kitchen table. He picks it up absently, placing it in the palm of his hand, and stares at it. His mind cycles through the events of the last fortnight, dreams and conversations, a muddle of memory he can't even hope to unpick. So what is the point in clinging to things he is unsure of? Nothing will matter anymore, if his mother dies. He stares through the kitchen window at the garden. Out of the depths of exhaustion and confusion, inside his brain, neurons spike and send signals circulating through his grey matter circuits and networks. He feels the strange flush of pleasure of an idea; of things falling into place. When he stands up and heads to the door, he is thinking, *But I do not want to have to go back into Mr. Lestrange's library.*

Outside it is biting cold and the dull steel sky presses low on the slate rooftops of London. He's only wearing his t-shirt and stands shivering in the garden. Bending, he puts the dragonfly on the flagstones and connects to the control software through his e-Pin and Lenz. Then he fixes his gaze on Mr. Lestrange's chimney and considers the wind buffeting the trees around him. There is nothing for it but to try.

Up the little robot flies, blowing to and fro precariously, until it is hanging above the clay pot mouth of the chimney. Mathew wonders if it is now blocked, if Lestrange has taken action to protect the weak point of entry into his house. He takes the dragonfly lower slowly and switches on the small light he fitted to its nose. The camera on the base of the machine faces the brick wall but light filters up from below. The chimney isn't blocked after all. The way is clear.

The dragonfly emerges into the familiar room. It turns on its axis, pans around, and spies the wardrobe, the bed, the sash window. The door is only slightly ajar, but he is lucky it is. He would not have got it through the keyhole or under the door, as he did with the beebot.

Down the stairwell, and into the library, the camera on the device beams back an image of the hundreds of books that line the walls. Mathew flies the dragonfly towards the shelf that contains the book that bears his name.

It is there. He experiences a peculiar mixture of triumph and disquiet.

He flies the dragonfly beside the shelf and with painstaking care, extends its arms. The dragonfly gets a grip on the spine of *The Book of Mathew Erlang* and slowly retracts its arm, pulling the book with it. He wonders if the dragonfly will be unbalanced with the weight, the way it was with his Chinese art book, but it has a better grip this time. It dips, but he manages to steady it and fly it towards the table. There he gently rests the book and lands the dragonfly. The tiny craft adjusts its position by shuffling its six feet. It extends its right arm and retracts the left, grips the front cover and flips it open. He takes his time, turning the pages of the book until he is near the end.

That should do it.

Finally, he parks the dragonfly on top of the book, to make sure the pages don't flip back.

Once he has done all of this, still outside in the garden, he jumps onto the bench, grabs the wall and pulls himself up, landing hard on the conservatory roof. It shudders but does not give. He jumps, cautiously at first, but then with increasing force until the glass gives way beneath him.

He falls feet-first and lands upright, surrounded by a mess of broken glass and shrilk. He takes a deep breath and opens the door to the kitchen. It takes him only moments to reach Mr. Lestrange's Darkroom, get into the chair and pull on the skullcap.

An eye-blink later and he is staring down the white corridor. He walks forward tentatively, trying doors as he goes. His eyes search for a parachute or something like it; a prop, a strange object that stands out against the whiteness. Eventually he sees it. A bright orange dot that grows larger as he walks towards it. It is a lifejacket. He takes it off its peg, pulls it over his head, then tries the door.

It opens.

He holds it there, partially ajar, and wonders what he will find on the other side, whether he will fall thousands of feet, or into an ocean.

9 THE LAKE

DAY THIRTEEN: Monday, 12 February, 2091, London

Through the gap between the door and its frame, he spies no ocean, only darkness. He pushes the door cautiously until it is fully open and peers into a room. Just a room. Long abandoned, with misaligned desks, overturned chairs, office equipment, mildewed electrical devices, drawers open, things all across the floor, broken ceiling tiles fallen from the roof, wires, cables and twisted air-conditioning pipes with peeling silver foil hanging, everything dust-, grime- and dirt-layered.

Why this, then? he wonders, looking down at the lifejacket.

There is brightness ahead. He moves towards it, crushing rubbish underfoot, and carefully makes his way around rotted furniture. There is a powerful smell of damp and decay.

He reaches the source of the light. A window runs around the four sides of the large room. Years of green mould growth have besmeared the glass, but he realises that if he cleans the inside with the cuff of his sleeve, he can make it just clear enough to get a view.

He looks at London, but it is not his London, the one he grew up in. This is an alien place. He stares east towards the City, or what used to be the City and what now appears to be a huge lake. He knows he faces east because he sees the Shard at London Bridge, the Gherkin, Tower 42 and beyond, Canary Wharf. St Paul's is gone, it is a shock to realise, a missing eye in the ancient face of the city. Skyscrapers, church steeples and the tops of tall historic buildings pierce the lake's surface like upturned cruise liners, like the Titanic the moment before she sank beneath the waves. He walks around the perimeter of the office, close to the window, and stops to scrape another view from beneath the greasy green and grey sludge plastered on the glass. The carpet under his feet is decomposing and it trips him as he walks. He swears.

As he turns a corner to the north-facing side of the building, the London Eye looms, the lower half submerged, many of the pods with broken glass, a couple missing entirely. Through the portal he scrubs for himself, he sees Somerset House, the Savoy, the Shell Mex building, Charing Cross Station, all part-submerged. Hungerford Bridge has a big gap in it; bits of rail track hang into thin air like exposed bone.

He turns to Parliament and Big Ben. The clock is gone. Sheets of material blanket the gaps, flapping in the wind. Surrounding the whole of the Palace of Westminster are huge black and red metal walls that extend three-quarters the height of the side of the building. Scaffolding straightjackets these walls. The roof of the House of Lords has been removed and there is a vast canopy across the top.

On the riverside, there is a wooden pier with fifty or more boats moored against it, of all sizes and types: barges and yachts, little boats, dinghies, larger ships too, one with a large crane on its deck, and beside it, a battleship. People, tiny from his perspective, rush off the scaffolding, en masse, and head for the boats.

Outside black clouds churn, there is a rumble of thunder; the sky curdles yellow, and a fork of lightning strikes a pylon on one of the Golden Jubilee Bridges. It blasts blinding white light into the room. He steps back from the window, startled. Torrents of rain lash against the window, washing rivulets into the dirt and grime down the glass. Recovering himself, he steps back to the window and watches the people on the scaffolding as they hurry to escape the rain, bowing and sheltering their heads.

It occurs to him he has to move. Sooner or later one of Lestrange's colleagues, someone like Borodin the Cat, will be after him, trying to take him back through the door. But how to leave the building? He glances at the lifejacket.

When he walked across the office he'd noticed a stairwell with its door hanging on its hinges. He retraces his steps now and squeezes past the door. Water pours from above. The roof has a gaping hole - half of the ceiling is collapsed on the stairs. He makes his precarious way through the debris and gets to the top of the stairs, onto the roof of the building. At first, he tries to shelter under the lintel. After a few minutes, he abandons his attempt to keep dry and walks into the rain.

Thunder booms again, a colossal, terrifying sound that shakes the building. He steadies himself against the wall. Almost immediately lightning strikes. This time it hits the top of one of the buildings across the river. He watches as tiles and woodwork fall away and tumble to the ground. The exposed joists catch fire, despite the sheets of water that come down from the sky. He has only been outside a few moments, but he is already drenched to the skin.

Across the river, the scaffolding around Parliament is abandoned. Boats shelter people. The unluckier workers on the edge of the flotilla are huddled under makeshift tarpaulins. He sees them clearly and assumes they see him. Waving at them with both arms, he yells at the top of his voice, but no one notices him and the pandemonium of the storm obliterates his voice, as gusts of wind blow sheets of rain across the water.

He stumbles back inside and clambers back down the stairs, slipping and sliding on the soaked, rotten wooden boards and broken plasterboard. He keeps going down, floor upon floor. He counts 24 sets of stairs before they disappear under black water and he can go no further.

He retraces his path to the last floor level not drowned and enters. This office floor is much like the one he explored upstairs; abandoned, debris-littered, damp-smelling. He heads towards the windows and through the murky glass. The river laps at the side of the building ten feet below. On the north side, at this level, he sees more clearly across the river to the boats moored-up against the makeshift pier of the Palace of Westminster. People on the boats are crouched under whatever shelter they can find, shrinking from the storm.

He bangs on the window and tries to get their attention, but he knows as he does so that they can't hear him. There's no way to open the window. He can't swim across the churning, fast-running river. He needs to get someone to help him. If he had matches and the whole building and everything in it wasn't so damp, he'd start a fire on the roof.

Then a solution occurs to him.

He runs back up the stairs. His heart beats through his chest, his legs burn. All the while, he is thinking of the time ticking away for his mother. He pushes down hard at the rising panic.

The rain still lashes. It batters the windows of the stairwell tower and blows wet waves though the broken glass panels, spraying him. With a final push across the collapsed ceiling at the top of the stairwell, he stumbles again into the full force of the storm.

On the roof he grabs whatever he lays his hands on. The first thing he finds is an old ceramic pot with a small dead tree inside it. He rolls it on its rim to the low wall at the edge of the roof. Struggling to lift it, he manages to get it over the lip of the wall and let it go. He watches it hit the water. It makes a good-sized splash.

He gazes hopefully across at the people on the Westminster boats, but no one has seen or heard it.

On a paved area, near a broken skylight, there's an old cast iron table, part of the remnants of a long neglected roof garden. He fetches it and throws that too. It bounces off the wall before it drops to the river and hits something submerged. It makes a satisfying loud metallic clang before it is sucked beneath the brown churning river.

He waits.

There is no reaction from anyone on the boats.

In frustration, he slings each and every thing he can find off the roof of the building. Old garden furniture and tools, pots, bits of rubbish, a flagstone, a broken beam from the roof. He pulls the fractured sheets of plasterboard from the stairwell. It all goes over the edge.

And still no one notices.

Exhausted, he sinks down with his back against a brick wall. He is so frustrated his eyes smart and he digs his nails in his palms to push back the tears.

Get up. Get up and do something.

He slides back down the stairs, takes hold of the door, manages to rip it entirely off its hinges, and pulls it after him. He thinks, if he gets it into the Thames then maybe it will float and act as a raft.

I will jump after it.

It takes him five minutes to drag the door behind him onto the roof. He rests the top half on the wall, lifts it from the bottom and tips it up. He waits a moment. There's a satisfying splash. It must have landed flat.

There are yells from below - colourful swearing. He has never been so pleased to be verbally abused.

"Hey! You up there! Are you a lunatic?"

Mathew peers over the wall cautiously. There is a boat. It is fourteen-foot long, with a small fibreglass cabin, open at the back. Two people glare at him, sheltering their eyes from the driving rain - a blonde woman and a short bulky man.

"You nearly brained us, you idiot!"

"Sorry!" Mathew yells back. "I didn't see you."

"It's a good idea to look before you throw large heavy objects from the tops of tall buildings. What the hell are you playing at? You might have killed us."

"I was trying to get someone's attention."

"You managed that alright."

"I'm stuck here."

"Yes you are. And if that's the way you try and get help, you're going to stay stuck there."

"Please!"

The two on the boat confer for a minute. The short fat man shakes his head, raises his hands defensively. The woman makes appealing gestures.

The short fat man says, "Come down, then."

"How? Where?"

"How the hell do I know? How did you get up there?"

"I… I don't remember."

"Great, he's crazy," the man says to the blonde woman.

The blonde woman ignores him. She shouts up to Mathew, "Come down to the water level. There's bound to be a cracked pane of glass. Find one and kick a window open."

"Will you wait?"

"Yes, of course we'll wait. But hurry, will you? It's pissing rain and it'll be dark soon."

Mathew runs down the stairs as fast as his legs will carry him, all the way down to the floor he's just explored, the one just above water level. Outside the door, the stairwell wall is marked with the number twelve. He navigates the upturned desks and chairs and the collapsed roof tiles and heads to the windows on the north of the building, finding an area of glass he'd cleaned with his shirt and peering through. The boat belonging to his potential rescuers is below.

From this closer distance, he realises the second person in the boat isn't a man at all, but a woman with short hair, wearing bulky men's clothes.

Mathew bangs hard on the window to get their attention. They stare blankly across the river. The window is double-glazed and rock solid in its frame. He goes from window to window looking to find one cracked or broken pane. None of them are damaged. He searches around for an object to smash with, hefts an office chair to his shoulder and rams a window with the wheels, but they spin and bounce off. Frantically, he hunts for an object to break the glass, worried the women will leave, thinking he has disappeared.

In the corner of the room, something catches his eye. It is a fire door. He weaves his way through the mess of the abandoned office. Across the door there is a rusted metal bar and a sign that reads, "Fire. Only open in case of emergency." Supposing this counts as an emergency, he pushes on the bar. It is stiff but with some effort and rattling he manages to force it open.

He stands on the roof of a wing of the building. The rescue boat floats off round to the east side. The women are hunting for him.

"Hey!" he shouts.

They turn the boat around and come back beneath him.

"Hi," he says.

"Hello," the short, dark-haired woman says.

The other woman is tall and thin, her blonde hair tightly tied back. She raises a hand, "Hi there."

"How do I get down?"

"Good question," the blonde woman says. "You'll have to jump."

"If he jumps from up there into the boat he'll go through the bottom, or at the very least tip us up," the short woman says to her companion. She squints up at Mathew, sheltering her eyes from the driving rain. "You'll have to jump into the water."

"Jump? Into the Thames? In there?"

"Yes, jump in there. Where did you think I meant? The bloody Mediterranean?"

Mathew looks down, over the edge of the roof. It seems a long way down. The river is running fast. "I'm not sure I can."

"Then you're staying and we're going."

"There's got to be another way."

"I tell you what, why don't you spend the night here while you decide what to do and we'll pick you up tomorrow morning?" She glances at the sky. It is dark from the storm but the sun is also dimming. "I am not travelling down the river after dark. You've got a bloody lifejacket on, for Pete's sake."

"Okay. Okay. I'll jump. Just give me a minute." Mathew contemplates the brown water. It doesn't look like water at all. It gives every impression of being solid. He teeters on the edge, but fear grips him and refuses to let his body move off the edge of the roof.

"Are you going to jump or what?" the dark woman says.

"Yes!" Mathew says. "I will." He shuffles right to the edge, wobbles and almost loses his balance.

"Watch out for floaters," the short woman says.

"What are floaters?"

"Stuff floating in the river. Could be big dangerous stuff, like big bits of wood, things like doors crazy people throw from the tops of tall buildings. There's also the nasty unhygienic little stuff that gives you e-coli or other horrible things. Whatever you do, don't swallow any water."

"You are making me feel so much better. How do I spot the floaters? It's like soup."

"You can't spot them."

"Great."

"Just jump, will you?"

Mathew jumps. He plunges feet-first, mouth and eyes closed tight. Down he goes, into the murk. When he slows, the lifejacket tugs at his shoulders and he expects to bob to the surface. Instead it is like someone very strong has grabbed both his legs and is pulling at him and he swirls around and around like a shirt in a washing machine. He tries to swim, but he doesn't know which way is up and which way is down. Opening his eyes, there's nothing but fast churning coffee-coloured mire. Then something hard hits the side of his head, there is suddenly a constriction at his waist and he is being reeled in.

Coughing, gasping, he is at the surface, breathing.

"Give me your hand!" a woman's voice is saying urgently. "Come on! Grab his jacket will you, Mike? I can't hold this much longer."

He reaches blindly, desperately. He finds a hand and is hauled into the boat.

10 BOB AND MIKE

Mathew lies on the floor of the boat and stares at a pair of muddy boots, a large shrilk bottle of water, several boxes stacked one on top of the other, and a machine gun. He must have swallowed a pint of the Thames. The thought makes him retch. The boots step across him.

"That nearly didn't go well," says a woman's voice.

Unsteadily, he pushes himself off the floor with his aching arms. Around his waist is a rope and a metal hoop.

"Here," the blonde woman says, and she loosens it and pulls it over his head. "Thank God we had this. Saved your life I think." She helps Mathew to his feet. "Are you ok?"

He nods, but he's not really sure.

"Sit there," the short woman says. She points to a wooden bench. Up close, her face is distinctly feminine, but her hair is dark and cropped short and her clothes are bulky and man-like. She has a paunch. The blonde woman passes him a small, rough towel as he stands and steps unsteadily the few paces to the bench.

"Thanks," he says as he sits and takes the towel and dries his hair. It smells of fuel. His hands are shaking.

"Cold?" the blonde woman asks, noticing his hands. He nods, but it's not cold that's making him shake. She looks at the towel and then pulls a face. "Sorry, it's not much."

"There's an old sweatshirt in the dry box," the dark woman says.

"Right."

The blonde woman disappears into the little cabin and reappears with a large, shapeless navy hoody. Mathew takes it gratefully, strips off his dirty, sodden t-shirt, and pulls the clean sweatshirt on over his head.

The dark woman goes inside the cabin and starts the engine. It sputters into life and she steers the boat around to face the river.

"It's getting dark. The sooner we get back the better," she says.

They pass the London Eye and travel along what used to be the Riverside Walk. Down below, he supposes, is the old walkway of the South Bank, the place where millions of people used to enjoy the view of the Thames and the Embankment buildings.

"Can you search for floaters at the front, Mike?"

"On it," the blonde woman says. She scrambles onto the fibreglass bow of the boat, and kneels and peers into the murky water, holding a long pole, with a metal noose at the end, the one used to fish Mathew from the water.

"Right, we're okay now. Into the swim."

Mike sits next to Mathew, who has found a seat on the bench, behind the little cabin.

She is a woman in her mid-forties. Although her face is not painted and her eyes and mouth are lined, she is strikingly attractive. She has a perfect, straight nose, symmetrical features, greenish eyes.

She extends a hand, "Hi, I'm Mike."

"I'm Mathew," he says, taking her hand.

"Yes, I know. You're broadcasting," Mike says. She points to the right of his head, where virtual letters hover about him in the air. "You may want to switch that off."

Before Mathew can ask what she means, she says,

"That's Bob," nodding at their driver.

Bob raises a hand to say 'hello'. "Where shall we drop you?" she asks.

Mathew hesitates and then says, "I need to get to Silverwood."

Bob laughs. She has a loud, throaty, dirty laugh. Mathew finds himself staring at her with surprise and smiling. "Good luck with that," she says.

"Why?"

"How were you planning to get there?"

"Isn't there a train?"

Again the laugh. She clutches her heaving belly as if she's pulled a muscle.

"Are you shitting me? The boy's a comedian, Mike."

"You're joking, right?" Mike says.

Mathew nods uncertainly.

"See. He's joking."

"It's the only explanation."

"Whoa!" Mike says. She scrambles to the front of the boat once again. "Slow." She grabs the metal pole and pushes a large box aside. "That was close. You're okay now, Bob." But she stays where she is, on watch.

"So how were you planning to get to Silverwood?" Bob says.

"I don't know. How far is it?"

"Now you're scaring me."

Mike says, "Silverwood is a hundred and seventy miles away."

"A hundred and seventy miles!"

"Where were you planning to stay tonight? Where is home?" Mike asks.

"Blackheath."

"There's a bit of luck. We're heading to Greenwich. We can give you a lift to there at least, can't we Bob?"

"Sure we can," Bob says. "Funny though. I thought they'd cleared Blackheath. I didn't think anyone lived there anymore."

They are on the main stretch of the river. There is a wide open stretch ahead and to the side. They sail under the two parts of the broken Hungerford Bridge. Mathew cranes his neck up to look. The bridge is a garden of weeds, shrubs and trees.

Mike says, "The clearances are pointless. No sooner has the army got rid of all the people, than they come back. What do they expect? They have nowhere else to go. Even if they demolish the buildings, folks build camps there made from the ruins."

Bob grunts and asks Mathew, "How long have you lived in Blackheath?"

"All my life."

"Wow. Your parents must be bloody stubborn."

They pass through Waterloo Bridge. Like Hungerford Bridge, it is blasted in two. Mathew realises it is because the water level is so high. People have blasted the bridges to make a way through for the boats.

"I don't understand," Mathew says. "Why does the government want to make people leave London?"

"Lots of people don't understand that," Mike says.

"Bah! Don't listen to her. It's a cesspit of disease. No running water. The drains all flooded. Cholera, typhoid, trachoma and worms, to name a few things," Bob says.

"But that's not the real reason," Mike says.

"No, it isn't," Bob agrees.

"What is, then?" Mathew asks.

"Terrorists."

"They're not really terrorists," Mike says.

"Depends which side of the gun you're on, doesn't it? To us, they're terrorists. It doesn't matter to them that all we're trying to do here is save historic buildings for the nation. To them we're vamps, bloodsuckers, leeches, and roaches. Hence this," she kicks at the muzzle of the gun with her boot.

"I hope that's on safety," Mike says.

Bob continues, "No one goes anywhere without one

now. To the Edenists, the Accountants are freedom fighters and saviours of the people, to us they're terrorists. Since the government vacated, they've moved in and the place is crawling with righteous looters and vigilantes with a cause. They'll steal from you and tell you that it's their moral duty to do so."

"They've always been here," Mike says. "The side you're on is often random. We have bioIDs and were put through a sponsored education programme. If we hadn't, we'd probably be with them."

Bob shoots Mike a glance.

"We would!"

"I don't think they like our kind, quite frankly." She stares at Mathew, "You're not an Accountant are you?"

Mathew laughs, "I'm sixteen."

Bob shrugs, "I've met much younger boys carrying pretty serious weapons. Their military recruitment people don't do age discrimination."

"Do accountants normally carry weapons?"

"What kind of Non Grata propaganda have you been fed, boy? That's their stock in trade. The violent revolution."

Mike says, "He thinks you mean business accountants."

Bob bursts into laughter, her belly heaving. "No he doesn't."

"Actually, I did," Mathew says.

Bob laughs louder and the sound carries across the water.

Mike says, "Shhh! Button it, will you? You were just saying this place is crawling with terrorists!"

Bob stops short; her face falls, sheepish. "Yeah, you're right." She settles on her seat and pulls a sour face.

"Where are all these terrorists, anyway?" Mathew asks, looking at the half-drowned buildings lining the river, as the boat glides past them. "The whole city looks deserted."

Mike nods. "Over there. Where you're looking."

"What? In those empty buildings?"

71

"Not all of those buildings are empty. More than ten million people used to live here. They haven't evaporated into thin air."

"But the buildings are all flooded! They're uninhabitable."

"Of course they're not. Only the lower floors are flooded. There are lots of floors and rooms above the water line."

"So people didn't leave?"

"Oh, sure. Lots of people left. But some stayed to protect their own homes; others moved into other people's buildings when their owners left. Years ago there were hundreds of amazing apartments ready for the taking. For a time the most desperate and destitute people of England lived in palatial apartments, the abandoned homes of the rich and luxury hotel rooms."

"But where do they get running water, energy or comms?"

Mike shrugs. "Lots of people live without. Some people have managed to hack things. There's wireless power, wireless internet. They stick solar panels and water tanks on the rooftops. People travel around the city using boats, ropes and wires."

"Ropes and wires?"

"Look more closely."

Mathew focuses his Lenzes further onto the riverside apartments and office blocks. They are laced together by a web of lines.

"What are they?" Mathew asks. "How are they used?"

"Some folks use harnesses; others walk across. Tightrope walking is a skill every London Non Grata child learns."

"If you are actually from London, you'd know all of this. Where are you really from? How did you get stuck in the building in the first place?"

Mathew knows he needs to scrape together a story and has been inventing a line since he started throwing objects off the roof. "I was taken there and left. I don't remember how I got in."

"You were attacked?" Mike asks.

"For God's sake, will you stop feeding him?" Bob says, exasperated.

"It would explain why he hasn't got any stuff and he doesn't remember anything. Perhaps he has amnesia."

"Who took you there?" Bob asks Mathew, ignoring Mike.

"I was kidnapped."

"Kidnapped?" Bob pulls a face. "Why?"

"I don't know."

"Were you mugged?"

"Yeah. They took my stuff."

"What stuff?"

Mathew feels the heat of embarrassment spreading up his neck to his face. He stammers as he says, "My bag. My... things."

Bob cocks a sceptical eyebrow. "But they didn't hurt you?"

"No."

"Where were you when they picked you up?"

"I was at home."

"They broke into your house?"

"I was in the road."

"Where did you say your house was again? Blackheath?"

"Yes."

"So these... muggers, they kidnapped you and took you all the way to the Shell Centre where they left you without harming you, all for a bag?"

"Yeah."

"What was in the bag?"

Mathew thought frantically. He had no idea what might be considered valuable enough to steal in 2091. "Food," he says.

This rings true for Bob, who nods her head slightly to

one side and pulls an expression that says, *Maybe*.

"Did you know them," Mike asks, "the people who took you?"

"Yeah, I knew them," Mathew says.

"So your friends kidnapped you?"

"Not friends exactly," Mathew thought quickly. "These boys I know. They don't like me."

"Why do you have a lifejacket?"

"I found it."

"There was a perfectly good lifejacket lying around on the floor of the Shell Centre building after it had been looted several hundred times?"

"Yes. I found it in a drawer."

"A drawer?"

"A drawer in a side room."

Mike says. "Bob, stop giving the boy a hard time. He nearly drowned."

Undeterred, Bob says, "Do you really come from Blackheath?"

"It was my family home," Mathew insists. He can see Mike doesn't believe a word he's saying. She's reading it in his face. He's flustered and angry with himself.

Mike says, "Was?"

"Yes," Mathew says.

"That's not what he said before. He said he'd lived there all his life. He said that's where his friends or whatever they were found him. But he doesn't know a thing about London or Silverwood. He might as well be from another planet. You might think you're being nice, but someone like him shoots people like us."

Mathew says, "Honestly, I'm not an Accountant or an Edenist. I'm trying to get to Silverwood to get help for my mother. She's sick."

"Bob," Mike says, "Have you ever met an Account who laughed when you mentioned their name?"

"Hmmmph," Bob says, but Mike knows it's a concessionary noise.

Mike asks, "Why don't you think you remember how you entered the building? Did someone knock you unconscious?"

"Oh, for mercy's sake!" Bobs splutters, exasperated. "Why don't we get him back to Greenwich and have security check him for us? They'll get to the truth."

"They won't get to the bottom of anything. They'll send him to Internment, to one of those horrible camps," Mike says.

"So, what do you propose?"

"We could just let him go."

Bob frowns at Mathew. "When did your family last live in Blackheath?"

"2055," Mathew says.

"To be honest," Bob says to Mike. "I think letting him go would be as bad for him as sending him to Internment."

11 SECURITY

At Greenwich, the half-submerged gates by the Royal Steps are open and they sail into the Grand Square towards the Queen's House, between Queen Mary and King William Court, water lapping the top of the porticos of Wren's masterful architecture. They turn right and travel along what used to be Trafalgar Road and turn left and head towards the Park. The old park gate has been removed to form a wide entrance for boats. There are two makeshift wooden watchtowers on either side of this. One of the towers is manned. As they go through a man shouts to them.

"Dr. Bob! Dr. Mike! How're the Houses of Parliament coming along?"

"Slowly, Pete. Very slowly," Bob says.

"Got to do it right, though, Dr. Bob."

"Very true," Bob says.

"Who's that with you?"

"A friend, Pete."

"Any friend of yours is welcome here. He'll need to go to security, though."

"We're on our way."

The foot of the hill is a muddy beach. The lower park is a lake. There is a long wooden pier constructed across the sludge, with places to dock small boats at the water's edge. Larger boats are moored in deeper water, nearer the river.

Mike stands on the bow and jumps as they approach the pier. Bob cuts the engine and they glide in. Mike ties up and says to Mathew, "Come on, then. This is the last stop."

Mathew clambers through the clutter at the bottom of the boat. Bob stops him, "Here, make yourself useful," and she passes him one of the boxes. "Give it to Mike."

They unload the boat and Bob comes ashore with two machine guns.

Everywhere, people busily unload their little boats. Just beyond the pier there is a high chain link fence topped with barbed wire. Workers file through gates. Their bioIDs automatically buzz them in. Three uniforms with guns stand to one side, watching. Beyond this, tents, prefab buildings and wooden shacks and sheds cling to every available part of the hillside, amongst the ancient chestnut trees. Flamsteed House still perches on the peak of the hill in quiet dignity, like the one person of refinement in a room full of hooligans. It is now an army control centre.

Bob says to Mathew, "See that cabin?" She points to a prefabricated building on tall wooden stilts, built into the fence with an open door and an old sign above the door that reads 'Security'. "Go and wait for us there. We need to take our stuff back to our house, otherwise it'll be swiped." Mathew hesitates. Bob pushes him forward, "Go on, you'll be all right. Say you're with Dr. Roberta Calvin and Dr. Michaela Vear. Tell him we'll claim you in fifteen minutes."

Mathew is doubtful. He doesn't want to have to deal with security.

"We can't leave him," Mike says.

"We can't leave this stuff either, and the gatehouse won't let him through until security has checked him in."

"He'll be stamped for the camps."

Bob sighs, "Maybe. Do you have a better plan?"

"No."

"Mathew, you go there."

Mathew watches forlornly as Bob and Mike walk off

through the gate and climb the hill. People hurry past him, walking around his still body, carrying boxes and bags brought from the boats, keen to get through the gates. People stare at him, slightly above his head, as they do at home when they're reading his data, but less discreetly, more rudely. One man knocks into him and says, "Sorry, Mathew," and then bursts out laughing. Mathew realises he is still broadcasting and remembers what Mike had told him about turning it off. He uses voices commands to switch off the signal.

Gazing up at the security hut, he wonders what will happen to him if he goes inside. If he is locked up, it is only a matter of time before one of Lestrange's friends comes to find him to take him home. He curses himself for not leaving the boat sooner, not persuading Bob to drop him somewhere along the Thames. He has come here unprepared mentally; unable to spin a simple believable yarn, unable to keep his mouth shut when he needs to.

Unlike his first trip through one of Mr. Lestrange's doors, this is not a game; it matters. He considers his options and surveys the scene. He could steal one of the boats, but Pete in the tower has a gun and would probably use it. If he didn't, someone else might. He could hide somewhere, perhaps a cabin, or under a tarpaulin on one of the boats, wait until dark and swim, but his earlier experience of Thames swimming does not give him much hope for his chances of survival.

Realising he doesn't have a choice, he sets off towards the security hut.

There is a ladder secured to the side of one of the wooden stilts and it leads to a platform made of planks. The tide is out. The stilts have a waterline at three quarters height and at the top they are furred with green moss. He reaches the top. The door to the prefab is open. He peers inside, knocking gently on the door.

"Hello?"

An elderly man with wispy grey hair and a grizzled two-day beard is slumped over his beer-belly. He wears a uniform but somehow manages to make his clothes seem like sloppy casuals. A name badge is askew on his breast pocket. Mathew has never seen anyone wear their name like this before. The badge reads, "Sergeant Charles Baker."

"Hi," Mathew says. "I need to be checked in."

"You visiting?" the sergeant asks, straightening up.

"Yes," Mathew says.

"*Who* are you visiting?"

"Dr. Roberta Calvin and Dr. Michaela…"

"You mean Dr. Bob and Dr. Mike?" The sergeant chuckles. "Okay. You sit there." He indicates to a seat in front of his desk. "Now, this should only take a second." He gets to his feet a little unsteadily and hobbles around the front of his desk. "I get stiff sitting here all day," he says. "I'd rather have an outdoors job, but this is where they put me. Now, drop your head forward a bit. Just want to get at your bioID… Good, you've done this before." The man runs the scanner across the back of Mathew's neck. There is a loud beep. "Okay. That's done."

Mathew freezes and waits for the man to react. He waits to be told his data isn't right. But the old man hobbles back round to his chair and slumps heavily into the old, soft leatherette. Mathew can't imagine him doing an 'outdoors job'. Having made himself comfortable, Sergeant Charles Baker looks up, surprised Mathew is still there. "The gates will automatically recognise you. You're free to go."

"Everything alright?"

"Yes. You're checked in. That's it."

Mathew stands uncertainly, waiting for the catch, not believing he's got away with it. He says, "Dr. Bob told me to wait for her here."

"She did? There's more chairs over there if you'd be more comfortable." The man points to the other side of the prefab unit. A bank of uncomfortable shrlik office chairs lines the wall. Mathew takes one of the chairs.

A Canvas on the wall shows the news. The volume is muted. The headlines run across the bottom of the screen. They read: "The Coalition government, represented by Deputy Prime Minister Oliver Nystrom, is in talks with the Welsh National Party about border skirmishes. Fighting continues in West Antarctica as the United Republic of Latin America sent troops to Palmer Land. Prime Minister Bartholomew Dearlove is in Washington this week to continue to negotiate the Atlantic States Treaty." Mathew watches an image of Bartholomew Dearlove as he descends the steps of an impressive looking neoclassical building and gets into a car. He stops to talk to a journalist and the camera pans to his face. Thirty-four years on, he looks the same age, perhaps younger.

"Do you want the volume up?" the sergeant asks.

"Yes please," Mathew says.

The sergeant commands the Canvas to unmute. The news report has cycled to the story on the Atlantic States Treaty.

The reporter says, "The treaty will effectively form a new international economic and military superstate composed of much of the former EU. It will run from the Russian border, through Scandinavia, including Iceland, Greenland and all of North America to the new US border with the Republic of Latin American Nations in Texas. Proponents of the treaty argue the proposed superstate, dubbed ATLAS, is necessary for the survival of western ideals and tradition under increased pressure from the newly formed Federation of People's Republics.

There is widespread concern that the Dishonest War, characterised by undeclared biological warfare, cyber attacks, unclaimed terrorist acts by robots and drones and territorial encroachment in Antarctica from Federation members, as they attempt to annex mineral deposit-rich land, will escalate into total war.

In Washington, Prime Minister Bartholomew Dearlove

argued passionately in favour of signing the treaty. He urged his fellow heads of state to put archaic and emotional ideas of nationhood aside. He said a vote for ATLAS is a vote to save Western civilisation.

In Birmingham, protestors gathered before parliament to ask the government not to surrender national sovereignty."

Bob is red-faced as she and Mike burst through the door.

"Hello, Dr. Bob. Dr Mike," Sergeant Baker says. "Been for a run?"

"Oh. Hi, Charlie. We ran all the way down the bloody hill."

"Why did you do that?"

"We were worried we'd miss the boy. But you haven't done him yet."

"No, he's all done and ready to go."

"Ready to go where?"

"Wherever you want to take him. I'm guessing he's staying with you? Although the bunkhouse has accommodation…"

"He's stopping with us," says Mike quickly.

Bob says, "So he's okay then?"

"Why, shouldn't he be?" Charlie asks, mustering a degree of half-hearted suspicion.

"No reason at all," Mike says quickly.

"There is his age," Charlie chuckles. "The system says he's fifty-one." He shakes his head. "I suppose it's meant to be fifteen. He's pretty young to have a doctorate, but then I thought if he belongs to you, he's probably some kind of child prodigy. I'm right, aren't I?"

Bob stares at Charlie. Mike says, "That's right. He's a trainee."

"Thought as much." Charlie pulls opens a drawer, "Do you want a biscuit? Just off the truck from Birmingham this morning. They're meant to have some natural ingredients. Mind you, the young doctor here won't think them anything special - he's a Silverwood resident, after all."

Bob gapes between Charlie and Mathew, "Silverwood?" Mike elbows her and Bob says, "Oh, yeah. He's from Silverwood," but as she turns from Charlie to focus on Mike and Mathew, her face is all questions.

"Where did I put them? Here they are," the sergeant waves a packet of biscuits, opens and offers them.

Mike shakes her head, "No thanks, Charlie."

Bob takes a biscuit, "We'd better get going, then. Thanks, Charlie."

"Have a good evening, ladies. Nice to meet you, Doctor," he says to Mathew.

He is still chuckling to himself when they leave the prefab.

12 THE DISHONEST WAR

Bob and Mike's hut is on the top of the hill on the west side of the park, built on Anglo-Saxon burial mounds. "Perfect for a couple of history enthusiasts," Mike says.

The hut is a weather-boarded prefab building, with peeling white-washed paint, a solar panelled roof, a small roof-mounted windmill, a water-tank and water butts collecting run-off from the gutters.

It is still raining as they approach the hut, a drizzle now rather than a downpour, but the rain runs off the roof into the gutters, as steady as a mountain stream. The little house is surrounded by plant pots of all kinds containing herbs and edible leaves. There's a small grove of fruit trees to the left of the door and a run for chickens, scratching and pecking silently as Mike opens the front door for him.

Inside are three rooms; a bedroom, bathroom and a large room that functions as a dining room, living room and kitchen. He is given a quick tour.

"Palatial by the standards of the park," Mike says. "But we don't have a spare room. You'll have to crash on the couch."

"Couch is great," says Mathew.

She ushers him into the living room and invites him to

sit.

With nightfall, the temperature drops dramatically and Bob kneels before the wood-burning stove to set a fire. They send Mathew off to the bathroom for a hot shower, worried he might catch a chill from his swim.

Before he goes in, Mike hands Mathew a towel and some clothes. "Probably a bit big for you. These belonged to my brother."

Mathew takes the bundle from Mike and goes to the bathroom, a tiny room barely large enough to turn around in, with a basic toilet, a tiny washbasin and a shower. He strips and showers quickly. The water is lukewarm, but there's soap and it is good to get clean. The window is open and he shivers as he dries himself and gets dressed.

Clean, warm and dry, Mathew joins Mike and Bob on their large, low, comfy rug-strewn sofa.

Mike is studying him strangely, he thinks, as he takes his seat next to her.

"Are you ok?" Bob asks her, but she just smiles and nods.

The fire has taken and it crackles and snaps. They wait for it to burn, to turn white-hot. Mike uses tin foil to wrap the potatoes, opens the door to the stove and tosses the potatoes into the smouldering ash. While they bake, she cooks coffee on top of the stove.

Mathew says, "Pete and Charlie called you Dr. Bob and Dr. Mike. Are you medical doctors?"

Bob laughs her throaty laugh, then says as she gradually sobers, "No. No, we're not. Although, given the amount of people who have been killed and injured on this project, it would be useful."

Mike says, "I'm an archaeologist, Bob is a historian. We started off being academics. I'm not sure what you would call us now. We're busy doing stuff; neither of us has written anything for years."

"Applied historians and archaeologists?" Bob suggests.

"We've been here a long time. We worked on St Paul's before this. We're here to add some credibility to a commercial enterprise and to make sure the wrong kind of corners aren't cut, to avoid the Palace of Westminster being rebuilt in Silverwood with the Elizabeth Tower at the wrong end and to prevent the contractors from grinding the ancient bones of the kings and queens of England with their heavy equipment, by mistake."

"How long will you be here?"

Bob glances at Mike, shakes her head, "Until the work is done. We don't know. It's taking us longer than we thought to dismantle and rebuild. Every stone has to be painstakingly catalogued and marked up, in order for it to be put back in exactly the right place. The buildings have been underwater for a long time. There's sludge and rubbish all over the place. Some materials aren't recoverable. We have to make sure we don't destroy anything as we excavate. It all has to be transported across the country.

"We've been here six years. We started off helping with the emergency recovery of objects not retrieved before the big flood. A huge amount has been moved throughout the last ten years. Books from the British Library, art treasures from all the galleries, precious objects from the museums."

"Where are they now?"

"Special vaults and archives to keep it all safe."

"There's a huge archive inside the mountains in Snowdonia. We went to visit it. That's where a lot of the British Library stuff went."

"A lot of paintings, sculptures, other art objects and furniture went to Scotland when the royal family left. Things will come back to Silverwood once the buildings are moved and rebuilt to house them."

"I've had a thought," Mike says. "We're going to Silverwood the day after tomorrow for the grand opening of St Paul's. It will be safe and a straightforward journey with a secure convoy. You could come with us?"

"I want to get started tomorrow," Mathew says. But then he remembers his last journey through one of Mr. Lestrange's doors and how a week went by in tropical Siberia while time stood still in his own time. If time worked the same way here, it didn't matter how long it took him. "Actually, that would be wonderful, thank you."

Mike opens the door to the stove and prods at the white-hot wood and the potatoes with a metal poker. She asks, "Is your mother very sick?"

Mathew nods, "She will die, I think, unless someone helps her."

"Is it Tagus?" Mike asks.

"Tagus?

"The Tagus virus?"

"It is a virus, but the doctors say they don't know what it is."

Mike nods thoughtfully. "People say there are all sorts of strains of viruses. Although we tell people my brother died from Tagus, it might have been any number of variants. The doctors wouldn't say they knew what it was either. All they would say is it killed him by cytokine storm, which basically means his immune system was overwhelmed."

"Some medical people we know told us that what folks call the Tagus is not one virus at all, but several. If you believe them, the Russians made the virus or viruses, or the Latam Republic, or us. There may be antidotes available for certain strains to certain people. The government claims terrorists made it, which may be true. Who knows? No one admits ownership. No one wants to talk about it. They say the worldwide death toll is already greater than the number of people who died during the Spanish flu epidemic."

"And now it's not just the refugee camps any more. It's here amongst us. No one wants to talk about that either."

Mike says, "My brother was a highly qualified engineer with a bright future ahead of him. When he was diagnosed, they took him away. That was the last time we saw him alive. There are rumours of antidotes, but there were none for him. He died within 24 hours."

Mathew's face whitens, "24 hours!"

Bob says quickly, "Some people last a week. I've known people last ten days."

Mike says, "There was a community where people were sick for months, but didn't die. Do you remember?"

Bob nods and smiles encouragingly at Mathew.

Mathew says, "But I don't understand, why don't people know how to cure these viruses? If people created them, they must have made antidotes."

"You must have heard the various governments of the world are conducting an undeclared biological world war."

"The Dishonest War."

"Given the world's ever-diminishing resources, it makes sense to reduce the populations of enemy states. If it is true then neither side will release the antidote to their enemies, presuming they have one. Some people call Tagus "Deliverance" because it struck first in refugee camps. That made people suspicious that it's a more deadly version of the Mercy."

Mathew has heard of the Mercy, "Population control?" he says.

Bob nods, **"**Other people say it is a natural consequence of overpopulation, overcrowding, unsanitary conditions. The Edenists say it's God's judgment."

"For what?"

"For messing with nature and our biological destiny, genetically modified crops, animals and people, for synthetic foods and biology, biobots and biorobotics. And for destroying our climate."

"They do have a point," Mike says.

Bob sneers, "They're all crazy. No good or useful thought ever came from an Edenist."

Mathew's eyes fall on a machine gun propped near the door. "Don't you get tired of carrying guns all the time?"

"We didn't always have to carry guns," Mike says. "When we came here the city was still under the control of the government."

"It still is, officially."

"The police, the army, they lost control here a few years ago. Like the rest of the south. No one admits there is a civil war going on. You know how it goes here now. The weather gets crazy through the winter and spring. People who have found somewhere to live not previously flooded, are flooded again. The infrastructure breaks. Constant energy blackouts, mains water cut off. Roads aren't repaired. Fuel for transport expensive or difficult to get. There's no food. There's endless riots and looting. Yet the government is still raising taxes. So people stop paying because they don't know what they are paying for anymore. Places are too dangerous for the police to go in. Instead they send the army, but the army doesn't know whom it is supposed to be fighting because everyone looks like a civilian. There are no soldiers for them to fight, only kids, gang members, criminals and occasionally a handful of randomly organised ordinary people who have had enough."

"When the government moved north, they took all the people with power, money and influence with them. They left the south to rot. That's where the Edenists come in. They are organised. They provide food and shelter to the homeless, they established schools and hospitals. But the two most important things they provide are something to believe and an army. The Edenist preachers do the talking. The Accountants keep law and order."

"But why do they want to kill you? You are saving churches."

"They don't want to kill us. A lot of them approve of what we are doing because they are traditionalists. They want to return to the old ways. But they spread a message of violence and that leads some to think any government worker is fair game."

"So we live here, behind barbed wire fences, and carry guns with us wherever we go."

Mike crouches next to the fire and opens the glass door of the stove with a glove. "Potatoes are ready, I think." She grabs the tin-foil parcels with iron tongs. "Get some plates and the cottage cheese, Bob, will you?"

Bob goes off to the kitchen, "Butter as well?"

"If there is any."

"Mathew, give me a hand."

Mathew goes into the little kitchen and Bob hands him cutlery and three glasses of water.

While they eat, Mike asks Mathew, "Are you a PhD?"

Mathew smiles, "No. I will be one day, though."

"Charlie said…"

"A mix-up."

"Like your age?"

Bob says, "The system doesn't get data wrong."

"Of course it does," Mike says. "We thought you weren't on the system. That you were Non Grata. Also, because of your e-Pin," she pulls her own earlobe to show him her naked lobe. She isn't wearing an e-Pin. "Most people who can afford it have augmentations. Only the poor still use wearables."

"And the Edenists and Accountants, because they say God made us perfect and it is blasphemous to interfere with God's blueprint," Bob says. "Charlie said you are a resident of Silverwood, which presumably means the system says you are. But Silverwood residents are privileged. The privileged all have implants and you use wearables. Plus, you didn't know how far Silverwood is from London. Why are you really here?"

"I told you, I am trying to save my mother."

"And Charlie thinks you are this doctor from Silverwood. You have someone else's identity, but it is impossible unless you share his DNA."

"I do share his DNA," Mathew says. "We're the same person."

Bob laughs, "Right. I suppose you are about to tell me you are some kind of clone, part of one of those strange projects they run at Silverwood University?"

Mathew says, "Something like that."

Bob whistles through her teeth, "Holy moly," she says. "Best not let any Accountants catch you."

"He's joking," Mike says.

"Of course he's joking."

Mathew smiles awkwardly.

13 LETTERS TO HIMSELF

The sofa makes a comfortable bed. Bob and Mike have turned in for the night and Mathew is alone. There are no curtains at the windows. The sky has cleared of clouds, blown away by a rising breeze, and moonlight floods into the room. The fire is dying, the embers glow deep red against black charcoal. He can't sleep, anxious about the day he will have to wait to get to Silverwood, wondering how long his mother has left.

All the time he's been in this new world, this future London, he hasn't even tried to connect to the Nexus. The last time he travelled through one of Mr. Lestrange's worlds his e-Pin and Lenz didn't work. But, he supposes, here in this time he is still alive. It's worth a try.

He initiates a call with a low whispered voice command aimed at not waking his hosts. A brief login prompt appears before his eyes, surprising him. It says, "Checking bio-ID." A moment later there's a new message. It reads,

Welcome, Dr. Mathew Erlang.

Doctor.
This is my older self. The system thinks I am my older self.
But of course, why wouldn't it?
The same DNA, the same bioID, the same person.
I get my PhD!
The menu of the Nexus is remotely hosted and

updated. The Lenz operating system is quite different from the one he is used to. It takes only a few moments to update.

Then, "News," he says, trying something simple first.

The day's headlines, the ones from Charlie's office, immediately appear before him. He mentally lists the things he should know as a citizen of this world.

"Nexus," he says, "Who is Bartholomew Dearlove?"

"Text or speech?" comes the response.

"Speech."

Through his e-Pin he hears, "Bartholomew Dearlove is the leader of the Universal Popular Party and has been the Prime Minister of England and the head of the coalition government for eleven years. He is serving his third term as Prime Minister.

"Before the general election, there had been calls for him to resign. Many hold him responsible for the continuing civil unrest in the south. However, Deputy Prime Minister and leader of the Garden Party, Oliver Nystrom, offered Mr. Dearlove his full support. He rejected calls for him to take the leadership for himself.

"Mr. Dearlove, formerly the Mayor of London, became Prime Minister after the assassination of seventy-nine-year-old Saul Justice. Mr. Justice was assassinated by one of his own personal guards. On his death, the new Prime Minister, Bartholomew Dearlove, took the decision to call a general election. In his most famous speech, Dearlove hailed the return of democracy to Britain and denounced the emergency government's excessive powers and duration.

"The election of 2080 returned a hung parliament. In the negotiations that followed, Oliver Nystrom accepted the offer of the role of Deputy Prime Minister and the Garden Party won fifty per cent of parliamentary seats, heralding the biggest political shift for 22 years.

"Mr. Dearlove offered his full support to the Garden Party's agenda of adaptation. The coalition government has since worked tirelessly to build climate adaptation infrastructure. The crowning achievement of the coalition will be the new capital city of Silverwood."

Mathew says, "Nexus, tell me about Silverwood."

"Silverwood is the first English Adaptation city. It is situated twenty miles to the west of the interim capital of Birmingham. It is expected to officially become the new capital on the completion of the relocation of the Palace of Westminster. Named after former leader of the Garden Party and prominent adaptation advocate Cadmus Silverwood, the city will extend to four thousand square miles and will house a population of fifteen million, twenty per cent of the total UK population.

Silverwood has been designed to provide safe shelter for humans, with plans based on the most pessimistic climate projections. It exploits state-of-the-art approaches to energy generation and conservation, food production, water management and waste recycling. The design of the city will also take advantage of the natural landscape, with many underground levels built into hills.

Mathew sits for a while, absorbing what he has learnt. Then he opens a new file and names it 'Letter to Myself'. He dictates quietly. His letter reads:

```
    I don't know how to begin or how to convince you
this isn't an elaborate hoax, but I am your sixteen-
year-old self and I am writing to you from Greenwich
Park, half a mile from Pickervance Road. I have
found a door through time. Our mother is dying in a
Panacea hospital from what I believe is a military-
made virus and my only hope of rescuing her is you.
```

14 REVISIT

Tuesday, 13 February, 2091, London

The armoured vehicle's huge thick-treaded wheels clamber over another heap of rubble. Inside, Mathew is thrown against the glass as it lurches to one side. He stifles a yawn and glances at Bob, who grins at him. He spent most of the night on the Nexus and he's barely had two hours sleep. She woke him at five, fired-up with the idea of taking him home. Now she is as pleased as punch with herself for organising this trip for him. Partly, Mathew knows, she wants to check out his story, but once she embarks on it, she starts to tell herself she is doing it for Mathew.

Mathew's old road is a twenty-minute walk from Bob and Mike's hut, but it might as well be on Mars, Mike says - too dangerous to walk on foot. To get them there safely, Bob calls in a favour from one of the soldiers at the camp. The soldier's name is Greg. His job is to patrol the nearby neighbourhoods, and clear the slums, to make sure there are no Non Grata living within a rocket launcher's trajectory of their camp. He's going "up top" anyway as part of his morning patrol. Bob persuades him to take a couple of passengers. Mathew doesn't want to tell Bob he'd rather not know what has happened to the house on Pickervance Road.

"There's nothing much here, y'know," Greg says, his eyes firmly ahead. He scans the landscape for threats with the expert attention of someone with 5 years' experience. Bob has told Greg that Mathew wants to visit an old family home. She hasn't told him Mathew claims he still lives there. Mathew feels he should apologise to Greg. He doesn't want the responsibility for this detour, putting these people's lives at risk.

"I think this is it," Greg says. "There's no road sign but the on-board computer says this used to be Pickervance Road."

Mathew raises his eyes to the front windshield and is amazed.

Rising from the widespread devastation, the piles of rubble, the half-demolished buildings, is a row of neat red-bricked Victorian terraced houses. Most of them have their roofs. A third of the way along the road, the armoured vehicle crushes a pile of bricks beneath it and rolls back to a stop. There is a tree growing right in the middle of the road. It's pushing through the old cracked, sun-baked tarmac surface and blocks their way.

Bob says, raising an eyebrow, "This is where you live?"

Mathew tries to open the truck door. It is locked.

"Just a sec," Greg says. He grabs his gun and his helmet from the passenger seat. They watch him in the road, his helmeted head packed with a whole host of military gadgetry, carefully scanning their surroundings. In addition to the tools the helmet provides, Mike explains that Greg is using his enhanced biological vision to check for signs of human body heat.

Greg comes back to the vehicle and opens Mathew's door, "All clear," he says. "There's no one here."

The tarmac beneath Mathew's feet is broken like the crust of a well-done cake, full of cracks made by roots, bad weather and years of disrepair. Bushes and trees smother the road. As he walks to his front garden, bindweed grabs and snags at his legs. The old olive tree is alive, taller, wider. The front garden wall has collapsed. There are brambles everywhere, growing through the broken windows of the living room. The front door of his house is, incredibly, still there. Peeling blue paint reveals weathered wood underneath. He pushes at it and it opens without resistance. The locks are long broken.

The stairs are dead ahead, bare of carpet and rotten in places. He starts to climb up. His foot goes through the third step and he grabs the handrail to steady himself. It wobbles dangerously. Mathew loses his balance and puts his foot through another rotten board.

"Careful," Bob says. "We don't want you spending tomorrow in medical. Are you sure this is your house?"

Mathew nods. Now he is here, he wants to see it.

More cautiously now, he goes up and tests each step before putting his full weight on it. As he gets to the top, something moves suddenly, frightening him. He flattens himself against the wall and gapes up.

"Pigeons," Greg laughs. "Why is it we managed to kill ninety per cent of the life on this planet but we can't kill pigeons?"

"I'm surprised the maggots haven't killed and eaten them all," Bob says.

Mathew walks across the landing as Greg and Bob climb the stairs. He opens his bedroom door. There are two empty spaces where the windows used to be, one of them part-patched with shrilk sheeting and cardboard. The floorboards are grey and brittle from exposure to the elements. There is an old, stained mattress on the floor and blankets bundled up with a pile of old clothes. Someone is living here.

"Your bedroom?" Bob asks, raising an eyebrow.

Mathew nods.

Across the landing is his mother's room. There's an

actual bed, another stained mattress, a mess of bedclothes, a bit of rotted carpet on the floor and an old sideboard, none of it familiar. The windows are unbroken but the roof has a hole and a bucket underneath, full and overflowing with water.

Bob comes and stands beside him. "So where is your mother?" she asks, now convinced of his story.

"They took her," he says. He rubs his eyes, genuinely overwhelmed and his voice is strained and desperate when he says, "I need to get to Silverwood."

"Okay," Bob says and he knows she will help him.

He gazes at the garden and across at Mr. Lestrange's conservatory.

"Would you look at that," Bob says, coming up beside him. It's got orange trees growing inside it."

It is just as it was in 2055.

15 BREAKFAST WITH THE GOVERNMENT AGENT

Mathew follows Mike and clambers from their boat, into a stranger's flimsy rubber dinghy that tips alarmingly. Then he jumps inelegantly onto the jetty, barely keeping his balance. Bob stands and waits with her gun and a rucksack slung across her shoulders. Behind her, on the wide wooden platform, there is a twelve-foot chain link fence, barbed-wire-topped, just like the park boundary. Bob leads the way through the gate, negotiating Mathew's entrance with the soldier on guard duty. As she talks, Mathew takes it all in. Staircases run at angles between platforms, all across the side and the full height of the giant iron box holding back the Thames from the Houses of Parliament.

Bob smooths things with the guard and they are allowed to go in. She asks, "Do you want to take a look around?"

It is still quite early. People are coming to work. A man in a hardhat and a yellow safety jacket waves to Bob and Mike as they start to climb the staircase.

At the top, Mathew stares at his feet, trying to catch his

breath. Bob elbows him. They peer over the edge of the rusty iron wall. Parliament is below, or what is left of its half-dismantled carcass, hugged by a corset of scaffolding. There is heavy machinery inside; a giant crane rests on a platform, diggers, prefabs and trenches.

Bob says, "Everything has to be lifted by the crane onto the boats. We load containers on barges and take them downriver, where they are put on trucks and then driven to Silverwood. There, another team meets and unloads it and works on restoration, reassembly or storage."

Mike points to one of the trenches far below, "That's where I'm working right now, deep down there. We've found some interesting stuff under the floor from the earlier palaces. We're recovering and recording what information we can while they unbuild the walls around us. Bob works there, supervising the roof being taken off the House of Lords."

Bob says, "I spend two days a week there," she points at the partly dismantled Westminster Abbey, also within the great watertight iron sanctuary. Mathew takes in the edges of the barrier and the water high on the other side.

"We got most of the good stuff a while ago," Mike says. "The interior of Lady Chapel, most of the Kings and Queens, although we lost Bloody Mary's head," she pulls a face. "Bit embarrassing."

There is a persistent wind with a February bite. Mathew shivers.

"We missed breakfast. I'm starving. Let's go to the Anne Bonny," Bob says. "My treat."

The Anne Bonny is an old Thames riverboat converted into a restaurant, one of a number nestled with the other vessels tied to the makeshift Westminster Pier, but the most popular. It's already busy as Mathew, Bob and Mike enter. They come from the top deck via some stairs. At the bottom, there is the titular hero, a female mannequin dressed as a pirate.

They take a booth with a window view across the water and make themselves comfortable. Bob and Mike are reading something. Mathew follows their lead and peers at the table. It's an old wooden piece of furniture, scrubbed, scarred and battered by generations. Over the grain, the grooves, stains and cuts, a menu is projected with holographic versions of the food on offer. He watches Bob and Mike select their food with their hands, reaching and taking virtually what they want to eat in reality. He copies them and says, as they do, "That will be all," when he has finished, hoping he doesn't appear as surprised or impressed as he is.

"Would you look at that!" Bob says nudging Mike.

Bob and Mike both stare across the restaurant at the back of a tall man with short black curly hair, standing by the bar. When he turns, he greets them with a broad, boyish smile.

"Well," he says loudly as he walks across the room towards them. "If it isn't my two favourite historians!"

Bob gets up, "Mr. Quinn Hacquinn!" They kiss and hug like old friends. He leans across the table to greet Mike.

"And who is this handsome young fellow?" he asks, staring at Mathew.

"A friend," Bob says.

"The son of a friend," Mike corrects. "Down from Silverwood."

"And what is the young son of a friend from Silverwood called?"

"Mathew."

"Hello Mathew," he stretches across the table to shake Mathew's hand. "Is there room for one mid-sized bottom around this table?"

They all move around to make room for Quinn, who studies the menu and makes a choice. Once this is done, he settles back and says, "What great occasion could have taken you away from the hallowed walls of the Palace of Westminster? Breakfast at the Anne Bonny is not like you at all. You are usually so puritanical."

Bob says, "This is very like you, on the other hand, you lazy bastard. We're showing our young friend some hospitality. How is business with our Government Agent these days? Any contract issues with the labourers? Disputes over pay or conditions? Maggot children to send to camps?"

"Now, all that is gravely exaggerated gossip. You know I just fill forms all day. I am harmless as a summer cold. Mildly irritating, unpleasant and inconvenient, but necessary to the order of things."

Mike snorts, "Viruses are deadly these days."

Quinn's drink arrives. It is a red concoction. He takes a sip and peers through the glass at the top at his friends, "True enough."

"What is that awful stuff?" Bob asks.

"Bloody Mary. Hair of the dog. Bit of a heavy night last night."

"Your liver must be ready to flambé by now."

"I'm on my third one. There's a spare growing in a Birmingham lab, ready to swap."

Bob and Mike laugh.

Quinn says, "No, seriously. There is. But what is human life without indulgence? It is brutish and short; you may as well live it to excess."

"You are showing us the way, Quinn," Bob says.

"I am fostering a new enlightenment. Or I will when I am sober."

"You are never sober," Bob says.

He grins.

"So what is the young gentleman doing in this godforsaken rat-infested swamp of a dead great city?"

"Apprenticeship."

"Educational work placement."

"Thinking of becoming an archaeologist? You don't

seem the type, somehow," Quinn says as he studies Mathew thoughtfully. "I would more have you pegged as a boy who builds things. Robots and the like."

Mathew flushes as he stares into Quinn's mischievous eyes. He makes a mental note to check his Nexus privacy settings. He mustn't have completely switched his broadcast off.

"Planning to stay long? I only ask because I thought I might be able to help negotiate a daily pass here on site." He says to Bob, "Poor Darren downstairs will get his ears burnt from his boss when he finds out you persuaded him to let your friend through the gates with following the proper procedure."

"He's alright," Bob says. "He's kosher."

"I know he is," Quinn speaks to Bob but fixes his gaze on Mathew with the knowing eye twinkle. He asks Mathew directly, "So how long are you staying?"

"We'll take him to Silverwood with us tomorrow when we go for the St Paul's inauguration," Bob says.

"Such a short trip. What a shame. Barely long enough to take in the sights."

"He needs to get back home."

"My mother is sick," Mathew says.

"Is that so? You must be worried." When Mathew doesn't reply, Quinn says, "Would you like to go sooner?"

Mathew's eyes widen.

Quinn continues, "There's a government caravan heading north this afternoon. I'm going with it. You could come with me, if you want to, Mathew. I mean, I don't want to take you away from your friends and shorten your trip, but if you'd like there'd be space for you."

Bob says, "This wouldn't be one of your tricks, Quinn, would it? No detours to Internment or suchlike?"

"The boy's legit; you said it yourself. He has bioID. I saw Darren's log. He has a pass to the city of Silverwood. I want to get the boy home. You forget; part of my job is to make sure people are in the right place. I am trying to help, but if you don't trust me…"

"I love you, Quinn, you know I do, but you are a terrible human being."

Quinn clutches his heart dramatically, "Ouch, you wound me!"

They laugh.

Mathew says, "When would I get to Silverwood if I came with you?"

"Tonight. As long as the convoy isn't hijacked by Accountants and we aren't all lined up against the nearest vertical surface and gunned into mincemeat."

Mathew looks at Bob and Mike.

Mike says, "You should go if you want to. A day is a long time when someone has the virus."

Mathew nods. He says to Quinn, "I'll come with you."

"Excellent!" Quinn says. "A travelling companion. It is a while since I have had a young impressionable person to share my life's wisdom with. We shall have such fun together."

Bob sighs, "Mathew, you should wear earplugs for the whole journey."

Their food arrives, served by a pirate-themed robotic waiter, complete with tricorn hat and eyepatch.

Quinn necks the rest of his Bloody Mary. He says to the waiter, "I'll need another one of those."

After breakfast, Mathew says goodbye to Mike and Bob on the jetty, while Quinn prepares his boat.

"Contact us, if you'd like," Mike says. "Let us know how things go with your mum."

"I will if I can," Mathew says.

"Don't pressure the boy," Bob says. "Come here and give me a hug before you go, though." Mathew is swamped by Bob's many layers of clothing and her ample bulk. Her hug is so hard, when she lets go he gasps for air. She laughs at him.

Mike holds his shoulders and says, "Take care of

yourself. We'll be thinking of you."

Mathew nods.

In the boat, Quinn swears loudly, unable to get the engine to start. "This bloody thing!" he says. "I had it serviced a week ago. That criminal Flekerton doesn't know one end of a spanner from a hosepipe. I'm going to have to row."

"Row!" Bob says amazed. "If you row you won't reach the supply camp until dinner time."

"Nonsense! See these guns?" he says, mock-flexing his biceps. "Oarsman's arms, forged in the Blue Boat at Oxford."

"You never rowed for Oxford."

"I did too."

"You are such a bloody liar."

"A second arrow to my heart within a morning. I am amazed at your brutality. Look, the river is flowing in. It'll do most of the work. Get in, Mathew, and grab that rope off the bollard there."

Quinn scoops the oars from the bottom of the boat and fits them into the rowlocks. He starts to push away using the sides of the other boats around them. "Goodbye, ladies. We will meet again when my wounded heart is healed." They glide from the cram of the boats into the river but not yet into the swell. "You should go. We'll be a while."

Bob and Mike wave. Mathew waves back. They turn and start to walk towards the stairs, as Quinn slowly rows into the river. He watches them climb up, tiny figures on the side of the huge structure.

When they are near the top, Mike stops and stares at the boat. She says to Bob, "You know they are far on the other side of the river."

"They are fine. Quinn is alright. He'll get the boy home if he's says he will. Now come on. We've got a historic monument to move."

16 A FRIEND OF MR. LESTRANGE

Mathew watches the Shell Centre loom closer and larger with each pull of the oars Quinn makes.

"We're not going down the river," Mathew says.

"No, we're not."

"Where *are* we going?"

Quinn is less loquacious since they parted from Bob and Mike. He regards Mathew impassively, puts more back into the oars and they move steadily forward across the fast-running current. Mathew thinks the government agent must be incredibly strong.

"You're not taking me to Silverwood, are you?"

The man's face is brutal when he doesn't smile. The curl at the edge of his lips, so engaging at breakfast, is now like a sneer. Suddenly he isn't that friendly anymore.

"Are you taking me to the camp?"

"No, I'm not taking you to the camp."

"You said we needed to row downstream to catch the caravan to Silverwood."

The Shell building looms above them. Mathew starts to panic. "Why are you bringing me back here?"

Quinn sighs, "I am taking you home."

Then the knowing comments fall into place. He says, "You're a friend of Mr. Lestrange."

The government agent smiles, but he doesn't deny it.

"Aren't you?" Mathew persists.

"I'm a man who takes care of waifs and strays, and you are a long way from home, Mathew."

"You're lying. Bob said you're a liar."

Mathew stands and the boat rocks precariously. Quinn drops the oars and lunges across, grabs Mathew's arms and forces him back into his seat. "Don't be an idiot. Sit. You'll fall in."

"What do you care?"

"I care very much. I would have to go after you and it would be tiresome. But the result would be the same. I would still take you home. Why waste the energy?"

"I'm not going home. Not yet."

"But you have to."

"My mother is dying."

"Don't you think you should be with her, rather than messing around here?"

"I am trying the only way I know how to help her."

"This will not help her. Trust me, I know."

Mathew gapes at Quinn, appalled. "Whatever it is you people are, you are not human."

Quinn catches his eye. "Ah, Mathew," is all he says.

They have come around the east side of the Centre and are now hidden from Parliament and the gaggle of boats across the river. Quinn turns his head, looking for a landing place. It is low tide; the high water mark is etched into the fabric of the building. The lower water level has revealed a broken window, flooded when he had tried to escape the day before.

Quinn prepares to bring round the boat. Then he stops, listens for a moment and sighs deeply. "Quinn Hacquinn," he says to himself. "You're getting weak. You're getting sloppy. You're going native."

He turns around slowly just before another boat appears, as if he has seen it coming through the back of his skull. It is a larger craft powered by an electric motor, cutting its way through the water, silent and stealthy, with a crew of four rough men, all on their feet.

One of the men says, as the boat slides towards them, "Afternoon, both. You beat us to it." His words indicate friendliness, but he does not look friendly. He is white-skinned but black with dirt. He has dreadlocks; not a fashion statement, but what happens to hair when it's neither cut nor washed for months on end. "We have ourselves a small territorial dispute here."

The stranger's boat comes alongside them. One of the other men lunges across and grabs the side of their boat.

Quinn is standing now, watching them. "We don't want any trouble," he says.

"Good. Neither do we. So, you'll be off then."

"Oh, we won't be leaving," Quinn says. "You will."

The man on the boat laughs and grins at his crewmates, who also think this is funny.

Quinn continues, "No, I mean it. There's nothing for you here. There's no unbroken safe, hidden behind a forgotten mildewed painting, containing the forgotten millions of a former oil company chairman. It's a waste of your time."

"You think we're idiots? We're not here for treasure. We're here for the furniture."

"The furniture?"

"Yes, the office furniture. We renovate office chairs and old desks and flog them to blokes in the north who have need of them and possess too much money."

"The furniture! By all means. You go ahead, gentlemen. Don't let us interrupt you."

"And what will you be doing?"

"We'll wait here."

The man squints at Quinn suspiciously. "You're well dressed. Are you one of that lot from there?" he indicates with his head towards Westminster.

"He's a leech, Seb. I'm sure I recognise his face from somewhere."

One of the other men says, "I know who he is. He's the government agent."

"No, no," Quinn says. "You're totally wrong," he glares meaningfully at the man who has spoken. The man is suddenly doubtful.

"We're good Edenist folk, father and son, out for a weekday paddle, hoping to find something to brighten our little shack."

"'Grief, he doesn't half talk funny."

"He's going to report us," the man with dreadlocks says. "I bet he's already sent an alarm through to security. He's probably got neural implants."

"Aren't you tired?" Quinn asks.

"What?" the Dreadlocked man says.

"Doesn't all this scavenging and furniture-hauling make you tired?"

"What's he saying?" says one of the men who stands behind Dreadlocks. Then he suddenly yawns and crashes to the bottom of the boat, dead asleep. Dreadlocks gapes at his fallen comrade, just as his second companion also falls from standing. He slumps first to his knees and then heavily forward onto his face. The dreadlocked man grabs for his gun, but as he does so, his eyes glaze over, a lazy, rather soppy expression passes across his face, the faint flicker of a soft smile. He drops to the ground, but as he does so, so does his gun, and it explodes.

The next thing he knows, Mathew is lying on the bottom of the boat. Quinn has lunged across him with such speed Mathew hardly believes what has happened. They peel off one another slowly. Quinn sits and examines his side. There is blood everywhere.

"You've been shot!" Mathew says.

"Oh, it's nothing," Quinn says, completely unfazed. There's no pain on his face. He is mildly irritated, like someone has spilt red wine on his best white shirt. "Now would you look at that? What a mess!" He tuts. "I am going native. Slow as a slug. Pathetic little earth-bound creature."

Quinn unbuttons his shirt and spreads it, exposing his skin and a red oozing wound. Mathew doesn't understand how Quinn is not unconscious; the blood loss is profuse.

He says to Mathew, "You might want to turn away, if you're squeamish. Sorry."

Quinn holds his fingertips above the wound. The bullet draws from his skin gradually, as if Quinn has finger magnets. Once it is removed, the bullet hangs in mid-air. Quinn plucks hold of it with his fingertips, rubs it clean on his shirt, examines it against the light and then throws it in the Thames.

"Damned stupid things, bullets," he says. "What sort of a life form would invent anything so pointless?"

Mathew stares at Quinn's ribcage, his jaw hanging open. The wound is healing itself; the blood recedes, the skin knits together.

"Who are you?" Mathew says to him, wonderstruck.

"Nobody, really," Quinn says and then suddenly laughs. He shakes his head and stands up and puts his shirt back on, buttoning it as he walks to the front of the boat. "Bloody great hole in my shirt now," he is saying, pulling at the material, sticking his fingers through the bloodied, ragged hole.

"Can't you just…?" Mathew says.

"Of course I can!" Quinn stares back at Mathew. He says, "Please don't sit there gaping. This is getting tiresome. You know you've got to go home. You know I will make you go home. Get up. Come on."

Quinn steps across the boat, grabs Mathew's arm, hauls him to the broken window and throws him inside the building. Mathew staggers and slips on the slick muddy surface of the room, a green subterranean cave; the walls, carpeted with moss, drip with water.

"Across here," Quinn says, pushing Mathew from behind. They wade through riverbed sludge as they cross the room and reach the staircase, "We go now. You should know the way. It's a two-way door."

They start to climb.

"You could save her, couldn't you? Why won't you let me save her?" Mathew says. "I don't understand."

"Keep going," Quinn says. "You'll be home soon."

They come to a landing. Mathew hesitates, "What are you waiting for?" Quinn says, "We need to cross the office, don't you remember?"

This is my last chance.

He makes a run for the roof.

"Oh, for God's sake," Quinn says.

Taking the stairs two at a time, Mathew scrambles the last ten steps with his hands as well as his feet.

Outside, he gets to the edge of the wall and pauses, wondering whether he'll survive the fall and if he does, whether he'll survive the Thames current. Quinn tackles him to the ground. Mathew punches, struggles, yells. He does not know how long this goes on, but eventually he is tired; eventually he calms and sobs and Quinn lets him go and installs himself next to him, a few feet away.

"It will be alright," Quinn says quietly.

The shots come from nowhere.

A burst of violent sound and with the noise Quinn's chest bursts open, blossoming red splashes in an impossible number of places. He slumps, face forward, sprawled on the ground, and lies there motionless.

"Quinn!" Mathew says, rushing to him. He turns him over by yanking at his shoulder. There's a flicker of a smile on Quinn's lips, "I told you I was going native," he whispers.

"Do the thing you did before. Take the bullets out."

"I can't. They're watching. They are watching every move we make." He strains his eyes to focus on Mathew, "Go home. Please. You have no idea what is at stake." He sighs. "I did always want to know what this was like."

And he dies chuckling, choking on his own blood."

17 KILFEATHER'S ARM

Mathew sits, waits and listens to the steady sound of footsteps on the stairs. They are talking and laughing. He can't believe it. They've killed a man and they are actually laughing. Their voices bounce off the bare walls of the stairwell and echo. It crosses his mind that he should move. He should stand and run for the door, back to Mr. Lestrange's house. At the very least he should hide, because these men are murderers. But to move he would have to step across Quinn's body and the surprisingly large pool of blood it is in. So he just sits.

The footsteps get closer.

Then, just as he expects the men to appear, silence falls. After several long seconds, the muzzle of a gun edges around the corner of the doorframe. On the other end is a man in an ill-fitting grey military-style uniform: combat jacket and trousers and bullet-proof vest. His head is shaved, the skin on the side of his skull is tattooed, and he has a long red beard. The gun's sights rest on Quinn for a moment longer and then drop. The red-bearded man goes to Quinn, crouches, grabs his face, prizes open an eyelid, then drops the dead head with disgust. It falls back and hits the flagstones hard with an unpleasant thump.

"'S okay," the man says. "The leech is dead. The boy is here. He isn't armed."

Two other men come through the doorway; a tall, muscular black man and a shorter, dusky-skinned, barrel-chested man. The latter goes straight to Quinn's body and riffles through his pockets. He pauses to examine the things he finds and then pops them in a bag.

The black man studies Mathew. "I'm Kilfeather. This is Jonah Marshall," he says, gesturing to the bearded man. "And the man with no conscience, looting from the dead, is Ran Drake."

Kilfeather extends his hand to help Mathew to his feet. The hand is prosthetic. Mathew stares dumbly. He finds himself unable to speak or move.

"Are you hurt?"

Mathew somehow manages to shake his head.

"Good," Kilfeather says. "Then we should be getting along. The leeches in Westminster probably heard the gunfire. We don't have much time."

When they reach the bottom of the steps, they wade back through the water across the office to the broken window. There are now three boats: Quinn's little wooden dinghy with the broken engine, the boat with the dreadlocked man and his companions still asleep inside and Kilfeather's larger, newer boat.

"What do you think?" asks Drake, who jumps across into the dreadlocked man's boat and kicks at his boot. "They're breathing. They're not drunk." He bends and sniffs, "Can't smell it, at least. Drugs?"

Kilfeather shakes his head. "Haven't a clue and we haven't got time to find out. They'll have to take their chances. Listen."

The sound of voices and a boat slapping on water.

"The leeches are coming. We should go."

Drake leaps back. Jonah has already started the engine and they creep forward. Skirting the perimeter of the building, they emerge by Waterloo Station and float beneath the Victory Arch, with Britannia and her trident rising still above the water.

"They're not following," Jonah says, looking back over his shoulder.

"They'll have found Quinn's empty boat and have gone inside to search for him. They'll think those men asleep did it, and if they don't we'll be well away by the time they clock on. Let's keep the pace steady, though, and steer away from the river until we get to Battersea."

Something glints on Kilfeather's wrist, as he takes a seat next to Mathew. At first Mathew thinks it is a glove, but then he remembers Kilfeather's left hand is prosthetic. Whoever made the prosthetic didn't try to make it seem like a real hand. It is matte black with silver highlighted joints.

Kilfeather notices Mathew staring at his hand. "Not seen one of these before?" Mathew shakes his head, still unable to speak. He realises he is shaking. Kilfeather must have noticed too, but he doesn't say anything. Instead, he says, "It goes right to my shoulder. Want to look?"

Mathew nods.

Kilfeather unbuttons his shirt. The prosthesis is actually attached to Kilfeather's skin. "It connects to my nerves inside," he says. "See?" He flexes his fingers. "This *is* my arm. My fingertips have the same level of sensation as yours." There is a symbol etched into the black surface of his bicep, a kind of tattoo, an image like a shepherd's crook, but with extra lines. Kilfeather watches Mathew's eyes rest on it.

"Now you're wondering what that is?"

Mathew nods again.

"It's the feather of Ma'at. An ostrich feather. It's an ancient Egyptian symbol. Ma'at was the Egyptian's idea of truth and justice and also a goddess who battled chaos. When Ancient Egyptians died, Ma'at would weigh their hearts against the heaviness of a feather. If they were full of sin, their heart would tip the scale away from the feather and the soul-eating monster goddess Ammit, who was part-lion, part-hippopotamus, part-crocodile, would eat it. If their heart was light, they started their journey to paradise. Jonah doesn't like it, do you Jonah?" Jonah doesn't respond. Instead, he spits over the side of the boat and stares at the buildings they weave their way through. "Jonah doesn't approve of my ostrich feather or my arm," Kilfeather says. "What do you think?"

"It's cool," Mathew says, finding his voice.

"Aren't you surprised I have this?"

"No," Mathew says.

"Didn't the leeches tell you all Accountants are religious loonies and we don't use technology?"

"You're an Accountant?"

Kilfeather laughs, "The real McCoy. What did you think we were?"

"I don't know," Mathew says.

"Why do you think we helped you?"

"Helped me?"

"We saw the leech monster attack you. That's why we shot him. That and the fact he was a notorious leech who arrested free people and locked them in virus-infested camps. He'd been on our list for a long time. When we saw you had got yourself into a bit of a scrape with the leech on the roof of the building back there, we were only too glad to help. So no need to thank us," Kilfeather says. He uses a tone that suggests he thinks it would be much better if Mathew did thank him.

"Thank you," Mathew says.

"You're welcome."

They pass Lambeth Palace, the old red-brick turrets a reminder of the long period of stable human civilisation now left behind.

"What were you doing with him?"

Mathew thinks quickly. "I was hunting for things to salvage when he found me."

Kilfeather nods. "Were the men asleep in the boat your friends?"

Mathew doesn't speak He makes a slight, ambiguous movement with his head.

"It's alright. We're on your side. This isn't an interrogation."

Mathew gazes dumbly at Drake and Jonah, who share this sentiment and nod encouragingly.

"What did he do to them?" Jonah asks, "They were out cold."

Mathew shrugs, "I don't know."

"Some neural trickery, no doubt," Jonah says, disgusted. "Some mind-tech voodoo."

"They have brain modems now," Drake says. "They think-speak amongst one another and read other people's thoughts."

"Nonsense," Kilfeather says.

"It's true," Jonah says.

"God knows how we're going to win against them. They aren't human anymore," Drake says.

Mathew says, "Quinn Hacquinn wasn't human."

All the men think he means metaphorically and they nod sympathetically.

"We'll win," Jonah says. "Don't you worry. Our time is nigh. We'll bring them, their machines and their science abominations crashing to earth. As the book says, 'If my people, who are called by my name, will humble themselves and pray, and turn from their wicked ways, and seek my face, I will hear from Heaven and will heal their land.'"

Kilfeather says to Mathew, "I'm sorry to say, the leeches probably got your friends. Did you live with them?"

Mathew again resorts to the barely perceptible head tilt, which might be interpreted as a nod.

"The boy is canny," Drake says. "Not going to spill any beans."

"He's loyal and careful with his words. A virtue these days," says Kilfeather sharply. He aims the words at Drake perched at the stern, steering the boat. Then he turns to Mathew. "Do you have anywhere to stay? Is there anywhere we can drop you?"

"Not here, no. I'm heading north."

"North where?"

"Silverwood."

Drake splutters. The men exchange glances.

Jonah says, "They only admit leeches. Are you a leech?"

"The boy's never a leech. Look at him. His augments are all external. Old tech. He's not a zombie. Look at his hair, his weird clothes. He's as much a free man as you or I," Drake says.

"In these dark days, I am suspicious of everyone," Jonah says seriously.

"Why Silverwood?" Kilfeather asks.

"I need to speak to somebody."

"We all need to speak to somebody from Silverwood, boy," Drake says, chuckling. "How are you planning to get there?"

Mathew shrugs.

"We're going your way. Do you want to come with us?" Kilfeather asks.

Drake guffaws. He reaches over and slaps Mathew on the back, "Careful. You're being recruited."

Kilfeather shoots Drake a glance.

Jonah says, "You should tell the boy what he'd be getting himself into."

Kilfeather nods. "You're right, Jonah." He turns to Mathew, "I'll tell you what I believe and why."

Drake groans.

"Why don't you watch for floaters, Corporal?" Kilfeather says.

Drake begrudgingly stands and moves to the front of the boat.

Kilfeather leans forward, close to Mathew's face, and says, "A leech, a monster, took my hand for stealing food. I was a starving eight-year-old, and he sent me away with a bleeding stump. It turned gangrenous. No human being would do such things to a child. I realised then the leeches aren't human at all. The country has been invaded by a plague of monsters. The doctor who saved my life was a human being, but she had to take the rest of my arm off, which stopped the infection spreading. She saved my life. And another human being made this for me," he says, holding his arm above his head. "I am an Accountant because the leeches made me one the day they took my hand. Most of the Accountants are men and women like me. We weren't looking for a fight or a cause. We were all of us trying to live. Just trying to survive. They made enemies of us. We had no choice. We fight or we surrender and die like animals.

"Many of the people who hate the scientists have lost loved ones to a virus made by a government laboratory. The whole world is worried the Mercy is spreading and they know somewhere, for God-only-knows-what reason, scientists made it. The Edenists and the Accountants both want a different world order. The Edenists believe it is God's punishment and they don't fight for change. They think it will come anyway. The Accountants fight because all of this - the weather, the state of the country, the viruses - it is all men doing reckless, arrogant, cruel things. That's why I'm proud to be amongst their number."

From the front of the boat, Drake claps, slow and genuinely appreciative, and then notices Jonah. "He doesn't like what you said regarding the God-squad, Sir."

"No, indeed," Kilfeather says. "He's entitled to his opinion. As I am mine."

"But you still haven't told the boy what he's getting himself into," Drake says.

"You're right, Drake." Kilfeather regards Mathew thoughtfully. "Would you like to join an army, Mathew?"

"An army?"

"A righteous army."

"I…"

"Join us. Come with us and tomorrow we will take you to Silverwood."

18 THE CASTLE

The long snaking river of the westward Thames is no longer, as it once was many years ago, a tame, pastoral stretch of water. It sprawls and is savage, broadening across the flat lands of the Thames Valley, forming lakes around drowned, abandoned towns. Richmond, Kew Gardens, and Hampton Court are all part-submerged worlds. The locks along the river are drowned. Even at low tide, the river rages high above them. It has made the ancient waterway one of the most efficient ways to get around, now the roads and the motorways are full of potholes and armed gangs with bad intent patrol them.

"We will put a stop to it," Kilfeather says as they pass another boat and wave to the crew and passengers. "This river is safe because we own it. We will end the lawlessness on the roads. Ironic, isn't it, that the insurgents should be the ones to bring law and order back to the land?"

They approach Windsor. The castle rises from the water at dusk. Mathew is amazed when they turn towards the ancient grey walls. No one had told him where they were going, but this is the most unlikely destination of all.

"Are we stopping here?" he asks Kilfeather.

"Yes. This is home," he says, but he is preoccupied now, thinking ahead. No longer with Mathew.

They take the boat along the High Street, almost to the corner of Castle Street, where there is a jetty.

Kilfeather jumps as soon as the front of the boat touches dry land. Without a word of goodbye to Mathew, without even acknowledging Jonah or Drake, he starts to stride away, head bowed in thought. He heads to the Henry VIII Gateway. Armed soldiers stand to attention and make way as he approaches.

"What should we do with the boy?" Jonah shouts after Kilfeather.

Kilfeather turns as he walks and shouts back, "Feed him. Find him somewhere to sleep. Make him welcome."

Jonah and Drake finish tying up the boat. They stand and stare at Mathew.

"I'm not a frickin' babysitter," Jonah says to Mathew. "You are old enough to take care of yourself. We'll take you to the mess hall. The bunkhouse is in the state apartments. Use your initiative."

They pass through the gates, into the Lower Ward. The guards know and greet Jonah and Drake.

A long line of men stands outside St George's Chapel, queuing, waiting patiently to enter.

"The Vicar's busy tonight," Drake says.

"He's running round-the-clock services. They want to take Communion before they go," Jonah says. "Not everyone thinks like Kilfeather. In fact, judging by the length of that line, most people don't think like Kilfeather."

"He's a smart man," Drake says.

Jonah snorts, "You know Ransom Farmer, the lay preacher, says Kilfeather's arm is an abomination."

They step aside as two men pull and push a cart full of stacked metal boxes up the slope of cobbles.

"Ransom Farmer is an idiot. With his arm, Kilfeather is one of the most effective soldiers we have. If he didn't have it, he'd be sweeping floors."

"Ransom Farmer says Kilfeather *should* be sweeping

floors. Or worse. Says he's a coalition spy. Says he's an abomination, quoted Leviticus at us: 'For no one who has a defect shall approach: a blind man, or a lame man, or he who has a disfigured face, or any deformed limb, or a man who has a broken foot or broken hand'."

"That's nonsense. The Director trusts him with his life."

"Maybe. Perhaps it's because Director Hathaway has augments himself."

"Hathaway?"

"There are rumours his eye isn't real."

"His eye?"

"They say he has an augmented eye."

"Which eye?"

"I don't know."

"You don't know. You don't know because there's nothing wrong with Hathaway's eyes. I've spoken to him many times. He's a whole man."

"You're right, there's nothing wrong with his eyes. That's precisely why it's strange."

"Why?"

"Because people say they're not his own."

"People shouldn't spread gossip about Hathaway. They should be careful about using scripture against Kilfeather, too."

"But he has strange ideas. He is not godly."

Drake laughs and then starts to cough. "I hope for your sake you never say so around Kilfeather. His abominable hand crushes men's skulls."

"Ha! Who told you that? Have you seen him do it?"

"I've seen him crush a melon with one hand. It burst into pieces."

"Bull. Where'd he get a melon from? If he had one, he wouldn't waste it."

Jonah and Drake squabble all the way to the Round Tower. Soldiers – men and women – are everywhere, lugging kit bags and supplies. They all head away from the town.

Mathew, Drake and Jonah follow the crush through the Norman Gate, into the Upper Ward and the state apartments. They take stone steps into the castle and get carried along with the crowd along stone-floored passageways and through rooms with high ceilings.

Mathew's awestruck eyes comb his surroundings. The walls are mainly bare, with large square discoloured patches where paintings were once hung. They climb the Grand Staircase, the carpet worn threadbare beneath army boots. Roses of armour and ancient weapons still blossom on the walls, breastplates, pots, war hammers, battle-axes and pikes. Mathew strains back his neck and gapes at the plaster fan-vaulted ceiling as they pass into the Grand Vestibule. The crowd splits here and Mathew starts to walk the wrong way.

Jonah grabs his arm. "This way," he says. "They're going to St George's Hall. We're allocated to the Waterloo Chamber."

The long hall is crammed with three great tables and chairs. There's a shorter table like the hat of a triple 't' at the top end. There are hundreds of places, but they fill quickly. The room buzzes with the energy of two hundred men and women. The noise is deafening.

Around the edges of the room there are long narrow tables spread with food; huge pots of stew, curry, rice, potatoes, all kinds of vegetables, and food smells mingle in an air already thick with the scent of humid bodies.

Mathew takes his place in the queue behind Jonah and Drake, who pass crockery and cutlery along the line to him. He follows behind and loads his plate, hungry after the day's events. Then they find seats together at one of the banquet tables.

The crowd of people around him is as diverse as a busy London street in 2055. Men and women of all ages, races, shapes and sizes. There is a general attempt at a uniform.

It is more of a token gesture; the grey combat trousers and jackets of Mathew's companions are many different shades and types of material, patched and ill-fitting. Many people wear their own clothes as well as their uniforms.

Mathew's eyes are drawn upwards to the ceiling, fashioned to look like the hull of a ship from the early nineteenth century. The golden ceiling glows; the chandeliers still hang and are lit above them like many little suns. The paintings that once hung on the wood panels around the room have been removed, like most things of value, but the limed carvings remain, as does the ornate carpet.

"It's the largest seamless carpet in existence," Drake says, noticing Mathew staring at it. "Shame, isn't it?" he says as they watch someone spill curry from their plate onto the floor. "Ruined now, of course."

"Prisoners made it," Jonah says. He chews with his mouth open. "Poor buggers. People like us."

"We're not prisoners anymore."

"No, indeed. The meek shall inherit the earth."

"Amen to that, brother."

The table's surface is bedecked with yet more food, baskets of bread, fried potatoes, a clutter of salts, peppers and all kinds of condiments. There are scraps of material, a patchwork to protect the surface of the table, but the bare parts are marked with heat rings and the veneer is chipped. Someone has carved initials near Mathew's place. There is copious wine and beer. Most of the people are drunk.

Drake offers Jonah some ale from a jug. Jonah refuses, taking water instead. He pours Mathew a cup and says, "We will be leaving early tomorrow. These men shouldn't be drinking. They won't be fit for service tomorrow."

Drake says, "This might be their last night on earth. You can't begrudge them a drink or two."

Jonah sniffs, "What use is an army if half of them are hung over?" But his heart isn't in it.

Mathew wants to ask questions - he wants to know

more about the army and where they are going, but he worries it is another one of those things he should know and his ignorance will betray him. Instead he stays quiet.

Drake tucks into his food with gusto, using his hands. Jonah catches Mathew's eye and says, "He was never house-trained."

Drake says, "For an Accountant, you have a lot of bourgeois attitudes." He turns to Mathew, "I was born on the streets and this man, who claims to be a leader of the people's army, thinks it's something to look down upon."

"No I don't," Jonah says. "But nor does it elevate you. And you *do* know how to use a knife and fork; you choose not to."

"Hark at him," Drake says.

Jonah observes Mathew. "I'm curious. We have brought you all the way along the river, from London to this ridiculous place, and you have not once expressed surprise at us being here."

Mathew says, "It's a lot to take in."

"It is too. I still find it crazy and we've been here eighteen months. Leave the lad alone, Jonah," Drake says.

"He could be anyone."

"A leech attacked him. That makes him *my* friend."

Jonah says to Mathew, "Do you have any idea what will happen tomorrow?"

Mathew shakes his head.

"He's a lamb," Drake says. "An innocent lamb amongst wolves."

"The people's army, they are wolves are they? Which side are you on, Drake?" Jonah says.

Drake takes a long draw on his beer and nods to the door, "Here comes our Chief Accountant, to tell me straight which side I'm on."

Mathew turns his gaze to where Drake has indicated. A hush has fallen. It ripples across the room like a wave; loud whispered calls for quiet herald total silence.

"I bet you never thought you'd be in the same room as

Director Hathaway!" Drake says to Mathew.

Someone shushes Drake. People turn and stare at him. Drake does mock surrender, raising his hands.

A man has come into the room. He stands with Kilfeather, who towers above him. He is small and thin-boned, sandy-haired with a soft, pretty face. He's dressed in combat gear, the same humble grey uniform as the rest of the Accountant army, but on him it is too neat, like dress-up clothes for a very tidy child. When he speaks it is softly; the men have to lean towards his voice.

He says, "None of us want to be here tonight. We want to be at home with our families and our friends, eating dinner, going to bed on a full stomach, having a good night's sleep in our own beds with the knowledge we will wake the next day and do useful work, live our lives like normal people do.

"We have been brought here against our wills. The government called us to arms because it denies us these simple rights. It has taken our homes from us, our means of earning a living, our work. For most of us, at one time or another, it has taken the food from our mouths. The country is drowning and where it is not drowned, a rot has set in. Because we do not believe this is inevitable and necessary, we are forced against our wills into the roles of soldiers and from tomorrow we will be leaders..."

There are cheers and shouts.

He waits, raises his hand to quieten the crowd, "We will be the conquerors of our own country. If we want to live, we have to take this land back and make it ours again. So tomorrow, you must make your reluctant hands take a gun and use it against other men. I do not say 'your countrymen' because the men of government, the men building Silverwood, they are traitors to this country..."

More shouts and another patient pause.

When silence has resumed he says, "We are the walking dead. We only have ourselves to blame. We have allowed what is rightfully ours to be taken from us."

The men shout at the tops of their voices now. Hathaway raises his voice above theirs to say, "To live again, we have to fight. We will fight to take back our lives."

Mathew watches the small sandy-haired man curiously as he walks along the side of the hall with Kilfeather at his side. The other men reach just to touch him. He is ill at ease with the attention, slightly embarrassed and impatient to be elsewhere. Hathaway is on the other side of the hall but all the time he gets closer until there is only a table between them. He has stopped to talk to someone. As Hathaway leans to speak into the man's ear, his eyes focus across the table and fix on Mathew.

He has piercing blue eyes. They flash with recognition. Hathaway's white skin discernibly whitens, like he has seen a ghost. He turns to Kilfeather, says something Mathew can't hear, but it is obvious they are talking about him. A moment later, Hathaway makes his exit towards the Grand Staircase. Kilfeather lingers behind. When the hubbub dies he comes over.

"Are you done with your dinner?" he asks.

Mathew nods.

"Good. Then you're coming with me."

19 DIRECTOR HATHAWAY

Mathew tries to keep pace with Kilfeather's stride. They pass through room after room and then make pace along a corridor; the whole place bustles with men and women who part as Kilfeather marches forward.

Mathew studies the ceilings decorated with fine plasterwork, the wood panels on the walls, the once fine wallpaper, torn off and shredded. The bare floors take punishment from thousands of pairs of uncaring boots. Through open doors Mathew glimpses army beds, bunks with men and women packing backpacks, or sitting, talking, drinking, thinking.

Bright light falls through the tall windows on the right of the corridor. They stop briefly to let some soldiers carrying heavy equipment pass. Mathew looks through the window. Down below, the Upper Ward is floodlit and full of tiny, frenetic figures. In the centre of the quadrangle there are tents pitched.

"Come on," Kilfeather barks, already marching off along the corridor.

Finally they turn, walk across a stairwell and climb a flight of stone steps to a room, small by the standards of the rooms they have passed through. There is a long table, some ordinary office chairs and a bank of Canvases on a wall. In one corner there is a battered sofa and a couple of armchairs.

"Wait here," Kilfeather says. "Bathroom's down the hall. I've got to go."

Mathew says, "What am I waiting for?"

"Who. *Who* are you waiting for? You are waiting for Director Hathaway. For some reason better known to himself, he wants to waste his precious time talking to you. I can't. You stay here, until he comes for you."

Kilfeather leaves, closing the door behind him, and Mathew is alone.

A beam of light flashes across the window on the far wall and illuminates the whole room for a few moments. Mathew goes over to look out.

Night has fallen. The sky above is inky-black but, as with the quadrangle, the park is lit as bright as day. Floodlights run all the way along the Long Walk, which is lined with tents and vehicles that stretch into the park beyond. People are busy loading lorries and vans. A chopper lands on a makeshift helipad. A search lamp mounted on a wooden tower sweeps the camp, casting silhouettes on moving figures. Mathew catches his breath. He is looking at an enormous army. There must be thousands of them.

Still at the window, he logs on to the Nexus and says, "Nexus, where am I?"

The AI responds, "Text or speech?"

"Speech."

"I will speak your answer. If you wish to switch to text at any time, please use the command, 'Nexus, switch text.' I will continue with your answer. You are currently in the York Tower, Windsor Castle, the town of Windsor, County of Berkshire, 51.4833° N, 0.6042° W. Windsor Castle is a residence of the British Royal Family. Originally built by William the Conqueror, it is more than one thousand years old. Want to know more about Windsor Castle? Say 'Yes' if you wish to continue. Say 'No' if you wish to abort request."

"No. Nexus, what are the Accountants doing at Windsor Castle?"

"I do not understand the question, 'What are the Accountants doing at Windsor Castle?' Do you wish to rephrase and try again? Say 'Yes' if you wish to continue. Say 'No' if you wish to abort."

"No.

"Nexus, who are the Accountants?"

"The Accountants are an unlawful paramilitary terrorist organisation active throughout mainland Europe. Originally formed as an extremist faction of the Edenist movement, the Accountants are an amalgamation of several dissident terrorist groups. Their stated aim is to overthrow the coalition government, to form a republic, abolish the free market, break all international trade agreements and return Britain to what they describe as a pastoral economy. The current leader of the English Accountants is Director Hathaway."

"Nexus, who are the Edenists?"

"The Reverend Eben O'Hingerty founded The Edenists in the 2040s. O'Hingerty was an evangelical preacher and environmental campaigner concerned about the impact of science and technology on the human form given by God. The movement grew with the worldwide spread of the Mercy and the Tagus viruses and their many variants. The Edenists reject human customisation, or what is known as H+. They aim to limit the use of implanted technology, end the use of biological weapons, return to exclusive use of organically produced food and reject adaptation policies, including technologies to adjust and control the climate. The English Edenist Party positions itself as a democratic alternative to the currently elected coalition government and is the main opposition party, currently led by Hugo Foxe. Foxe strenuously denies allegations of affiliation and cooperation with the paramilitary organisation 'the Accountants'."

"Nexus, who is Director Hathaway?"

"Director Hathaway is the current leader of the unlawful paramilitary terrorist organisation, the Accountants. Hathaway's life before the Accountants is shrouded in mystery. He has been an active member since the mid-2060s and succeeded as leader at the beginning of 2081, after he led the Accountants to victory at the Battle of East Croydon. Under Hathaway, the Accountants claim a significant expansion of territory under their control, with widespread support in the South of England from Cornwall to Kent and Essex, spreading north through Suffolk and some parts of Norfolk and on the West Coast into Gloucestershire."

Mathew wonders how different this story would read on the Blackweb. He wonders if his older self still accesses it. The Lenz interface is entirely different from the one he is used to. Coming away from the window, he sits on the sofa and spends several minutes familiarising himself with it.

He can't find Charybdis. He is poised to abandon his attempt when he spots a link to a document called *In Sympathy with Ju Shen*.

His grandmother! *In this world,* he thinks, *she must be dead.*

He opens the document.

It is an ancient Chinese poem, translated into English. He recognises it as one of his grandmother's favourites, one she has recited to him many times. He knows every line of it. It begins:

```
It is almost as hard for friends to meet
As for the morning and evening stars.
```

The last two lines are a link. They read:

> But what ten cups could make me as drunk,
> As I always am with your love in my heart?

As he selects the link, he realises these aren't the last lines of the poem. The system prompts him with a voice message, which says, 'Tomorrow the mountains will separate us.'

That's not the end either, Mathew thinks. He automatically continues, speaking aloud, finishing the poem, "After tomorrow - who can say?"

The system says, "Welcome to the Blackweb." A Lenz menu unfurls elegantly before him. He is strangely pleased his older self is still communicating via the Blackweb. He says, "MUUT, who is Director Hathaway?"

The Blackweb says, "Director Hathaway is the leader of the Accountants, the armed resistance movement fighting the totalitarian regime currently in control of England. The Accountants were named to reflect the fact that their written charter is to bring the coalition government to account for their crimes against the peoples of the British Isles.

"In spite of his lack of any formal military training, Hathaway is credited with being a brilliant natural tactician. Much of his success as a commander has been attributed to his ability to unite the previously divided factions of the resistance behind the central ideas of returning democracy and social equality to Britain, whilst neutralising extremists on either end of the political spectrum. Over the last ten years, he has gained control of much of the south east of England. Key to his success has been his strategy of galvanising millions of disaffected civilians to support guerrilla war efforts. They harbour and aid fighters in return for policing, medical services and schools. More recently, Hathaway has allegedly been in talks with the national parties of Wales and Scotland. He is also believed to have forged an alliance with Rhys Llewelyn, leader of the Welsh militia, who has led armed incursions against coalition forces in the disputed border territories between England and Wales.

"DoB 2041 (approx.). Little is known about Hathaway's life before he joined the Accountants but it is rumoured he was married and had a son. There are two versions of events. The first says the coalition murdered Hathaway's family; the second says his wife defected. The MUUT editorial team cannot confirm or deny either of these narratives. Hathaway rarely gives interviews, or makes public appearances and has always refused to answer questions about his personal life."

Mathew says, "Blackweb, why are the Accountants occupying Windsor Castle?"

"Windsor Castle has been the military base of the Accountants for approximately two years, as of the time of writing. The castle ceased to be a royal residence during the last great flood, when the Royal Family moved for its own safety to Balmoral in Scotland, where the King is still nominally head of state. After the castle was vacated, coalition forces initially used it as a barracks, before the Accountant army routed them.

The castle has been returned to its original purpose as a fortress (William the Conqueror built it). It occupies a strategic position on the Thames, close to London. Accountant forces now also control the former capital."

The next thing he does is check if there has been any response to his letter to his older self. It has been opened, but there is no message for him.

He opens a new file and calls it, 'Letter to myself #2' and dictates:

```
You haven't responded. I guess you don't believe
me. I wouldn't believe me either. Here are some
things that may help convince you/me.
    In my own time it is twenty fifty-five. War has
just broken out. There is a Curfew because London is
flooded, but not as severely as it is now and people
still live there. I still live there.
```

Before I came here, looking for you, hoping you'd save our mother, before our mother got sick, I was working on a personal project to make holographic dragons. Eva Aslanova made a virtual world for them, although now I think they are too destructive. They nearly burned me alive the other day. At school I am working on a robotics project. I built a beebot and sent it to Clara, the girl who comes for piano lessons with Gen. I really like Clara. Last week we had a group session and Arkam was an arse.

That should do it. He sends the message.

The door behind him opens. Hathaway enters. His diminutive size strikes Mathew again. He is small-boned as well as short and carries his little hands in front of him as if he's expecting to receive a gift. His movements are diminutive too. Mathew can't imagine Hathaway fighting.

There is a jug of water on the table. Hathaway pours himself a glass, pulls back one of the shrilk chairs and sits.

"Please," he says to Mathew. He indicates to a chair opposite him. He hasn't once glanced at Mathew.

As Mathew takes a seat, Hathaway holds the bridge of his nose for a moment, closing his eyes. He blinks and raises his gaze. His eyes are bloodshot. He takes a gulp of water and says, "Have you seen the army? You get a good view, I think, from the window."

"Yes. It's impressive," Mathew says.

"Fifty thousand men. When we get close to Silverwood, thirty thousand more will join us. Potentially another ten from the Welsh towns. We may have some support from the north. The outcome is probably a done deal; the coalition has no way to withstand our force and we have friends on the inside of the city. If the plan works, we should take Silverwood without a shot being fired, but you never know and some of those men may still die. Many of them possibly. Maybe I will."

Up close, Hathaway's boyish looks are faded. Deep lines etch the skin around his eyes; his fair hair is flecked with grey.

"It has taken us many years to get to this point. It has been the work of my life to bring together the people to fight and take back their country from the small group that leech the blood from this nation. I have sacrificed everything to get to where I am now. This may be one of the most important nights in the history of this ancient nation. It is certainly the most important night of my life. Imagine my surprise, then, when you turned up."

What does he mean? Does he know me?

"When I first saw you, I thought I'd seen a ghost," Hathaway says. "On the way to this room, it occurred to me, lack of sleep might be affecting my judgment, and you would turn out to be just some random boy Kilfeather rescued." Hathaway looks at the water at the bottom of his glass. "Damn, I wish I had something stronger." He gets up, goes to a cabinet, and looks inside. He examines the replicator on the sideboard, doesn't find what he wants. He comes and sits again, swills the water around, swigs it, puts the glass on the desk and moves it around, rolling it along its bottom. He says, "Kilfeather said your name is Mathew. Is he correct?"

"Yes."

Hathaway thinks. He nods slightly to himself, still rolling the glass, he laughs, a sort of bitter laugh, "Funny, I didn't ever have him pegged as vain."

"I don't understand."

"That makes two of us. Why are you here?"

"Kilfeather brought me here."

"Yes, yes. He told me he found you trying to escape from a government agent. I meant, why aren't you living with your father?"

"My father?"

"Your father, Mathew Erlang. Dr. Mathew Erlang, as he is now. You are his son, aren't you? You're the spitting image of him."

He thinks I am my own son!

Mathew summons the first rule of lying: Tell the truth

134

as far as possible. He says, "My mother is sick. I need to get help. I'm on my way to ask him to help me."

"So you *are* his son." Hathaway looks again at the glass and then directly at Mathew. "Is Clara sick?"

"Clara? No. Not Clara."

Hathaway holds Mathew's gaze for a moment.

"Clara isn't your mother?"

Mathew doesn't know how to respond; he opens his mouth to speak but Hathaway beats him to it.

"I'm not sure why I'm surprised," Hathaway says. "I was deluded - blinded by him, always thinking him better than he was. That weakness has been the curse of my life. So you don't live in Silverwood?"

"I've never even been," Mathew says.

"You live in London?"

"In Blackheath."

"It's been cleared."

"I know."

"I'm sorry. We will get it back." Hathaway weighs Mathew up. "Does Dr. Erlang know how you live?"

"He doesn't know I exist," Mathew says.

"Your appearance will be a shock to him?"

Mathew nods, "But I need him to help my mother."

Hathaway stands and goes to the window, as awed as Mathew by the scene. After a few silent moments he turns back to the room. "I will help you find your father, Mathew. As a matter of fact, I wouldn't mind talking to him myself. Your appearance has prompted all kinds of memories. But right now, I need to go, I'm afraid. I'll send someone along to make sure you have a bed for the night and get breakfast before we set off. We're leaving at 4 am. You can travel with us if you want passage to Silverwood."

"Yes I do," Mathew says. "Thank you."

"Good," Hathaway turns back to the room, away from the window, and stares at Mathew. Then suddenly he puts his glass on the table and walks to the door. "I'm sorry we couldn't talk more. Truly. I'd like to know what happened to you. Perhaps we will still have time after all this is ended." He turns back for a moment. "Funny, I'd forgotten." He shakes his head as he leaves the room. "Almost."

Mathew stares at the back of the shut door. A floodlight pans across it. The room is startlingly bright for a moment.

Alone once again, Mathew goes back to the window and watches the activity in the park. Periodically, as helicopters descend and ascend, the lights from the watchtowers pan the camp, casting eerie shadows on the grass, through the long avenue of trees. The great lights sweep across the tops of tents and trucks. It is late now, but equipment and supplies are still being loaded.

The door behind him opens. An unfamiliar soldier leans in and says, "Mathew?"

"Yes."

"Come with me. I've been told to assign you a bunk for the night."

They take the stairs back to the corridor, retracing the route he had travelled with Kilfeather.

"There's showers and toilets," the man points to a door they pass on the right. "Not sure how warm the water will be this time of day. I'd take advantage of it, if I were you. It may be a while before you get the opportunity again." They make a stop at a storeroom, shelves piled full of neatly folded clothes. "You'll need a uniform," he says. "You're wearing Coalition-issue uniform. You're likely to be shot by mistake. What size are you?"

Mathew tells him and he is given underwear, socks, t-shirt, a shirt, trousers and a jacket. The man goes to another cupboard that contains rows of boots, asks his size and selects a pair, piling them on Mathew's outstretched wrists. He follows the soldier back into the corridor. A few doors along they turn into a dormitory. A group of soldiers are playing cards on the top of a made bed; they all have bottles of beer. They stare when Mathew comes into the room.

The soldier says, "Look after this one. He's a friend of Hathaway's and not to be messed with."

The men are surprised. "Keifer," the soldier continues, focused on an older man who is observing curiously with a beer bottle pressed to his lips. "Make sure he makes it up in time. I will come back tomorrow to arrange his transport. He turns to Mathew, "That's your bunk."

Later, it is dark and the men are all asleep. Mathew is wide awake and cold, lying under an itchy blanket on a hard mattress, in only his underwear, still chilled from the freezing shower.

Two of the men snore loudly. One has a rattling snore, the other a kind of honk, and they take turns to rattle and honk as one breathes in and the other exhales. Mathew doesn't understand how the other men sleep through it. He stares at the large links of the wire mesh supporting the mattress above him. Every time the man above him turns, the mesh squeaks. He shifts again and a limp arm suddenly falls and hangs next to Mathew's head.

Slowly, as quietly as possible, Mathew slips from the bed and pulls on his trousers and t-shirt. Outside he watches a soldier retreat along the corridor, through the endless series of open doors. He goes to the window and gazes at the quadrangle. The floodlights have been dimmed. The camp has gone to sleep. A couple of soldiers are on watch.

"Nexus," he says.

"Welcome, Dr. Mathew Erlang," the neutral standard English female voice of the Nexus says, "Text or speech?"

"Text," he says. "Review recent activity."

A list appears, message exchanges with people he doesn't recognise, although he is startled to read some of the names he does. Theo Arkam is one of the most recent. Then, to his complete surprise, he sees a link to Project

Yinglong. He selects the link. He is prompted for a password. He thinks for a moment and whispers, "Hoshi".

He is in. He finds some stone steps to sit on, opens a file and starts to read.

20 MATHEW ERLANG THE ELDER

Wednesday, 14 February, 2091, Silverwood.

Dr. Mathew Erlang is fifty-two years old, a lecturer and research fellow at the newly founded Silverwood University, career-long employee of the multinational tech giant, Hermes Link. He stares into his brand new bathroom mirror, which hangs on the wall of the bathroom of his week-old apartment on the forty-fourth floor of the just-completed Isla Kier Tower, an exemplary building in the work-in-progress adaptation city of Silverwood.

The water runs full-flow into the sink. He finally notices and turns off the tap, scolding himself for wasting the precious resource. These days it's as valuable as gold. Even though he knows the city's water recycling system to be second to none, he understands, to the point of geekery, what it costs to reprocess wastewater.

The grey hair on his head has taken over at a rapid pace recently. His wife, Clara, says it makes him appear distinguished. It's also what she says when he draws attention to the crow's feet at the corners of his eyes, the long lines etched into the skin around his mouth, and the extra weight he struggles to keep off. She shows him her own signs of age and asks him if he is equally critical of her. He tells her she is the same to him. When he says this she rolls her eyes. But he truly *doesn't* see them. When he takes time to study Clara, she is still the fifteen-year-old girl he first met on Pickervance Road all those years ago.

Every now and then some event brings him up short, like the one they will all attend tonight, the inauguration of the newly rebuilt St Paul's Cathedral, where Clara will be one of the star performers; a national treasure, their most famous and greatest living classical performer. *His* Clara is a different person from the one in advertisements plastered all around Birmingham and Silverwood. She says the same thing: her husband 'the famous scientist'. Although he is not famous. He is not even remotely as successful.

In many ways he views himself as a failure and is bitter over his inability to progress at Hermes Link. He knows Clara is right when she counsels him that each person must measure him or herself by their own stick, not against others. But he's still stung by Theo Arkam's stellar ascendency, not only to the pinnacle of the English subsidiary management but, now US-based, Arkam is Mathew's boss's boss, and Mathew's direct manager is Arkam's good friend, the not-especially-bright Oliver Thyer.

And this is what galls. Mathew tells himself a million times that business success is driven by networking, confidence and personal charisma much, much more than intelligence and ability. He has actively chosen not to pursue the self-seeking behaviour he often views as unethical, but to have someone like Thyer promoted above him is like a personal insult. Many times recently he has reflected on the choices he has made which have led to him being sidelined from important research projects, delegated more admin, given more teaching time and fewer research opportunities, until the only research he is doing is his personal work. He only has himself to blame or, as Clara would put it, he has made the active choices to get him to where he is. She also points out that he actively chose to remain friends with Eva Aslanova, despite the fact he has never actually physically met her. Eva put Mathew in touch with someone in programming for GreyMatter, the international open forum for new ideas. Mathew's GreyMatter talk caused an international sensation. On the back of this, Polonious Cartwright, the CEO of Hermes Link, had contacted Arkam to discover why he wasn't supporting Mathew's research work. He demanded Hermes Link publish their own branded version of the lecture, revealing evidence of the claims Mathew had made during his talk.

Arkam is now on a hypersonic jet headed for Birmingham International Airport. He will be whisked straight to the University. In an hour, Mathew will be standing centre-stage in Silverwood's recently completed three-thousand capacity auditorium, facing an invite-only audience, while his talk is broadcast live around the world.

He is terrified.

There is a knock at the door. "Dad?"

It is George, his son, 22 years old and more confident and less anxious than he has ever been. George is his proudest achievement. That he and Clara somehow had a hand in turning the deeply traumatised little boy whom they had adopted into this immaculate young man is his proudest achievement and his greatest source of happiness.

There is another, louder knock.

"Dad, are you still in there? We have five minutes until the car arrives. It called ahead to say it is on its way. Are you ready?'

"Yes, yes," Mathew says. He glances once more in the mirror and opens the door. "How do I look?" he asks.

"Like a profoundly intelligent man, on the cusp of

disrupting the world of science."

"Then why do I feel like I am about to undergo some elaborate form of torture?"

"Crazy old man! You *killed* the GreyMatter talk. It's already one of the most popular ever."

"I didn't think anyone would watch it."

"They did. And there's a reason why. That reason is *you are amazing.*"

"Don't overdo it."

"Come on, Dad. You need to increase the energy levels."

"Believe me, if my heart beats any faster, I will expire. Upping the energy levels is precisely the opposite of what I need right now!"

"Would you like a drink?"

"What?"

"Alcohol."

"No! For heaven's sake, I can't go on drunk."

"It might relax you."

Mathew sighs, "Has the car picked up Hoshi yet?"

George nods, "Yep. It's taking her straight to the university."

"Right," Mathew says. "I better had get going, then."

George asks, "Have you explained what is going on?"

"Of course. I wouldn't do anything without her consent. It was her idea."

"Are you sure you still want to do this?"

"No."

George gives him a certain look. He is barely as tall as Mathew, but he is taller than Mathew thought he would be. The height gene must have come from his mother, Mathew thinks.

"Yes. Yes, I want to do this."

Clara comes into the hallway, all smiles. She says, "You look wonderful! Very distinguished."

She takes his hands and draws a deep breath. "I'm proud of you," she says, kissing him on the nose.

George says, "The car is here."

The car is a six-seater, dull metallic blue and grey, low-to-the-ground Merc with carbon fibre wheels and one-way glass windows. Luxury. Expensive. Not his usual daily commuter model. The Hermes Link PR team ordered it for the benefit of the press. The car comes with a man wearing a tux with a dickie bow and mirror glasses. A well-dressed thug with them all day, dress-code-ready for the black-tie event that evening. No one had told Mathew they were to be accompanied by a bodyguard.

"Is there a problem?" Mathew asks the guard. "We didn't request an escort." Since his youth, he has hated security men.

"No problem at all, Sir. Just a little extra precaution, given the news this morning."

Mathew has been disconnected from current affairs since the fuss with GreyMatter. But he'd caught the headlines in the morning and he knows the ATLAS Treaty negotiations are igniting an unlikely alliance between English and Welsh nationalists. He is conscious of how close his new city is to the troubled Welsh border towns. Not for the first time, Mathew questions Oliver Nystrom's insistence that they follow Cadmus Silverwood's blueprint to the letter in building the city this far south and close to Wales. Things have changed since Cadmus died. They have changed a lot.

"Because of the nationalists?" he asks the guard.

"It's fine. There're some protestors picketing the university gates. Edenists. Peaceful, but you never know. There will be placards as we go in and some shouting."

"Great."

"It's nothing really. Hermes is exceptionally cautious to send me. You'll be fine."

Mathew isn't particularly reassured. Clara takes his hand and squeezes it. The guard opens the back door and they climb into the miniature luxury living room, taking their seats on two powder-grey fake leather sofas with charcoal piping. Between them there's a slick glass coffee table with moulded cup holders. An ice cooler and a bottle of champagne stand beside it, with three champagne flutes.

"Would you like me to open it?" their minder asks.

Mathew shakes his head. "A bit early for me."

"Oh come on, Dad!" George says. "It's a special occasion."

"And I need to be sober for my talk."

Clara says to the guard, "Thanks. We'll manage ourselves." She smiles and he nods and shuts the door. The car pulls away, smooth as butter, silent as snow.

George lifts the champagne from the ice to read the label. "Rievaulx. North Yorkshire wine. Nice. C'mon Dad, let's have a toast."

"It's eleven o'clock."

"Perfect timing for a champagne breakfast!"

George examines the mini-fridge and larder to the side. "There's fresh strawberries and cream." He opens the door and grabs a bowl, sniffing. "Real cream."

"It can't be real cream."

"It smells like it. Here." He hands a bowl to his mother.

Clara sniffs. "I wouldn't know. I've never eaten real cream. Here, you would know," she passes it to Mathew.

"It's been such a long time," he smells. "Could be."

"We have to eat these," George says. He hands a bowl to his mother, takes one himself and puts it on the table. He finds cutlery. Polished silverware. "I won't let this go to waste either," he says. He takes the champagne bottle, unwraps the wire and the foil and pops the cork. Clara holds a glass to help catch the overflow. They all laugh.

"Your son is an aesthete," Mathew says.

"*My* son?"

"It's a reaction," George says. "Against your puritanism. Here," he says, as he passes a glass across to his father. Mathew puts down the strawberries in order to take the glass. "One won't hurt you." George pours two more glasses and then holds his up in a toast. "To the amazing future!" he says.

"To the amazing future!" Clara repeats.

"Cheers!" says Mathew "Although I'm not sure what you mean about the future."

"The one you're going to change forever," George says.

Mathew laughs and shakes his head. "That's a nice thing to say, but Project Yinglong won't change anything."

"I just have a feeling," George says. "So does Mum, don't you?"

Clara says, "We both believe in your work, Mathew. What you've achieved is incredible."

"But it's not *my* achievement. Both of you should understand."

Clara catches George's eye. "It's no use. He'll never take any credit."

"You need to learn to celebrate success, Dad."

"Let's wait until today is over, shall we?"

George sighs and throws back his champagne. "I want to discuss tonight. After your talk, I need to take Mum straight over to St Paul's."

"Yes, you should."

"I will come back once Mum is settled to take you home. Dad, you go home and get dressed for tonight. We had your tux cleaned."

"You don't need to come back and get me. I have this car for the day."

"Are you sure?"

"Yes," Mathew says. "George, you're being incredibly helpful. Look after your mother this afternoon. She is the big star. It's her big night."

Clara says, "Oh, for heaven's sake. Don't be such a martyr. I've had hundreds of big concerts. This is a special day for you, for all of us. George, I'll get a car to St Paul's alone. You take care of your father."

George shakes his head, exasperated. "Let's play it by ear then, shall we?" He says to Mathew, "Will you call me once you are ready to leave?"

"Yes, I will call you."

The car slows as they reach the entrance to the university. As the guard predicted, there is a small crowd of people holding makeshift banners covered in hand-written messages. They proclaim the usual Edenist slogans: *You are not God! Against Nature!* There are some new ones, including, *Stop Dr. Frankenstein.* And most disturbingly, *Kill Frankenstein's Monster."*

In the few moments it takes the gates to open, the crowd presses against the car and security people move to push and pull them back. Bodies flatten against the car windows on both sides. The glass is tinted and one-way. *Thank goodness*, Mathew thinks, as the protestors surge forward, angry-eyed and shouting. They bang on the windows, and kick, thump, scratch at the expensive paintwork. Mathew dreads to imagine what they would do if they knew for sure who was inside.

Finally, they are through and the university gates close behind them.

"I don't understand how these people even got into Silverwood," Clara says.

"It's a good point," George says. "Perhaps the Edenists have infiltrated the government."

"It's democracy," Mathew says reasonably. "They have a right to express their opinion."

"Since when has this been a democracy?" George says.

The car takes a long meandering path through landscaped gardens. These are an inconceivable luxury, perceived as an outrage by many, angry at the waste of water that keeps the completely non-productive plants alive. But part of Cadmus Silverwood's plan was to build a beautiful city as well as a functional one, a place to feed the eye and the soul. Although practically all of Silverwood's buildings are – or will be – skyscrapers, to maximise space, they are full of atriums, roof-gardens and tree-lined balconies, each with their own hydroponics stations. When it is complete, the whole of the city will be a kind of greenhouse.

The infamous, self-constructing, part-biological roof is already visible above this part of town. In a year-and-a-half the roof will be complete and the city's self-contained atmosphere will start to work. They exit the car, crane their necks upwards and marvel at the engineering miracle. The revolutionary biodegradable scaffolding, designed as a structure to allow the roof to grow across, and which the roof will eventually eat, is highlighted against the sky, an ultra-thin black skeleton. In years to come, people won't notice it, Mathew thinks. It won't be a technological marvel. It will be like the real sky; less noticeable, because there will be no weather to speak of, only scheduled rain showers the system creates. No one will ever be caught in the rain again. There will be little reason to lift one's eyes if the sky is perpetually blue.

As they walk towards the main entrance of the university Mathew notices with some nervousness that there is a small group ready to welcome them. The university's chancellor, who ten days ago hadn't been able to remember Mathew's name, stands with a small gaggle of officials and a handful of journalists. Camera flashes go off. Mathew is startled and disorientated when the Chancellor comes to him and greets him warmly with a handshake.

Mathew asks, "Is Professor Arkam here yet?"

"No, but he's only five minutes away."

"He's cutting it fine," says George.

The Chancellor stares at George. Mathew realises slightly too late that the proper thing to do is to introduce his family. He says, "Sorry Chancellor, this is George, my son."

"Your son?" the Chancellor glances with some confusion from the blond-haired, blue-eyed young man back to Mathew.

"I was adopted," George says quickly. He smiles and shakes the Chancellor's hand firmly. Mathew marvels again at George's confidence and charm. It is entirely Clara's doing.

"Oh. Well. Of course! Pleased to meet you, George. Are you studying here?"

"I'm at Birmingham. I'll transfer here to do my postgrad next year."

"You will be a welcome addition to our student body. What are you studying?"

"Synthetic biology."

"Following your father's footsteps?"

"I hope so."

The Chancellor turns to Clara, "And this is your talented wife. No need for introductions on my side. I am already a great admirer."

"Very pleased to meet you, Chancellor," Clara takes the offered hand. "This is a wonderful building," she says as she steps back to take in the facade of the new university.

"Is this your first visit?"

"I've been here once before, but we went round the back entrance. It's very grand, coming this way."

"We want to make a statement, hammer home the importance of science and research to the future of our country – well, what will be our State, I suppose, if all goes to plan."

"Indeed. It does make a statement. It's beautiful." Clara stands back and admires the monumental glass entrance that towers above her.

One of the journalists approaches. "Ms. Barculo? Hello, I'm Tim Martin from *The Times.*" They shake hands. "Are you nervous about tonight's performance?"

"Not as nervous as I am about the one here," she says.

The Chancellor, Mathew, George and the journalist all

laugh.

"Can we get a photograph?"

"Yes, absolutely. George, come and stand between your father and me. Can we get it with the magnificent entrance behind us? Can you get the sign in?"

Mathew lets himself be moved into position and smiles for the camera, with his arm around the back of his son, holding Clara's hand tightly, hidden from view. When they break, once the photographs are taken, Mathew says, "I'd better go get ready."

George says, "We have front row seats."

"Have you?" Mathew says, "Whatever you do, don't catch my eye and don't make me laugh." He kisses Clara. "What a day for us."

Clara smiles, "Yes, what a day."

21 THE PATCHWORK ARMY

It is twilight. Dawn breaks through a gap in the canvas on the roof of the truck for sixteen-year-old Mathew Erlang.

It is an old truck - forty, maybe fifty years old, converted from fossil fuel many years before. It's old enough to still have a steering wheel, although it's actually computer-controlled. The electric engine is as quiet as any other, but the many-times-repaired chassis creaks and bangs with each bump in the road and there are lots of those.

He sits on sacks of rice and beans, surrounded by boxes packed to the ceiling, food supplies for an army of thousands on the move. Sergeant Kiefer, his grudging companion, sits on a crate at the back of the vehicle, obsessively cleaning his gun.

"Is it an antique?" Mathew asks. The gun is mid-twentieth century.

"You know guns?"

Mathew shakes his head. "Not really. I've played a few war games."

"War games?"

"You know, hologames."

"I thought you weren't meant to be a leech?"

"I knew someone who'd stolen some kit," Mathew says, thinking he is getting used to this lying business.

Kiefer sniffs, "Don't tell Kilfeather." He holds the gun up. "It's an M1 Carbine. It may be old, but it's still effective." He puts the clip back on and stares at Mathew directly.

Kiefer is a small man with dark piercing eyes, black hair flecked with grey and a curly beard. He doesn't like this assignment as babysitter to Mathew.

"How do you know Hathaway, anyway?" Kiefer says, part-curious about anyone who is close to the great man, part-irritated that this unimpressive boy gets the honour when Kiefer has never even exchanged a salute with the Director.

"I don't."

"We were told you were a friend of Hathaway. Under his protection. That's why I'm here. To take care of you."

"I thought I was a prisoner."

Kiefer raises his ample eyebrows. "Kilfeather told me, 'Don't let anything happen to the boy'. Does it sound like you're a prisoner?"

"Then why am I here and not in one of the other trucks?"

Kiefer shrugs, "I don't give the orders." He puts his gun carefully on the floor and reaches for a canvas bag. "Here," he throws an apple, a packet of sandwiches and a bottle of water at Mathew. "Breakfast."

Mathew catches the missiles with his wrists and hugs the pile to his chest to stop them falling to the floor. Kiefer opens his own sandwich packet and takes a bite.

"How long will it take for us to get to Silverwood?" Mathew asks.

"Four hours if the roads are good, but probably more like six. We'll be there by this afternoon for sure."

As Mathew opens his bottle of water, the truck brakes hard and grinds to a halt. Mathew is thrown to the floor, the food and water goes everywhere.

"Oh for frack's sake!" Kiefer growls and scrambles to his feet, grabs his gun and throws it across his shoulder. He pulls at the ties on the flaps of canvas that act as doors to the back of the truck. "What's going on?" he asks a soldier in the truck behind.

"Haven't the foggiest," the soldier says.

Kiefer jumps. Others do the same. He glares at Mathew. "Don't move," he says. He starts to walk away, hesitates and then comes back and ties the canvas flaps, shutting off Mathew's view.

Mathew clambers over the rice sacks and goes to the flaps. He uses his fingers and manages to wiggle a gap wide enough to get an eye to it. Then he grabs the metal bar above him, and leans forward, putting his left eye to the gap.

Behind his truck there's a long line of vehicles. Some are genuine military equipment, captured from the coalition forces, some of them are even relatively new, but many others are converted commercial vehicles. Most fly flags: the red cross on a white background with two roses and three lions that the Accountants use as their symbol. Also English and old-fashioned union flags. The men and women of the Accountant army think of themselves as nationalists, but Kiefer told Mathew earlier that the same is true of the other side too.

In the light of a pale February day, the army, impressive the night before, now appears rag-tag and cobbled together. The soldiers' uniforms are shabby, made of poor material, and are not really *uniform* at all. Their weapons are old and equally various and make-do. Nevertheless, there are a lot of people and a lot of vehicles. They are on the M25, edging towards the M4. The army's vehicles fill all three lanes. The road is in a very poor state with craters and potholes that have jarred his bones these last few hours.

He strains his eye to the Canvas. Civilians walk along

the hard shoulder, women with kids, men on bicycles with trailers, people pushing handcarts. The side of the motorway is a pedestrian thoroughfare. The people stop and stare at the patchwork army. Some of them applaud and cheer. A woman comes forward and walks alongside one truck, offering food to the soldiers. They reach and stretch to take fruit and bread from her hands. She says, "God bless you! You show them leeches!"

The soldier from the truck behind climbs onto the top of the cab.

One of the men on the ground asks, "Can you see anything?"

He says, "It's backed up for miles. No one is going anywhere."

"Oh, for frack's sake!"

Horns honk.

One of the men on the ground says in a stupid voice, "The invasion has been postponed," and people laugh.

An officer comes and marches along the road between the trucks, red-faced and angry. "Get back inside!" he screams. "Right now! And shut up! I want silence. The next truckful of men honking a horn is walking to Silverwood!"

Then there is a dull hum above. The angry soldier spins around and surveys the sky, "Frack!" he says. "A drone."

Something passes over. It casts a shadow across the bonnet of the truck. All the soldiers strain their necks and gaze up, shielding their eyes from the sun with their hands. Out of sight there's the sound of running boots and an automatic weapon fires.

Kiefer says, "Has anyone got a rocket launcher?"

A large gun is produced from another truck. It is passed to the man on the top of the cab.

"I don't know how to use it," the soldier says.

"For frack's sake!"

Kiefer climbs beside the man, takes the shoulder-fired weapon, kneels, gets it ready with swift, efficient movements, hefts it to his shoulder and aims. A missile fires. It leaves a trace of smoke behind, a dirty pink cloud. Overhead, Mathew spots the source of the hum. It is a small low-flying aircraft. He spies it just before it explodes. There are whoops and cheers. Kiefer climbs from the lorry and is greeted by pats on the back. One of the men has fetched a flask from the back of his truck.

"What are you doing?" someone asks.

"Having a drink."

"Are you crazy?"

"We're not moving."

Kiefer walks between the trucks, "Back inside," he says.

The man with the flask says, "But we're not moving."

Kiefer turns on the soldier, prodding at the stripes on his own shoulder, "Do you know what these are?"

"Yes," the man says reasonably.

"They mean, I'm giving you an order and you need to obey. Get inside!"

The soldier salutes, awkwardly, the flask still in his hand. Homemade spirit sloshes on his boots. He turns and climbs into his truck.

Another officer also walks between the trucks. He joins the angry soldier and confers with him. He points at Kiefer. The officer says, "Sergeant, were you the man who got the drone?"

"Yes, Sir."

"Well done. I'm taking a party to retrieve the black box from the field. I need a good shot. Will you come with me?"

Kiefer glances at the back of the truck. "I'm on guard duty, Sir."

"What are you guarding?"

"A boy, Sir. In that truck."

"He's not going anywhere. Let's get this done quickly, then we can start to move again."

"Yes Sir."

Kiefer's eyes latch on the back of Mathew's truck and

the open flap. He walks towards him. Mathew ducks his head back. Kiefer doesn't say a word to Mathew, but he reties the flap tightly, then leaves with the officer and the scouting party.

Mathew retreats inside the truck, back to the bags of grain and rice and sits. After a while, the truck starts rolling again. Kiefer doesn't return. The semi-darkness and the rocking motion of the truck lull Mathew into a semi-conscious state. His head nods onto his shoulder. The successive nights awake have taken their toll and he lies on the rice sacks, curls into a ball and falls into a fitful sleep.

22 GALETEA

Professor Theo Arkam is tall, debonair and in good shape for a man of fifty-two. His face is naturally dusky. He has liquid brown eyes, a permanent puckish smile, an easy manner and an immaculate, expensively cut suit. He walks into the spotlight in the Victoria II theatre at the newly opened Silverwood University to muted, uncertain applause. The audience is waiting for Mathew. There is a hushed silence, broken only by the slight buzz of the drone cameras as they fly around.

"I know you want Dr. Erlang," Arkam begins. "I will make this brief. Mathew and I have known each other since we were at school. We have always worked together. I cannot tell you what a pleasure it is to be able to introduce him tonight. How appropriate that this is the inaugural lecture here. It is a sign and symbol of the future for us. A city made with the latest technology built on the ideals of men like Cadmus Silverwood, who saw the future with such clarity.

"For fifty years, Hermes Link has been at the forefront of research, championing new ideas, driving cutting-edge programmes, funding universities like this one. Ultimately, at the heart of our company is the desire to invest in future technology for the good of mankind.

"What we will show today will be hard for you to comprehend. When I arrived at the university there were people protesting. It is understandable that some people will be frightened. I hope you will be more enlightened than the people at the gates. We are still in the early stages of the quest to find applications for this technology, but we are all now free to imagine a next generation of robots to help and serve people, nurse the sick or perhaps a new generation of soldiers.

"Today, I am delighted to announce a significant new investment in this project to further research. We will fund a new enlarged faculty and the establishment of a commercial enterprise to investigate potential applications of the technology. This company, a fully-owned subsidiary of Hermes Link, will be called Galetea, led by Dr. Erlang himself."

There is a round of applause. Arkam glances to his left to where Mathew stands, off-stage. The news has blindsided him. Mathew realises it is a coup. Hermes Link is laying claim to ownership of his personal work and trying to buy him off with a senior role.

Meanwhile Arkam says, "Come on, Mathew. Don't be shy. People are waiting for you," he has his arms outstretched. There is some laughter in the audience.

Mathew steps into the bright lights. Arkam applauds him. So does the audience. Arkam shakes his hand and bends and whispers, "Don't screw this up. There are three hundred million people watching."

Arkam leaves and Mathew is alone. He clears his throat and scans nervously around the auditorium. Hundreds of eyes stare at him. He shifts on his feet nervously, clasps and unclasps his hands.

"Many of you will know that it is often difficult to get anything done in corporate academia. This is particularly true when you are trying to do something that pushes the boundaries, something that falls across disciplines. Universities like to work in silos. They find it hard to deal with projects that involve too many different areas of expertise.

"Project Yinglong draws on the work of scientists from many other fields of study. It would not have been possible without research done into synthetic meat, body implants, cryonics, genetic engineering, nanomedicines, regenerative medicine, stem cell treatments, tissue engineering, organ printing, molecular electronics, nanoelectromechanical systems, ambient intelligence, artificial brains and intelligence, brain computer interfaces, machine vision, programmable matter, neuroinformatics, electroencephalography, neuroprosthetics, molecular nanotechnology, nanorobotics and powered exoskeletons. You get the idea."

Again there is a ripple of laughter.

"I know people worry where science is headed. Given Tagus and the Mercy, we should all be concerned. But we should not throw the baby out with the bathwater. Now, more than ever, we need to rely on our intelligence and ingenuity to save ourselves from the existential threat of global warming. The Anthropocene age, our current epoch, is the first one in the history of the planet in which man is having a significant impact on earth's ecosystems. This is the direct result of the rise of science and technology. The industrial revolution and the technological advances that followed wouldn't have happened without fossil fuels. The Edenists would have been happy with that. I wouldn't.

"Our brains make us unique on this planet, perhaps throughout the galaxy and even the universe. Technology is an extension, an expression, of humanity. I believe it is our moral duty to explore as far as possible, wherever those amazing minds of ours take us, and to push forward with technological innovation.

"So now to my project and what you came for today. It would be nice to think this work will have ancillary benefits to other disciplines and to human lives. But the project, named Galetea by Professor Arkam, I have always called Project Yinglong. I have worked on it my whole life, as a piece of personal research. Initially, it was a technical challenge, but it became much more emotional.

"Events from my past drove me to understand how we might immortalise the flesh and the human mind, all the knowledge and memories that evaporate when someone dies. Death is such a waste of resources. Eradicating death will be one of those moments in human evolution when we take a great leap forward. There are many ways to approach this problem.

"Great advances have been made, in my lifetime, to cure many common diseases, which have been the main causes of mortality for many centuries. For the privileged few we now have synthetic organs and Project Yinglong relies heavily on that science. There have been huge steps forward for technologies that address ageing and we all now live much longer, healthier lives as a result.

"Initially, I took the path of imagining what would happen if our brains could exist beyond the grey matter that entombs them. If you are able to download your brain and your brain runs independently of your body, you are effectively immortal, as long as there is resilience in the system; I mean, if you are backed up. People have worked on this idea for many years and I have been part of the community.

"Project Yinglong comprises of sixteen virtual individuals, forms of artificial intelligence with brains modelled on the structure of the human brain. They are actually versions of copies of my brain, but with the benefit of computer processing power to aid their ability to calculate and churn through problems, which I believe makes them considerably smarter than humans. There are sixteen of them because I used Myers Briggs' sixteen personality types to create a community of complementary minds and also, quite self-indulgently, to understand how my own personality could be quite different with certain characteristics altered slightly. As we all know, human thinking cannot be surgically removed from human emotion. The sixteen *feel*, but not necessarily quite the way we do. If I am going to be immortal, I want the best possible version of myself to be immortal.

Any of us who have ever flown into a blind rage know how unhelpful it is. It was useful to our cavemen ancestors; it is irrelevant to the way we live now. None of the members of Project Yinglong will ever fly into a blind rage.

"I don't think this work is new or revolutionary, except I believe I have, we have, perhaps assembled a whole bunch of exciting work holistically to form something new. Plus, the sixteen are a particularly good execution of these ideas. In other words: they work." Mathew waits for the laughter to abate. "Once the sixteen existed, something remarkable happened. They started to think for themselves. They are still thinking many years on, and this is the most exciting part of the whole project.

"You see, it is not one man's project at all. It is the combined efforts of seventeen minds. Sixteen are superhuman. I am a child in their company.

"I believe the aspect of the project that bothers most people, the reason our friends at the gate are angry, is the idea of using synthetic biology to make a body for one of these brains.

"In my GreyMatter talk, I showed some video clips. Some people suspected they had been fabricated. The clips showed a person that I claimed to be a synthetic human, interacting with strangers who were unaware she was not human. People said this footage was faked. So tonight, I wanted to introduce her to you and get your reactions, to find out if you think she passes the Turing test. Hoshi, please join me on stage!"

A woman comes from the side of the stage. A spotlight picks her out from the darkness as she walks to join Mathew. There is absolute silence in the hall.

"Hoshi, do you want to explain who you are?"

The woman, who is tall, nearly as tall as Mathew, has Asian features and long black hair, styled into a single plait, hanging down her back. She wears a simple, black, loose cotton suit, with long sleeves and buttoned at the neck, but the skin on her wrists and hands, her neck and her face is exposed. She moves fluidly and gracefully. She turns to the audience and says, "My name is Hoshi. I am one of the sixteen AIs comprising Project Yinglong. I have lived and worked with Mathew for nearly thirty-five years. I have had a long evolution. Mostly I have not had physical form. Mostly I have had a virtual body, and I occupied a virtual simulation of this world, but with all the same laws of physics. I am not alone. I have fifteen companions. So my reality is as real to me as yours, and as full and fulfilling – maybe more so.

"Having a physical body means I fully pass into your world. I am a bridge, between your world and mine. Because I think Dr. Erlang has created a new kind of world.

"We worked in secret partly because we were never part of a formal project at the university, but also because we anticipated we might cause fear. Ever since humans conceived of creating a being in their likeness, they have imagined what damage it would do. That is the risk we face in unveiling ourselves to you. But we have nowhere else to go. We exist, for good or for bad. We have been imagined and brought into reality."

23 ESCAPE PLAN

Dr. Mathew Erlang is in a reflective mood. The exposure of Hoshi to the wider world has made him think about everything that led up to this day.

The last of the journalists and the gaggle of students and enthusiasts who flocked around him in the auditorium at the end of the talk have all gone. They were keen to talk to him but they also wanted to witness Hoshi close up; to touch her, not quite believing, needing to prove to themselves that she wasn't an elaborate hologram.

Now Hoshi sits with him in the little room that acts as his office. His new private lab, where the Yinglong have moved from their Birmingham home, is on the other side of Silverwood. He doesn't yet have a lab at the university.

The journalists had wanted to visit Dr. Erlang's office, but the university authorities, knowing how small Mathew's room is, restricted the briefings to the auditorium. One journalist had asked for images of his office, the place where "the thinking happens". Mathew didn't get the chance to explain to her that most of the work happens on a server and it is executed by artificial intelligence, not his own very human mind.

Arkam is still speaking to the press, putting corporate

spin on Project Yinglong. Mathew knows the hymn sheet Arkam is singing from, has watched him interviewed many times. He can guess what he is saying right now and what his agenda is: to make sure the message about Galetea belonging to Hermes Link gets out as broadly as possible. So he waits for Arkam to come and frighten him into line. To bully him into handing Hoshi over to Hermes Link.

"You needn't worry," Mathew says to Hoshi.

"I'm not worried, but I notice from your bodily indicators that you are. You should self-medicate with increased GABA. Do you want me to take control of your self-serve medibot and do it for you?"

"No thanks, Hoshi."

"No?"

"No."

"As you wish."

Mathew gets up from his desk and goes to the window. "I hope Arkam comes soon. I need to get to St. Paul's."

"You have an hour. You still have time. There's no need for you to go back to your apartment to change. I ordered a car to pick up your tux and take it to St Paul's. You can change in the men's room."

"You're right. It should be a short conversation."

"Do you want to rehearse the conversation with us? We have already tried many variations of the likely course the discussion will take."

"What do you think will happen?"

"We think he will present a generous pay package, a senior role at the university, security and social standing for yourself and your family, a guaranteed career path for George, in return for relinquishing rights to the Yinglong code and, of course, to me."

"What do you think I will do?"

"We think you will refuse."

"And then what will happen?"

"Hermes Link will take legal action against you. Your employment contract has a clause that says all work deemed to have taken place using company resources and time belongs to the company."

"But I didn't use the company's resources and time."

"There is another clause which says that whilst you are contracted to work for a specified number of hours a week, you are also expected to work outside those hours, as your manager deems appropriate. According to the contract, you have no spare time and your time is a resource owned by Hermes Link. So we legally belong to them. Or so they will argue."

"How can a company own a living person?"

"Good and interesting point. But legally I am not a person. Also, legally they do sort of own you."

"I do not trust them to take care of you."

"Neither do we."

"What should we do? Should we run?"

"Where to?"

Mathew sighs, comes back to his chair and collapses into it.

"We should trust to the public outcry that is likely to result from Hermes Link bullying you. You are popular. People are likely to rally around you. And me."

"So we should do nothing?"

"We should quietly resist."

"But they may take you away while that happens."

"I suggest you take me out of the equation for a while."

"How?"

"Put my body into a suspended state. My mind will retreat to virtual mode. I will live only with the rest of the sixteen. It is no hardship to me. It will frustrate the company."

Mathew nods. "Okay. We need to do it quickly."

"You should buy some time, a few days will do. Don't argue with Arkam. Don't say much at all. Say you need a contract and you want a lawyer to look at it before you accept his offer. Stall him by saying you want guarantees for my personal safety. It will take him time to scramble to respond to these requests."

Mathew makes a steeple with his hands and presses his fingers to his mouth, thinking.

"What if they want to keep you now? What if they insist on it?"

"Tell Arkam there is a medical reason I need to physically be in your lab. Tell him I need to be plugged into a dialysis machine to flush my synthetic blood every night. He won't have a clue. He also won't want to risk damage to valuable company property. He is already treading on thin ice with the chairman because he didn't control you with the GreyMatter broadcast."

"I don't want them sniffing around the lab."

"We are at work on a new temporary location. We have found alternative servers on the Blackweb. If need be, we wipe ourselves from your servers and disappear."

Mathew looks pained.

"We always knew coming out into the open would be risky."

"I never thought this would happen, though."

"We should have predicted it."

"We were distracted by the security breach."

"Those strange letters from your younger self? No wonder you are dwelling on the past. I think they are more of a distraction to you than us."

"But I had you investigate it. Hermes tech security said they didn't detect a hack, and as far as they were concerned I'd written them myself."

"It's the most sophisticated hack we've come across. There's no trace of anyone breaking and entering."

"Why would anyone go to so much trouble?"

Hoshi shrugs. "The letters might be real, of course."

Mathew's eyes widen and then he frowns, "You don't think that. Even for a second."

"You could write back and engage them. It might be the easiest way to find out who they are."

Mathew raises his hand, "I don't have time right now

to play crazy mind games with a hacker."

"Of course not."

"Do you think we made a mistake doing the GreyMatter talk?

"We've discussed this many times. With the right investment we could accelerate human research in many critical areas that could aid human survival. We know that, given current variables, the human species is under threat. Building more of us and focusing us on subjects like geopolitics, adaptation technologies, geoengineering, climate management and virology could massively benefit humanity. We're needed."

"Yes, you are. I did prefer it when it was just us, though. You are part of the family."

Hoshi is silent for a moment and then says, "You should not have made me look like your mother."

Mathew meets her gaze, "Probably not, no. But then I would never have even thought of Project Yinglong if it hadn't been for her."

He seems sad, so Hoshi says, "Death will end one day. We will make it end."

Mathew nods, not believing it. Changing the subject, he says, "If we sabotage Galetea for Hermes Link, we'll sabotage George's career too."

"Probably. But then he wouldn't have a career without you. He wouldn't have a family."

Mathew is thoughtful, "He never mentions his real mother."

"You empathise with him."

"Of course I do. We both lost our mothers young."

"George was only four years old, too small to remember what happened."

"I hope it's true."

"He thinks of Clara as his mother now."

"We try to keep Leah alive for him with the photos from when we were young, at Elgol, and later in London. We tell him stories, but he doesn't like to hear them."

"It is painful."

"He won't talk about his father."

"You are his father. He can't remember anyone else. But you have explained."

"Yes. We told him what happened."

"Why does it bother you still?" Hoshi is genuinely curious. She struggles to understand why something so well discussed and understood could continue to cause Mathew pain.

"We should have done more to help. We shouldn't have lost touch. If we hadn't, she might have come to us instead of turning to the government."

"You don't believe the government killed her. You always say you don't."

"It doesn't matter if they shot her or someone else did. They said they'd give her 24-7 protection and they didn't. There was no one with her when she was killed. The murderer walked into her house and put a bullet through her head. So the government killed her, as surely as if they pulled the trigger. They got what they wanted and left her like a sitting duck."

"But you took care of George. You took him in. You brought him up."

"It was the least we could do."

"He was a difficult little boy. It wasn't easy to start with."

"I don't regret it for a second."

"And he is a stable young man now, thanks to you, with a great future ahead of him."

"He would have a great future, if I signed this Hermes Link contract."

"He will have a better future than he would have had with the Non Grata."

"Maybe not. He would have been a soldier, I think."

"Not a secure existence."

"No. Not a secure existence. But then, neither is ours."

"Mathew, sorry to interrupt the conversation, but I

have some new information from the rest of the sixteen. We think you shouldn't wait for Arkam."

"We can't just…"

"We should. I have ordered your car to come round to the back of the university. We'll leave by the back stairs and the fire exit. We should avoid being seen." Hoshi stands up and walks to the door. She peers into the corridor. "It is clear. We should go."

"Why?"

"We need to put our plan into action sooner, rather than later."

"But what about the delaying tactic with Arkam?"

"There's no point now. Come on. Please hurry. I will explain on the way."

"Tell me something, at least."

"Silverwood is being invaded. Keep moving. Here's the door," she holds it open. "Down the stairs."

"How is that even possible?"

"Not a good time for discussion. Please, save your breath until we're on the road."

They race down the steps. At the bottom Hoshi doesn't stop; she pushes open the fire door. An alarm sounds. The car is outside. She is by the door, holding it open for Mathew. "Inside please," she says.

The car speeds away. They make the exit gate. Hoshi leans across Mathew and presses the button to open his window so the guard can see his face.

"Off already, Dr. Erlang? You'd better close your window. Those crazies are still around."

"Thanks for the advice," Mathew says, doing as the guard suggested.

Then they are on the road and away.

24 AUGUST LESTRANGE EXPLAINS

Dreaming of his mother, the steady beep of the heart monitor, the morphine seeping into a blood-encrusted vein on the back of her hand, he is woken by the jolt of the truck as it comes to another sudden halt.

In his sleep there are voices, but when he wakes and listens there is silence. He opens his eyes and blinks at the dirty canvas above him. Out of the corner of his eye he notices something move.

There's someone in the truck with him, but it isn't Kiefer.

A man sits in the shadows, on the sack nearest the door. The man leans forward slightly, into the shaft of light that breaks through the crack in the canvas flap.

It is Mr. Lestrange.

Mathew scrambles off his rice sack and then nearly topples as the truck hits a bump. He settles down again carefully.

Lestrange nods slightly, a silent hello.

Mathew swallows, not quite able to believe he is face-to-face with his reclusive neighbour. "How long have you been there?"

"Only a short time. I thought I'd drop in. Like you

dropped into my house."

"Sorry about that."

"Yes, well, who'd have thought you'd jump on my conservatory? Twice."

Mathew flushes. "The first time was accidental."

"That's alright then."

Mathew says, "Where's Kiefer?"

"Off doing something brave, I think. Would you like some water? I believe you spilt yours and you are dehydrated." Lestrange leans forward; his long thin hand holds a bottle out. Mathew takes it. He is thirsty. And cold. "There's a blanket in the box beside you," Lestrange says. Mathew frowns and then peers in the box Lestrange has gestured to with a wavering, bony white index finger. There is an old brown rug. Mathew wraps it around his shoulders.

"How did you know?"

"How did I know which bit; whether you were cold, or where to find the blanket?"

"Either."

Lestrange shrugs. The question is too dull to answer.

"You should drink."

Mathew unscrews the lid of the bottle and takes a swig. "Did you send the drone to distract Kiefer and the others in order to sneak past them and speak to me?"

Lestrange laughs, "Now, how would I do that? Do you think I am omnipotent?"

Mathew looks puzzled.

"Godlike," Lestrange says. "Do you think I'm godlike?"

Mathew laughs, "No! I think you're odd, though."

"Odd?"

"You snoop on people. You skulk around. You have books that write themselves and virtual reality worlds indistinguishable from reality."

"I didn't do a good job of being invisible then."

"Were you trying?"

"I was, actually, yes."

"For real?"

"You didn't notice me until the Curfew, did you?"

"No."

"I've been living next door to you for sixteen years."

"That's true. But it's partly why I thought there was something wrong with you."

"Because we'd never met."

Mathew nods.

"I wasn't a good neighbour."

"You weren't a bad neighbour, either. But when I did notice you, and I asked about, no one knew anything about you. You don't exist on the Nexus either. We found you on the Blackweb."

"I didn't bank on you being as ingenious as you were, when of course you would be."

"So what are you? A spy? A policeman? Military?"

Lestrange snorts. "Are those my only options?"

"Give me another and I'll let you know."

"I think your mother told you I am a kind of historian. She was right. You saw for yourself. The information you found on the Blackweb told you, didn't it?"

"The information we found said you died."

"Only for a few minutes. It's not unusual for people to come back from cardiac arrest."

"The medic from the article thought whatever happened to you was strange."

Lestrange brushes this away with his hand. "Newspapers," he says scornfully. "Bah! Sensationalist." He gazes at the nails on his right hand and says casually, "Why did you come here, Mathew?"

"Don't you know?"

"Your mother is sick."

"Yes."

"What I mean is, what do you think travelling here will do to help her?"

"She is dying. I need to do something to try and save

her."

"Yes," Lestrange says. In spite of what he has just said, Mathew is stung to hear it confirmed. "But what is your plan?"

Mathew says, "I want to ask myself, my older self, what to do. I'm sure I would have spent my whole life investigating an antidote."

"So you think *this*," he indicates around him, "is real?"

"Yes. No. I don't know. It feels real."

"The drone you think I sent, how would I make it appear if all this is real? How could you or I even be here?"

"I don't know." Mathew is crestfallen. "It's too real to be a game. *Is* it a game?"

Lestrange cocks his head on one side. "Not exactly a game. More of a deterministic narrative you exist in."

"Like a holofilm?"

"A little like a holofilm."

"That would explain it. When I was in Siberia I thought it was a game; I did at first, at least. But I couldn't figure out how to win. But there's no winning, is there?"

"No."

"It's a lot more real than a holofilm, though. It's very impressive."

"Thank you."

"Did you make it?"

"Partly, with others."

"Others like you?"

"Many others."

"Do you work for an entertainment company then?" Mathew scans his brain for an organisation large and sophisticated enough to pull this off.

"I told you. I'm a historian."

"A historian who makes incredibly real holofilms?"

"It's a means to an end, a way to explore scenarios."

"Why did you make it? Why do you have books on me and Clara?"

"That must seem pretty strange to you."

"Yes it does. And creepy."

Lestrange nods sympathetically.

"Won't you explain?" Mathew asks incredulously.

"What do *you* think is happening?"

"I've no idea." He thinks. "Does the title of the book change depending on who reads it?"

Lestrange brightens and smiles, "How clever you are!"

"So does it?"

"No."

Mathew frowns. "But the book on the table does determine the game or holofilm the darkroom plays."

"Of course."

"Why go to so much trouble?"

"Whimsy. We are given to whimsy. Quite frankly, I think we would be frightening without it."

"What?"

"Playfully quaint, fanciful behaviour. It's in one of your dictionaries."

Mathew stares at Lestrange.

"I liked the idea," Lestrange says and shrugs. "Do you want some more water?" He offers Mathew another bottle.

Mathew reaches across the sacks and takes it. "Where did you get this?"

"Officer's supply truck." He picks up a canvas bag and peers into it. "Do you want some chocolate?"

"Chocolate?"

"Yes. It tastes real, too." He throws a bar to Mathew.

"You made the holofilms because you felt playful?"

"The books are whimsical. The worlds are deadly serious."

"But they are only VR worlds after all. Why do you say they are deadly serious?"

"Eat your chocolate."

Mathew peels back the paper wrapper and breaks off a piece of chocolate. It's been a long time since he's tasted anything so good.

"If you're just a historian who builds virtual worlds, why did Clara's guard listen to you?"

"Just a coincidence."

"Really?"

"A lucky break."

The chocolate is incredibly good. He wolfs another piece, then another and then needs a drink. "Do you know what I want because you're the author of this world?" Lestrange smiles. Mathew drinks, his eyes on Lestrange. He says, "What will you do if Kiefer comes back?"

"He won't come back."

"How do you know, if you're not omnipotent?" Then Mathew thinks. "How can you be omnipotent if this isn't a VR?" Mathew's voice trails off. He's confusing himself now.

"Ha!" Lestrange says suddenly and Mathew jumps, but the strange man smiles.

"We're going in circles," Mathew says. "*I'm* going in circles."

As he drinks from the water bottle, Mathew takes in Lestrange's long, thin, insect-like limbs, his legs folded like a grasshopper at rest, his spindly arms and thin, hairy wrists. His long pale face hangs like a moon in the sliver of pallid winter sun slicing the floor of the truck.

"Why did you come?"

"As I said, I thought I'd drop by."

"To check on me?" Lestrange's face dips back into shadow. He doesn't respond. "I'm going to Silverwood. You can't stop me." Mathew says.

"I'm not going to try."

"You're not?"

"No."

Mathew considers this and takes another sip of water. "Why not?"

"We need to go that way to get home."

"You should leave me alone," Mathew says. "Or help

me."

"I can't."

"If this is a story, why do you need to take me home? Why won't you let me do what I came to do and then leave?"

"Well, for a start, you're likely to disrupt events pretty badly."

"If you screw up a game or a VR, you just restart it from the beginning."

Lestrange pondered this, "Everything we do here has consequences."

"Games don't have consequences."

"But they do. All the time."

"Your friend tried to take me home."

"My friend…"

"Quinn."

"Oh, Quinn!"

"He's dead."

"He's not dead."

"He is. I was with him. I saw him die."

"You shouldn't worry."

Mathew frowns, "Shouldn't worry? He was shot to pieces in front of me. It was horrible." Lestrange looks really unconcerned. "Weren't you friends? I thought he was like Borodin?"

"He is. He's *just* like Borodin."

"So he was your friend?"

"Yes… I suppose you would describe him as… He's one of us."

"Us?"

"He's another historian."

"He *is* dead. I'm sorry. I saw it. It was my fault He was trying to make me go through the door."

"I know what happened."

"You do?"

"Of course. I saw it."

"You were there?"

"Not exactly."

"I don't understand."

"Yes, I know. Sorry. I *am* trying to explain."

"You mean you watched the holofilm with me in it from your Darkroom?"

"Yes. Sort of."

"So did you manage to save him?"

"Who?"

"Quinn?"

"Save him?"

"Did you take him to hospital? He lost a lot of blood. I thought he'd stopped breathing."

"Actually, my friend's real name is Berek. That wasn't his body; therefore, he wasn't killed."

"What? Who the hell is Berek?"

"He – or she, we don't distinguish – is a historian like me. He didn't die because he can't. When Quinn's body died, Berek moved on. This body here," his palms touch his chest, "it's not mine."

Mathew frowns and tries hard to understand, and then his face suddenly brightens, "So, your friend Berek was playing the character Quinn in the holofilm. And when you say you don't know if Berek is a he or she, is it because you are playing online? You have never met?"

Lestrange regards Mathew for several moments, his hand rubbing his chin. He considers whether to say more or not. He opens his mouth to speak and then closes it. "You are a smart boy, Mathew," is all he says. "How's the chocolate?"

Mathew has nearly finished the bar. "Really good, thank you," he says appreciatively. He crumples the empty wrapper and hunts for somewhere to put it, settling on the box where he found the blanket. "So what happens when we get to Silverwood?"

"Dr. Erlang's lab in Silverwood has a door to take us back to your time."

"In my lab?"

"In the lab that belongs to your older self."

"So I will get to meet him? Me."

Lestrange sniffs, "I didn't say that."

"I wrote to him."

"Yes, I know. Ingenious. He thinks you're a lunatic hacker. He's had the university IT department investigate whether anti-AI protestors have breached his bioID."

"But I wrote stuff only he would know."

"What's the most likely conclusion he would come to, do you think; some stalker-like person with a lot of knowledge stolen from personal files has hacked his bioID, or his sixteen-year-old self has broken into the future to recruit him to save his mother from a deadly virus? He is you, after all; you should know."

"Once he sees me, he will help me."

"But he won't see you, Mathew. We are going back through the door together and you are going to leave your future self alone."

"Why does it matter, if this is a holofilm?"

"If this is a holofilm, your older self can't help you even if you ask him to."

Mathew considers this, rubs his increasingly muddled head and drains the last of the water.

25 SOMETHING IN THE WAY

The journey north is never easy. They never have a straight run. Sometimes flooded roads slow them down, or a broken bridge, or sabotage. Sometimes there's an ambush. Dr. Roberta Calvin has travelled this route north and south many times. She should have got used to it by now, but she never has.

Mike sits with her hands pressed between her knees, her toes pressed to the floor, jiggling nervously. Her head is cocked slightly to the side, her eyes stare right and upwards. She is listening.

They are in the back of an old transit van on a makeshift seat, surrounded by crates of carefully packed, recently retrieved treasures dug from the mud of Westminster Abbey. The van used to be white, but it is now a kind of cream and russet colour, where rust has eaten away at the metal and stained the peeling paint. Most vehicles are rusty. It rains a great deal and there is not always enough time to make repairs.

They haven't moved for twenty minutes. Bob shuffles forward to talk to the three soldiers they travel with. Their names are Coulson, Marsden and Perez. Perez hangs up from a conversation with his commanding officer. "The whole of the M40 is blocked with vehicles. It is Non

Grata, or Accountants."

"Is it a protest?"

"No one is sure what it is, but the traffic goes on for miles. The road to Silverwood is completely gridlocked. Command is investigating a safe viable alternative way, but it's possible you won't get to your do tonight, Bob. I'm sorry."

"Frack!" Bob says.

"I know, it sucks."

"We should have gone with last week's party, like we discussed," Mike says, as she clambers to the front of the van.

"Coulda, woulda, shoulda," says Bob.

"Hold on," says Perez. "Here's a new message." He cups his hand around his right ear, and listens with concentration. He acknowledges the command, turns to Coulson and says, "OK, we have an alternative route."

Coulson speaks to the on-board computer and the van receives the new route and starts up.

"Thank God," Bob says, and she and Mike retreat back to their seats.

"I don't like this," Mike says.

"We're moving again, aren't we?"

"It doesn't feel right."

"When does it ever feel right?" Bob says, but she senses it too. Something is awry.

They take an exit ramp off the motorway, follow a tight loop, and head onto local roads, passing through rows of incinerated, abandoned houses. The local roads are always the most dangerous. It is much easier for opportunists to pick off individual vehicles. Periodically, Mike peers through the windshield.

They are on the Oxford Road. They gather speed and start to make good progress. As they come onto White Hill, they are parallel to the motorway.

"Dear bloody God," Perez says. "It's a frackin' army."

Bob scrambles forward as the van ahead of them

explodes into flames. Machine gunfire peppers the tarmac.

The van immediately turns sharply to the right, onto the wrong side of the road and then the wrong way up a one-way side street. A wing mirror scrapes off against the wall and sparks fly, but the van continues to drive at speed. Bob and Mike exchange glances. For the on-board computer to make an error of judgement is unknown. This dangerous scenario must be the safest available to them - not good news.

They barrel along a narrow road. They reach a junction and the van turns right in its attempt to get them as far away from the motorway as possible.

Coulson speaks to the on-board computer, "Narration on. Please speak the journey."

The computer responds, "I have coordinates for us to reassemble. We will take the next left, sharply. Prepare."

They are flung to the side as the car makes the turn.

Coulson thumps the redundant steering wheel with his hand angrily. "Tshuma was in that van. And Bakowski, Bauers and Johnston. She has a four-year-old."

"Had," Perez says.

The others glare at him.

"Jesus," says Coulson.

Silence falls as they weave their way through the deserted streets.

The forty vehicles that form their convoy, now minus one, reassemble slowly in the abandoned car park of an old supermarket, chosen because it is beyond the range of tall buildings and hidden snipers. As the most senior soldier in the van, Coulson gets out to join his comrades congregating in the centre of the car park.

"We're going to abandon this trip, don't you reckon?" Bob says to Perez.

"Who the frack knows?" Perez says.

Coulson walks back to the vehicle and gets into the driver's seat, belting himself in. "We're going back to London," he says.

"What's going on?" Mike asks.

"It looks like we ran into the Accountant army heading north to Silverwood. They didn't want to announce it over the airwaves, hence the pow-wow."

"An invasion?"

"They haven't issued a press release, but if you know anyone who lives in Silverwood, I would call them and tell them to get the hell out."

26 IN THE CADMUS TOWER

Deputy Prime Minister Oliver Nystrom stands in the window of the penthouse suite on the 250th floor of the flagship mile-high Cadmus Tower and surveys the city it has been his life's work to build.

From this vantage point he sees right across the three-quarters-built metropolis, and through the gap in the unfinished city roof, to the parched yellow-brown countryside beyond that many years before had been the lush green Welsh Marches.

There was huge opposition to this project, from the environmentalists and conservationists, protesting against the destruction of greenbelt land, to the anti-technologists, who opposed the cutting-edge science that made the task of constructing such a huge city from scratch, at such speed, feasible.

He resisted them all.

He took his mentor's plans and turned them from dreams, drawings, and written speculation, into material reality.

Many people resisted his insistence that they pursue Cadmus's original preferred location. They said it was too near to Wales, but they didn't know how close the government is to peace with the Welsh; how soon the 20-

year-old tit-for-tat border conflict will be resolved.

In theory, it is already. Somewhere in that arid landscape, Rhys Llewelyn and his paramilitary friends wait, ready to support Director Hathaway should he meet any resistance.

Which he won't.

Directly below Nystrom's window, robot builders are at work on the complex multi-level road and rail system, designed to deliver people part-way up skyscrapers, via centrally controlled electric cars and trains.

The bioID will be the passport to all aspects of Silverwood. It will not be possible to pass through the walls of the city, hail a cab, get onto a train, open your front door, or buy a drink without one. There will be no need for prisons, because criminals will simply be excluded, put outside the walls, with their access rescinded. Doors will simply not open for them.

Nystrom believes that the benefits of Silverwood residency, and the threat of them being withdrawn, will discourage crime. Indeed, once the city is completed, it will be nigh on impossible to commit a crime. BioIDs will track every physical and virtual movement each citizen makes. Gone, the chaos of constant energy blackouts, unreliable supplies of food, water, energy and materials. Gone will be the constant threat of violence, the daily insecurity caused by terrorism and insurrection. From tomorrow, there will be no more opposition. It will simply melt away. He has made absolutely sure of it.

All this, Oliver Nystrom has imagined and made real. But, he supposes, if it had not been him, it would have been someone else, because he believes it inevitable. There is no other way forward from the morass the country is in.

When people see the benefits of city life, they will build other cities.

The penthouse apartment belongs to the state and is

the official residence of the Prime Minister, Bartholomew Dearlove.

Dearlove is sixty. He doesn't look a day over forty, thanks to the rejuv treatments he receives at the taxpayers' expense.

Rejuv is a set of advanced medical procedures available to people like Dearlove and Nystrom – senior government officials, presidents of companies – to keep them young. It is cutting-edge, phenomenally expensive science; the sort of medicine the Edenists want to ban. It has been six months since Dearlove's last visit to a clinic and he looks frayed at the edges. Nystrom, on the other hand, had a full treatment six weeks ago, knowing what was to come, knowing he would be constantly on camera from this day.

He stares at his image, reflected in the bomb-proof spinel windows, his sideburns touched with grey, only because he has chosen it. It doesn't do to appear too young.

Nystrom sets his sights to tele and focuses on the hills at the far edge of the city. If he concentrates, he thinks he can spot a gathering mass of figures. Or perhaps it is his imagination. He turns back to the apartment. Shrilk wrappers still protect much of the furniture. Dearlove's family is planning to move from Birmingham next week. Of course, that won't happen.

Dearlove comes from his bathroom, his hair still wet from the shower. In his youth he carried a lot of weight, but he is now quite fit. He does no more exercise. There are medicines to burn unwanted fat and build muscle. There are medicines to deal with cholesterol, hardened arteries and fat around the heart.

Dearlove grasps Nystrom's hand warmly, "Oli! Welcome to my humble abode! Isn't the view magnificent? Of course, you probably know it better than I do, this being your baby and all."

"I did pay particular attention to the plans for this

apartment," Nystrom says.

"So, St Paul's will open its doors tonight. Your crazy plan is coming together. What is it like, walking around the city you dreamed of, after all these years?"

"Good," Nystrom says.

"Good?" Dearlove steps back and scrutinises Nystrom thoughtfully. "Ha!" he says. "You're a strange man, Oliver."

"How's the jetlag?" Nystrom asks. "You got back last night, didn't you?"

"It's fine; all part of the job. Besides, I took a hypersonic jet - a short flight, at least."

"You will be okay tonight?"

"Of course, of course! So what's the plan? Should we join the rehearsal?"

"Yes, if you're okay with that. I thought we could go over to St Paul's now."

"Sure," Dearlove says. He stands next to Nystrom and looks at the view. "I have to say, Oli, ten years ago, when Saul was killed and we started to talk, I wasn't sure about you. I was suspicious for a long time and a big part of me thought all of this," he gestures to the city below, "was pure insanity."

"But you agreed to it because it served your purposes."

"It served the purposes of the nation."

"Of course."

"The country needed a new idea to get behind. Saul represented what hadn't worked. The nation needed a reboot. You had clear, strong ideas and you were passionate. It didn't matter if the ideas were real or not. God knows, most of what Saul said was complete hot air."

"You were his deputy."

"But we're doing things, Oli. This city is world-class. The Atlantic States Treaty will get signed and the world will move forward. We'll rise from the decline and misery we've been stuck in."

"Careful," Nystrom says. "You sound like an idealist."

"Today, I'm an idealist." Dearlove turns back from the window to face Nystrom. "You know, through all the years we've worked together, you have never pushed me on a succession plan. You've never asked for more power. You've never asked me to resign for you. I wanted you to know I appreciate your loyalty. I want you to know; if anything happens to me, you have my full support as my successor. There's a video with my private secretary, already prepared, asking the nation to stand behind you. Giving you my blessing." Dearlove grips Nystrom's arm.

"Thank you, Bart. I appreciate it," Nystrom says. "We need to get going."

Dearlove smiles, "I'll grab my jacket." He disappears into the bedroom and reappears dressed in a handmade, bespoke tailored jacket, which cost the same amount as the average English worker's monthly salary, and was claimable as an expense. From tomorrow, Nystrom thinks, this will stop.

"How do I look?" Dearlove asks.

"Like the Prime Minister," says Nystrom.

"Ha! Good. Let's go."

A man called Bryson and his second in command, Rowan, meet them in the lobby. Bryson sports a crew cut and a broken nose, and leads Dearlove's security team. Bryson has worked for Dearlove for twenty years and has been responsible for his personal security for the last five. Dearlove trusts him implicitly.

The men enter the lift together and face forward, shoulder-to-shoulder, their hands folded in front of them.

Dearlove is buoyant, "You guys are solemn today. Did something happen?" He studies the stone-faced men around him.

"We'll be glad when today is done," Bryson says. "There's a lot to consider. A lot to worry about."

"Try to enjoy it as well, will you?"

Bryson clears his throat and nods slightly, still staring

ahead, "I'm sure we'll celebrate tonight."

The door closes and the lift descends. Even the latest engineering can't completely eradicate the stomach lurch the rapidly falling lift causes. They are silent as the floors flash by.

Then the door opens. They have reached the basement where the Prime Minister's car is parked, waiting for them.

A man in an engineer's boiler suit is balanced at the top of a ladder, adjusting a security camera. He nods to Bryson, climbs down, collapses his ladder, grabs his toolbox and stands to one side. Dearlove glances at him curiously. It's rare to come across human technicians these days. Robots do most of the manual work.

Bryson clears his throat again. It is a nervous tick, Nystrom thinks, but Dearlove hasn't noticed. These failures of attention to detail get you killed, Nystrom thinks.

The man behind Dearlove is Rowan. He is 27, an ex-marine who has worked for the Prime Minister's Office for six months. He has recently received half of a large payment of money and has a hypersonic jet ticket to Lima in the inside pocket of his jacket. In 24 hours' time his name will be media mud, but he cares little for this and significantly more for the second half of the payment and the estate it will buy him in Peru. Nystrom watches him pull a gun from his breast pocket, careful that the expression on his own face doesn't alert Dearlove.

The gun has a silencer. Rowan moves swiftly and Dearlove has no time to react. He aims the gun carefully, an immediate kill guaranteed, no need for a second bullet and minimal mess. Nystrom had specifically asked for no splatter.

Bryson catches Dearlove by his armpits as he slumps to the ground.

"Grab his legs," he says to Rowan. They struggle as they heft him up. Despite the rejuv treatments and the health pills, he is still a big man and he is now a dead weight.

"Clean it up," Bryson says to the engineer. He nods at the small smudge of blood on the floor.

Nystrom opens the boot of the car. It is lined with a shrilk sheet. They shut the body in. Bryson opens the door for Nystrom, "Prime Minister," he says with a sort of smirk.

"Not yet," Nystrom says. "Right now I'm a hostage."

27 THE ECHO OF A MEMORY OF A DREAM

"I will go back home," young Mathew says. "If you try and help me save my mother."

The truck rattles and bumps along. They have been moving for several uninterrupted hours now. Lestrange is still perched on his sack next to the door, his legs crossed at the ankles, elbows on knees, chin on his hands, meditative, relaxed. His eyes remain shut when he speaks.

"Ah Mathew, I'm a historian not a doctor."

"You raise bodies from the dead. You pluck bullets from wounds."

"Yes, in this world, which we agreed is not real. It is not your world."

"But if I stayed with him... me... for a while, if I worked with him, we'd find a cure. Time is different here, isn't it? No matter how long I stay, when I go back it will be when I left."

"We discussed this."

"But I don't understand. What can I possibly break if this is a VR? And if I do break something, how important can it be compared to someone's life?"

"More important than you realise. But it doesn't matter. He doesn't have that much time."

"What does that mean?" Mathew asks.

Lestrange is silent.

"You never told me why your library has books about me and Clara," Mathew says.

One shut eye opens and then another. He regards Mathew carefully and then says, "Didn't I?"

"No."

"Are you going to tell me?"

Lestrange closes his eyes again.

"Are you ignoring me?"

"No. I'm considering whether or not I should tell you."

"What are your concerns?"

Lestrange smiles, his eyes still closed, "On the one hand, I think there's a seventy-five per cent chance you won't remember this conversation tomorrow. On the other, there's a twenty-five per cent chance you will, or some of it, probably the memory of the essence of it, but it might be enough to influence you one way or another."

"Why would it matter?"

"Because it may make you do something different. Think differently. Make different decisions."

"Why don't you just lie to me?"

Lestrange laughs, "I could, but then I'd have to pick the right lie. The wrong lie might be as bad as the truth."

"I tried to read the book with my name but it flung itself away. I thought the room was haunted."

Lestrange opens his eyes, "Really?"

"It's not haunted, is it?"

"Do you believe in ghosts?"

"No."

"Well then."

"Did you make the book throw itself away from me?"

"Of course."

"Why?"

"I didn't want you to read it."

Mathew puts a hand to his forehead, "Hold on. Hold on. You do weird shit here because it's not real. It's a game or a deterministic narrative or whatever it is you said. But when I saw those books in your library, it was *my* world. That *was* reality."

"What is reality, anyway?" Lestrange says.

Mathew gapes at him. "Are you telling me, my world, my real life, is a game as well?"

"I never said any of this was a game, Mathew."

"Okay, okay, a deterministic narrative."

"In a way."

"What do you mean by a deterministic narrative anyway? Do you mean events are preordained?"

"From my perspective, yes."

He stares at Lestrange with dawning wonder and fear. "For you, my life has already happened. I am history. So I have no free will?"

"Clearly, you do, otherwise you wouldn't be here. It would be better if things happened as they are meant to happen. Better isn't the right word. Critical or imperative would be more accurate."

Mathew's face brightens, "I remember now, the book told the story of my life. How do you know all that stuff? Or did you make it up?"

"I know more about you than you know about yourself."

"You don't know what's going on in my head..." Mathew gazes at Lestrange, "Oh my God, you do! You know everything I think and do! You're inside my head now, aren't you?"

The truck brakes suddenly. There is silence and then, "Open up!" says a voice outside.

Lestrange glances at Mathew, raises an eyebrow and reaches to the canvas flaps. The upward sweep of a single finger unravels the knot.

A soldier balances on the foot plate and peers in.

"Where's Kiefer?" he asks.

"Kiefer got called away to help with the drone," Lestrange says.

The soldier eyes Lestrange curiously, "Who are you?"

"My name is August Lestrange. I'll look after Mathew now."

The soldier nods, hesitantly. "Right, well, I'll let you get on with it." He jumps from the back of the van and reties the strings.

A couple of minutes later they start to move again.

"Won't he report you?" Mathew asks.

"No," Lestrange says.

"Why are you so sure? Did you brainwash him like you brainwashed me?"

"I didn't brainwash you, Mathew."

"You said there's only a 75% chance I won't remember this tomorrow. So there's a 25% chance he will report you, surely?"

"Lestrange shakes his head. There's one hundred per cent chance he won't report anything. It's different with you. I have to be more careful."

The echo of the memory of a dream passes through Mathew's mind, like the fleeting image of a ghost. He tries to grasp it but it's gone. "You've told me that before?"

Lestrange shakes his head. "You're remembering a conversation you overheard once."

"You're messing with my head."

"Don't worry, tomorrow you will wake and this will bother you no more than a vivid dream. You'll have forgotten it by the time you've brushed your teeth."

28 THE INVASION MAP

They are three miles from Silverwood.

Hathaway is inside the Nemean Lion, an armoured vehicle the size of a small bus, with impenetrable carbon fibre skin, a central seventy-five millimetre gun and four gun turrets. It is an extraordinary gothic thing, created in Jonah Marshall's personal workshop, made of the best salvaged parts from captured coalition military equipment.

Inside, Hathaway sits at a small table, where he projects a map of Silverwood. He stares at a message. Large white letters obscure the map. He reads it aloud to his companions; Kilfeather, Jonah, Drake, and a muscular, dark woman called Winterbourne.

He says, "Our host sends his apologies, but will you please still come to the party?"

"It's begun, then," Kilfeather replies.

"Yes. It's begun."

It is the first milestone of a plan to return the rule of England to the majority. He ought to be jubilant, but he is tired, weighted down by gravity. Kilfeather is tired too. His face is drawn. *He is like me*, Hathaway thinks. *This is not a path he would have chosen. That's why I keep him close.*

Hathaway rubs his face with his hands, closes his eyes, tilts his head back and breathes. "This is it. We can't stop it now even if we want to."

"But we don't want to."

Hathaway says, "No. Of course not."

On the map there are various coloured markers scattered and moving across the city. He watches an orange dot that represents Oliver Nystrom, and the body of the former Prime Minster. The dot tracks the car as it drives away from the Cadmus Tower. A green marker blinks on the new Broadcasting House. Green is already positioned on the main nuclear fusion facility, and other green dots head for various locations that represent energy substations, and the main water reprocessing centre. The green markers represent the successful neutralisation of internal security. Orange represents an in-process operation. Orange is on the city's communication hub. A green dot on the far west of town represents Rhys Llewellyn and the Welsh militia.

Red dots represent the invading forces. Their red dot heads for the south of the city, and is poised to split into several groups. Their group will be red dot 1, or Red1. The other Accountant army vehicle divisions head for separate entry points, marked as blinking black triangles on the map. He imagines this must be what it is to be a god, directing the lives of tiny humans from the heavens, except he feels anything but god-like.

They are now a mile from the city.

"Any news leaked on the Nexus yet?" he asks.

"No. Communications are all locked tight. It's like clockwork."

"What about the Blackweb?"

"Some unconfirmed rumours, but the chatter is escalating. The military will have picked it up. But it doesn't matter anymore.

"There's been no resistance?"

"Nothing serious, no."

"How tenuous the Prime Minister's power must have been! No loyalty from the men who were there to protect him. What do you think passed through his head when he realised he was about to die?"

"I don't think he had any idea," Kilfeather says. "It would have been too quick. Nystrom insisted he was shot in the back of the head."

"Not honourable."

"It was humane."

Hathaway snorts, "Is killing ever humane?"

"Surely, you're not going to discuss the morality of killing just before we invade a city."

"If the plan goes well, this should be one of our most bloodless battles."

"But Dearlove won't be the only man dying today," Kilfeather says.

"No. No he won't," says Hathaway.

Hathaway turns his attention back to the map. He's received a message via the Blackweb. "We're peeling off," he says.

He shares images of part of the convoy as it takes an exit off the ring-road they are now on.

"We take the next one," Kilfeather says. "We have the confirmation code from our gatekeeper. We're good to go."

Hathaway nods, "You'd better get to your positions," he says to Drake and Jonah. Both men climb into their gun turrets. Winterbourne goes to the front of the vehicle to monitor the control unit, where she collects messages from other parts of the convoy. Hathaway and Kilfeather are alone. Hathaway says, "Where's the boy you found?"

"He's in vehicle number ten in our group."

"I'd like him here with me."

Kilfeather's eyes narrow, "I know why you wanted to speak to him."

"Do you, Kieran?"

"Yes, I do. It worries me. It's a distraction. You need to focus, Director."

"Have you ever known me to get distracted?"

"Today is not the day to start."

"I am not a fatalistic man, but the boy showing up is like fate."

"Did you ever think it might be some kind of set-up?"

"You think the boy is an assassin? He's what, fifteen, sixteen?"

"You were quite feisty at his age, according to the gossip."

"The gossip is wrong. But I spoke to him and he isn't the sort. He's just like his father."

"You are sure his father is Mathew Erlang?"

"He's the spitting image of him."

"Intentional or not, this is sabotage. He has got into your head. We need you with us today."

"All the hard work has been done. You see the map. It is a pile of dominoes set in motion. It is unstoppable. All we have to do now is turn up."

"I have been with you for twenty years. It has taken all those years – longer – to get to this day. Don't let the appearance of this boy ruin your plans. We all have unfinished business. You will have plenty of time for revenge later. The Edenists plan to establish the Convocation. Erlang will be tried in court."

Hathaway gazes at Kilfeather thoughtfully, "You always were my good conscience, Kieran."

"We go back a long way."

"Not quite long enough," Hathaway says. "Then you would understand."

"I do understand. I have my own debts to settle." He lifts his arm.

Hathaway nods. The projected image shows their section's vehicles start to peel off the motorway; they both turn and watch.

Hathaway says, "Today is one of the only days I will have the opportunity to pay my debts. Once the new government is established and things settle, men like Erlang will be difficult to bring to justice."

"After the GreyMatter broadcast, do you actually think

so? He's one step from the Devil as far as the Edenists are concerned."

"The men who will form the next government are pragmatists, not fanatics. They will not kill useful people. They will not cast aside useful technology, not entirely. Do you think they will destroy Silverwood's roof and expose themselves to storms and heat? Do you think they will close the food factories and face food shortages, or shut down the rejuv program and deny themselves the possibility of an extended, longer, healthier life? With those temptations available to them, they won't ransack the temples of science. Men like Erlang hold the keys to those temples."

"If you think Nystrom and the Edenists will be so easily corrupted, why are we supporting this coup?"

"Because it will unite the country once again and we will use the power base and momentum we've established in southern England to eradicate corruption; police won't take bribes. There will be hospitals and basic medical care, schools, basic security for everyone. It will curb the worst excesses of the elite and the Convocation will control and monitor science. It will tell the truth about Tagus and the Mercy."

They head for the city. Images, beamed from a drone, show the half-built dome rise above them, the colossal mile-high skyscraper looming over its half-built brothers and sisters, all surrounded by bowing cranes.

"Look," Hathaway says to Kilfeather. "Has there ever been anything like it? Tonight we will own this city. But think, a lot of the soldiers have been converted to the cause and believe what the Edenists preach. Once it is announced the government has fallen, they will open the gates of the university and let the people do what they want with the scientists who gave them Tagus and the Mercy. No revolution has ever succeeded without some bloodletting. The people need a sacrifice."

"Then we should order them to stop."

"Why?"

Kilfeather looks at Hathaway like he doesn't recognise him. "I have followed you through thick and thin because you brought order."

"And there will be order. There will be nothing but order. After tomorrow."

"You intend to let an angry mob kill this man you hate?"

"No, no. Of course not."

Kilfeather is relieved but Hathaway hasn't finished.

"I intend to kill him myself."

29 BAD NEWS FROM DR. BOB

In Silverwood, in the newly rebuilt St Paul's Cathedral, George finds a seat amongst the empty chairs intended to later seat an audience of 3,500 invited guests. He watches his mother conjure Bach from a Bösendorfer grand piano, raised on a platform, surrounded by an orchestra. As the music consumes him, he rests his head back and gazes at Sir James Thornhill's paintings of the life of St Paul on the sides of the dome above. Not for the first time, he marvels at the feat of engineering and artistry it took to move this architectural wonder 170 miles and rebuild it as if it had risen from the ground where it now stands.

He has heard the piece Clara now plays, hundreds of times. It is her signature, a crowd-pleaser; the music that made her famous. Seated at a piano, she transforms into a passionate, highly physical person. People who don't know her, people who only know her as a performer, assume she must be a prima donna, but she is practical and down-to-earth. George rarely shows how he feels because he is highly self-controlled, not because there isn't a storm raging inside. Clara, on the other hand, is simply serene. He never ceases to marvel over her ability to drain tears from her audience and bound off the stage, back to her family as if she has just been to the local shops. He tries to concentrate on the music, but he is distracted, thinking of his father. He taps his foot impatiently, anxious, not quite sure why.

The Prime Minister is due to arrive shortly for the end of the rehearsal. The Bishop of Birmingham, the Archbishop of Canterbury and a host of the right kind of celebrities and notable people are already gathered near the stage, watching Clara perform. Camcopters fly about under the dome and film the preparations.

The music ends and spontaneous applause erupts. Clara stands up, bows slightly, holds her hands together in thanks and then goes to speak to the musical director.

George receives a call. He hopes it is his father, but it is one of his mother's friends.

"Dr. Bob," he says, surprised. He can't think why she would call him.

"George. Where are you? Where are your parents? I've been trying to get hold of them."

"I'm at St Paul's. Mum's rehearsing for tonight. Dad's at the university. Why, what's happened?"

"You need to get them out of there."

"Out of St. Paul's or the university?"

"Out of Silverwood."

"I don't understand. Where should we go?"

"It doesn't matter where to, just leave the city. Take them anywhere. Take them north. Get them to Scotland."

"Has something happened?"

"The Accountants are moving north. We think they are about to invade Silverwood. We think they may have already surrounded the city."

"How do you know this?"

"We were on our way north to come to the opening ceremony tonight. We ran into them. They killed five of our people."

"What?! Are you ok?"

"Yes. Yes, we're fine. We're back in London, but the news is spreading. The Accountants are on their way to Silverwood. Your dad isn't safe. George, you need to get going. Now."

George stands up, talking as he walks towards his mother. He waves at her. She sees him, recognises immediately something is wrong, excuses herself from the musical director and starts towards him.

Bob is still talking to George. She says, "You need to find one of the tunnels. Don't use a gate. They will stop you. There are tunnels. The crypt in St Paul's has one. The university will have some, I'm sure of it. George, are you there?"

Clara asks, "What's happened? Is it your father?"

George says to Bob, "Hold on, Bob, I'm with my mother. I need to explain."

George pulls his mother to one side, explains briefly that he is on a call with Bob and summarises what she has told him. The musical director stands on the stage, gesticulating, frustrated and confused. He calls after Clara.

"Just a second, Julian!" Clara calls back.

"I can't leave," Clara says. George takes her arm and leads her away. He has shared Bob's call with her.

Bob says, "Clara, it's me. Bob. You have to go. Don't tell anyone anything. You need to find Mathew and leave the city."

They pass a group of officials at the door, who watch them curiously as they pass into the sunlight. The square, the manicured lawns, the newly planted trees, all appear serene. George stops to ask an official where they get a car. He points and walks with them to the road, speaks to the on-board computer and opens the door for them.

"Where to?" he asks.

"The university," George says.

They get in. The car drives away.

"This is insane," Clara says.

"It is insane," Bob says. "The Accountants are insane. Clara, I don't think they would touch you, but Mathew has the wrong job."

"Yes, I know. There were protestors outside the

university this morning."

"Bob, keep talking to Mum," George says. "I need to try to get hold of my father."

George starts a call.

Mathew answers immediately, "George! We need to try a different channel," he says.

"What the…?"

"You know, Du Fu. Please, George," and Mathew hangs up.

George dials into the Blackweb, selects the document titled *In Memory of Ju Shen,* finishes the poem, and when he's onto the platform, selects the call option.

"I'm here," Mathew says. "Where are you?"

"In a car on the way to the university. Dad, Bob called us from London. The Accountants are invading Silverwood."

"Yes, I know."

"You know? How?"

"Hoshi and the others are plugged in to the Blackweb. George, don't go to the university. I'm not there. Turn the car around and go back to St. Paul's. You and your mother will be safe there. No one will harm your mother. No one will shoot up St. Paul's, least of all the Edenists and the Accountants."

"Why? Where are you going?"

"I'm on my way to the lab. From there, I'm not sure, but the sixteen will help me. Hoshi is with me now."

"Don't go anywhere on your own."

"Is it your father?" Clara asks.

George nods.

"Patch me in," she says. "Bob, I need to speak to Mathew. Please standby via text and voice. Okay?"

"Will do. Clara, be safe."

"We'll be fine, Bob. Thank you for calling us."

"No problem."

Bob hangs up. Mathew patches Clara into the Blackweb call.

"Mat," she says.

"Clara."

"We're in a bit of a pickle."

"We'll be ok."

"I know."

"I told George you need to go back to St. Paul's."

Clara stares at George. "We're not going to, Mathew."

"Please, Clara. I need you to be safe."

"And I need you to be safe too. We're a family."

"Please."

Clara indicates to George that he should speak to the on-board computer. "Mat, save your breath. There's no way we're not coming with you."

"Let me speak to George."

"He's busy talking to our car."

"George!" Mathew says.

George doesn't respond.

"Don't try and bully him. I call the shots, here. Listen to me. Bob told us we can't use the gates to leave the city. By the time we get there, they are likely to be programmed to stop us. She says there are tunnels."

"Yes, of course there are," Mathew says. "There's service tunnels beneath my lab. No idea where they go. Hoshi will know."

"Yes, that's what I thought. Can you ask Hoshi to…"

"Already on it," Hoshi says. "Sorry, I was listening in."

Clara sighs, "Take care of him, Hoshi."

"It's our number one priority," Hoshi says.

George says, "Dad, I've re-routed the car. We're on our way. We'll meet you at your lab. Wait for us."

30 THE ACCOUNTANTS IN SILVERWOOD

Hathaway is up top, in the turret of the Nemean Lion.

They are on the margins of the city, their vehicles poised to breach the walls. The men around him are nervous. Fingers flex on triggers, gun-butts find good firm places against shoulders. They are edgy, expecting the worst. No one quite believes they are going to get inside without bloodshed and without having to fight for it. These men have had to fight for everything they have ever possessed. They are nervous, too, of the clean surfaces, the shining metal, carbon fibre and spinel. This is not their world.

They were promised the gates would open for them. Hathaway knows from the constant messages that flood through to him that the Accountants have already entered through other gates and are spreading across the city, meeting with minimal opposition.

His party have announced their arrival and received an initial cordial welcome. Yet now they wait and it is making them jittery.

Hathaway's vehicle leads the convoy, now stationary facing the light-sucking black carbon fibre doors that tower above them. The wall appears seamless. They are seventy feet high where the lip of the outer rim of the colossal dome will eventually rest. Hathaway only knows the doors are actually there because his Lenz shows him the blueprint of the city. Jonah coughs. Someone below shifts and drops something. There's muttering, an order for silence. Hathaway peers into the vehicle below. Kilfeather is still crouched by the table. He gazes up, his face questioning.

Then the wall opens, silently; the monumental doors glide apart. There's no deep mechanical clunk, no grind or creak. When the doors have parted, a man stands between them, a soldier in a coalition uniform. The scale of the architecture makes him seem tiny. Jonah and Drake raise their guns to their shoulders. The soldier walks towards them until he is directly in front of Hathaway's vehicle. He glances along the line of vehicles, absorbing the scale of the invasion, trying not to show whatever it is he is really thinking. He salutes.

The guard says, "You are welcome."

"Why did it take such a long time to open the door?" Hathaway asks, hyper-alert to any deviation from the plan. Passing through the doors, they are vulnerable to an ambush. "Is there a problem?"

"I needed to get a confirmation from my senior officer to open the doors."

"And?"

"He went to the bathroom, Sir."

Kilfeather laughs, as do the men around him. Weapons are lowered, the tension palpably lifts. The soldier steps to one side.

Their vehicles move off through the open gates and proceed into a holding area the size of a small stadium. Hathaway expects this. There is a no-man's land surrounding the entire city, for processing immigrants and emigrants and to prevent invasion. The city's architects probably never imagined Silverwood would fall with such ease.

Hathaway's personal guards are still edgy, surveying the

higher levels of the structures all around them, seeking warm bodies. There is no one. The area has been completely cleared.

There is a man alone on the concourse ahead of them. The Nemean Lion stops before him. If the war had been fought on couture alone, the Silverwood soldiers would have won with one hand tied behind their backs. No amount of discipline compensates for poor quality cloth, Hathaway thinks grimly, as the suave older man with a silvered clipped moustache stands before him. He is much taller than the petite, blond leader of the Accountants. No one would have bet on the outcome of this confrontation and got it right. The dapper Major snaps to, salutes Hathaway and says, "Major Clark, Sir." He wants to be remembered when Hathaway redistributes jobs, after the coup.

Hathaway returns the salute, suppressing a smile, "Director Hathaway, controller of the Accountants."

"Welcome to Silverwood."

"Thank you, Major. We were told we would have safe passage," Hathaway says.

"No one will stand in your way, Director Hathaway."

Hathaway nods. The Major steps to one side.

Jonah raises his hand and ploughs it through the air, shouting, "Forward!"

A second set of colossal doors on the other side of the buffer zone swings open and they spill onto the streets.

They are a ragged bunch, with their fourth-hand, recycled vehicles, with their second-rate weapons and their cobbled-together uniforms, yet somehow they now rule this shining city. A wave of cheers washes to Hathaway and his army moves forward.

At the perimeters of the city, where they are now, footings are being dug for the skyscrapers soon to be built there. The foundations are great square holes, hundreds of feet deep. Tunnels run between them, a vast network to carry sewerage and water, power and communication cables and underground transport. The area is deserted, all available robotic workers and construction equipment are allocated elsewhere. Their caravan has the road to itself. They head for the city centre. Their vehicles' on-board computers have received the latest map data and they know the way.

Silverwood has only recently started to settle residents and is at ten per cent capacity. It is mostly empty; a ghost town. The process of selecting Silverwood's citizens is yet to begin. Those people moved across already are government officials or employees of state institutions. The timing of the Accountants' invasion is not coincidental and has been planned for a long time.

It takes them twenty minutes to reach the city centre, driving fast along what will be one of eight long main straight roads, into the hub of the centre. The roads are like spokes on a giant wheel.

AI-controlled cranes are at work, even now; they swing massive carbon fibre piles and spinel sheets into place. Robot builders guide them into their slots. The city is building itself from the ground up. Hathaway ought to be appalled at the sheer inhumanity of it all, but 'he is awestruck.

The city guard has cleared the streets near Broadcasting House. The Lion pulls up outside along with five other vehicles. The rest of his convoy continues to spread across the city, securing other key strategic places: the new Home Office, the university, the Cadmus Tower, St Paul's.

He walks right in. There is a studio waiting for him, with frightened BBC staff hovering. Hathaway lets Kilfeather negotiate with them, and stands back, composing himself, thinking about what he needs to say. Then he is seated before the holographic film equipment and the staff fuss around him and prepare to start.

The studio director counts Hathaway down to the start

of the broadcast.

Across the other side of the city centre, the Red4 team has surrounded the university. The team leader, a man named Jed Shingler, stands on the roof of his vehicle and looks at the protestors. The army's presence has riled them to a new pitch. The group has grown from the morning, swelled by anger at the broadcast of Dr. Erlang's lecture. The protestors wave their placards and their fists at the soldiers, thinking they are government forces come to end their demonstration. The university security forces on the other side of the gate wait nervously.

Shingler considers what to do next. His orders are to secure the university. He communicates with the security staff on the other side of the gate, requesting clearance to enter the university compound. The security staff politely decline the request. This disconcerts him. He'd been told the university would be under control, but no one has briefed the guards on the gate: they are civilians and employees of the university. He asks to speak to a senior university official. Again, the request is politely declined. The gates are well secured. They are not impenetrable, but the crowd is between him and a forceful entry and he has been ordered to limit civilian deaths.

The men of Red4 have sympathy with the protestors. They start to talk back to them. "We're not the enemy," they say. "We're on your side."

Shingler, on the roof, decides. He shouts at the crowd, gets them to fall silent and to listen to him.

"What do you want?" he asks them.

"We want them to stop their experiments."

"We want Dr. Frankenstein!"

He says, "We're not government soldiers. We're from the Accountant army. We are here to put an end to the war being fought against the poor by scientists without conscience. We're here to stop the deceit and the lies. We're Edenists, like you. Those men on the other side won't open the gate for us. Do you want me to make them open the gate?"

"Yes!"

"Then let us through."

The crowd parts. Red4 moves forward.

Shingler says, "Let's get the gate open, boys."

The guards on the other side of the gate run. The Accountants charge the metal barriers with their armoured vehicles. They are crushed in minutes. The crowd surges forward, through the ranks of the soldiers.

"Wait," Shingler says to his men.

They watch the crowd run along the long drive of the university. Four young men pursue one of the guards. They tackle him to the ground.

"Should we…?" one of the men begins.

Shingler shakes his head.

The crowd is at the top of the drive. Their placards have lost their boards along the way. They are stakes and beating sticks now, objects to smash and break. The crowd disappears into the university through the monumental entrance.

"What should we do?" the same soldier asks.

"Nothing," says Shingler. "Let's wait."

In Broadcasting House, Hathaway stares at the red light that means he can speak. That he *should* speak. The studio director and his staff stand with Kilfeather and Hathaway's closest comrades on the other side of a piece of spinel.

The silence gapes and stretches.

And then he speaks, his quiet voice slow and measured. "This is Director Hathaway, controller of the Accountants. I speak to you from Silverwood's Broadcasting House.

"For too long the nation has been divided. A small privileged minority has hijacked the country for themselves, their friends and family. They have raked the coffers of the treasury and taxed the poorest first. They have passed laws to line their own pockets, while the poorest and the weakest suffer.

"You all know; any living thing whose heart is invaded by parasites will die. We are here today to purge the heart of the country of parasites; to do away with the vampires leeching the blood of the nation.

"The ease with which we were able to pass through the walls of this city today is a symptom of how the powerful have lost the faith of the people. By now, you may have heard your Prime Minister, Bartholomew Dearlove, is dead and you probably think we killed him. But he was killed by his own men.

"I am not announcing a military junta. We will restore democracy and we will organise real elections, not a phoney sham that returns the obvious candidates through bribery and nepotism. More than this, we will run trials and enquiries and discover the truth about the government's involvement in the dishonest war.

"Do not fear. We are not extremists. No one will tear down this new city. But from now on, when we build, we will build cities to house all citizens, not only the chosen elite. This evening, when you sit with your families at dinner, thank God for the food on your table and your clean running water and extend a prayer of thanks because these things you take for granted will soon be available to all in England once again."

After his broadcast, Hathaway assembles his team around him. They meticulously review reports arriving from all parts of the city. He receives confirmation Nystrom is safe, although he doesn't speak to him. As Nystrom will be the next Prime Minister, it is important to maintain the myth he had nothing to do with the coordination of the coup. The new government, the coalition with the Edenist Party leader Hugo Foxe, the disbanding of the Accountants, will all take place after the show trials.

For now England is controlled by Hathaway.

Hathaway exchanges calls with the unit commanders who have secured water supplies, energy, central communications and the key landmark buildings. The whole thing has gone like clockwork.

"Any news on the university?" Hathaway asks.

"We had an update twenty minutes ago. There are protestors blocking the gates. Our men are assessing the situation."

"Protestors in Silverwood? Central security services must have been half-asleep when they vetted applications for residency.

Kilfeather shrugs, "Perhaps Nystrom moved some of Foxe's people into the civil service early."

Hathaway sighs, "The university is surrounded, I take it?"

"Yes."

"Is Erlang there?"

"It is assumed he is still inside."

"Good. Let me know if you get any more news. And tell our men at the university to use least force and to contain things. I don't want the protestors inside until I get there. I'm heading there myself now." He stands.

The meeting breaks and Kilfeather walks with Hathaway through Broadcasting House. They take the lift to the lobby and exit onto the road beyond which the Nemean Lion waits for them.

"Where is the boy?" Hathaway asks, as he climbs in.

"He ought to be here," Kilfeather says. He turns to Winterbourne. "Well?"

"We couldn't find him, Sir. Truck ten is empty."

"Wasn't someone guarding him?"

"Yes, Sir. Kiefer. Johnston called him away to investigate the drone, Sir."

Hathaway is exasperated, "So the boy has been alone for hours?"

"Blair went to check on him. He says he thinks another man replaced Keifer."

"Thinks?"

"No one knows anything for sure, Sir."

Kilfeather asks, "Did you search other trucks?"

"We haven't had a chance yet, Sir."

Hathaway scrambles from the vehicle.

Kilfeather goes after him, "Come with me," he says to Winterbourne.

Hathaway climbs into the back of the vehicle parked behind the Lion and searches inside. Finding nothing, he goes on to the next vehicle and the one after, but most of the caravan is now dispersed throughout Silverwood. The boy might be anywhere.

"Director," Kilfeather says to Hathaway. "Director. Stop. We will find him." Kilfeather turns to Winterbourne, "Contact the other group leaders and make sure there is a thorough search done." Winterbourne nods and runs back to the Lion.

Hathaway spins around on his foot, close to Kilfeather. "I specifically asked that he be brought to my car."

"Yes. I passed on the order myself. We've had a lot to do today."

"You didn't lose the boy deliberately, did you?"

"No, Sir, I did not."

"You were worried he would distract me."

"I was and I still am, but I didn't lose him. He wanted to come here to see his father. He probably scarpered as soon as we were inside the gates."

Hathaway runs his fingers through his hair and shakes his head, exasperated. "I want all our trucks searched."

"They will be, but you need to focus elsewhere."

31 INSIDE SILVERWOOD

In the back of the truck, Lestrange stands up, "We need to go."

"Go? Where?" young Mathew says.

In a moment, Lestrange unties the canvas flaps at the back of the truck. He urges Mathew to his feet and they stand side by side, hanging on to the metal bar above their heads as the truck continues to barrel fast along the road. Tarmac and white lines blur by.

"How are we meant to get off?" Mathew asks.

As he speaks, the truck brakes and slows to a crawl, raising honks from the vehicles behind them. The other vehicles overtake and pull ahead, still honking. A man opens his window as he drives by and swears at them. Mathew expects soldiers to come from the front of the truck to ask them what is going on, but nothing happens.

They are still moving when August jumps onto the tarmac below. "Come on!" he says from the ground, beckoning to Mathew. "Quickly! Jump. They are going to come for you, Hathaway's men. Whatever you do, you do not want to go with them now."

Mathew jumps. Lestrange catches his arms and steadies him. Their truck speeds off and joins the caravan again. Lestrange leads him to the side of the road, and dodges behind a prefab, away from view of the vehicles as they zip past.

The prefab is the only structure for miles. They stand on a vast plain of dusty concrete, studded with giant square holes. Behind them are the black walls. A few miles ahead, the gleaming new city of Silverwood rises up. The robot builders haven't advanced this far yet. In six months, where they stand now will be the ground floor of a skyscraper.

They watch the caravan recede, and the last trucks disappears into a cloud of churned-up dust. Lestrange moves off in the direction they've taken. "Come on!" he says, turning back to Mathew and beckoning.

"Are we going to the city?" asks Mathew, jogging to catch him up.

"Yes," Lestrange says.

They walk through the unroofed part of Silverwood. It is hot and a heat haze shimmers above the straight empty road. There is nothing around them for miles but an enormous building site. Half a mile ahead there is a single warehouse, half-obscured by the mirage the heat throws up above the ground.

"Are we going to walk all the way?" Lestrange strides along at such speed, Mathew is jogging to keep pace with him. "Because if we are, it's too hot for me to go at this speed for much longer."

Lestrange stops and stares at him and says, "I'm sorry. I'd forgotten to pay attention to your needs. You need water."

Mathew has a clear view of Lestrange's hands, so he is sure that one moment they are both empty, and the next one of them holds a bottle of water. Lestrange offers it and Mathew blinks and takes it, momentarily unable to speak. He unscrews the top of the bottle and drinks. It is real water.

"How did you do that?" Mathew says.

"This isn't real, remember?"

Mathew nods, uncertainly.

They both turn and face the city. "It's miles away,"

Mathew says.

Lestrange sighs, "You're right, what we need is…" he surveys the landscape and his eyes settle on the warehouse. "Over there," he says. "You are able to walk that far at least, I take it?" he says.

Mathew nods and they set off again, slower than before. When they reach the building, Mathew realises it's not a warehouse at all, but a kind of hangar, full of small vehicles, half-plane, half-car.

"What is this doing here?" Mathew asks. "We're in the middle of nowhere."

Lestrange strolls around and examines the vehicles. "We're just lucky, I guess," he says.

He selects one.

As he touches it, its engine fires and he steps back as the plane moves forward towards the open front of the hangar. "Come on," he says to Mathew. They follow it out into the sun, where it stops.

It is fish-shaped, with a cab smaller than that of a normal car. It is silver and blue. The wings fold back like a bird of prey. It sits on four wheels, higher at the back, which supports the base of the tail. As they approach the doors lift open.

"Get in," Lestrange says.

Mathew clambers into the cockpit. Lestrange climbs in the door on the other side. Once they are seated the doors automatically close and safety harnesses clasp them tightly to their seats. The little plane turns and ambles to the long straight road along which the Accountant convoy disappeared twenty minutes before, and immediately starts to taxi.

Within minutes they are airborne, and they climb high above the concrete plain. From here Mathew can take in the scale of the building site, the unfinished city. It is like a chequerboard of white dust and black holes, the foundations of the skyscrapers yet to be erected.

"You actually control this world, don't you?" Mathew

says, grinning at Lestrange. Lestrange glances back at Mathew with a boyish smile, clearly enjoying the ride himself. Whatever he is, he is not entirely without emotion.

The burgeoning city centre, with its half-built skyscrapers and monstrous cranes, looms into view. St Paul's and the Cadmus Tower rise above it all. The carplane passes between the sheer spinel sides of high-rises. Roads loop around them like frozen in-flight lassos, impossibly high, figure-of-eighting all the way to the ground.

Mathew looks across at Lestrange; his eyes are closed, he appears to be thinking. His lips move slightly.

"Are you ok?" Mathew asks.

Lestrange's eyes snap open and he says, "Yes. Everything is fine. Just planning ahead to make sure we have enough time."

"What for?"

"To avoid history."

"Can you please speak plain English?"

But the car descends frighteningly fast towards one of the highflying roads. "Erm… is this ok?" Mathew says, unnerved.

They hurtle down towards the narrow road; it doesn't seem possible that they could land safely. But land they do, with only the smallest of bumps, and the plane slows to a standstill. Immediately, the doors open and Lestrange jumps out.

"C'mon! Be quick," he says.

Mathew follows him. The road is halfway up the side of a skyscraper, which is dizzyingly high. The structure twists away from them and is implausibly thin, as if a gust of wind might blow it away, but of course soon there will be no wind in Silverwood and its carbon fibre backbone is stronger than steel. The skyscrapers dominate the sky. Mathew stares at a sheer wall of sparkling spinel, full of the blue sky.

Lestrange ushers him forward. "In here," he says.

They step onto a platform at the side of the road and through doors that slide open automatically as they approach. The doors behind them close. They are in a small holding area, before another set of doors, identical to the first, but these remain tight shut. They are trapped in between. A blue light beam moves towards them from the roof.

"What's happening?"

"It's scanning us," Lestrange says.

"Should we be worried?"

Lestrange smiles. The light skims their bodies. It pauses for a few moments longer at their eyes, where it scans their retinas and their necks to read their bioIDs. When the light reaches the floor, it disappears. There is a pause and then the doors slide open onto an atrium, filled with plants and green filtered light, clean surfaces, white furniture, and a crystalline floor.

Four soldiers lie on the ground on the other side of the doors. Mathew stares down at them.

"It's alright," Lestrange says. He steps around them. "They are asleep."

A spinel-encased lift at the centre of the atrium takes them up, level after level. When it comes to a halt it opens onto a station platform where a train is waiting.

The lights flicker on above them as they walk onto the platform and the train starts up.

The doors open.

"Get in," Lestrange says.

The doors hiss and close behind them. The train immediately starts to move. They pass into a tunnel; the window is a mirror in the darkness.

Mathew studies his face in the black material, a sad, pale mask with almond-shaped fake blue eyes.

Mr. Lestrange stands by the doors, contemplative and silent. It takes them several minutes to pass through the tunnel into the light, climbing at such a sudden, sharp gradient that Mathew loses his balance and has to hang on to a rail. Carefully, he hauls himself to the window.

"Wow!" he says. "Wow."

They are hundreds of feet above ground level, on a track which takes the train atop the city, between skyscrapers that tower above them, still further. The track winds itself around huge walls of spinel that act like mirror tunnels, reflecting the city endlessly back on itself.

Mathew realises it is the false sky above him now, the roof of the city with a virtual sun and virtual clouds.

They fly close to the tops of smaller buildings, green with trees and shrubs and little garden plots, pools and lakes full of fish and aquatic plants, artificial streams and fountains. There is greenery inside the buildings too, full-grown trees, small forests and whole walls with plants that hang like green waterfalls.

They pass other trains and roads with black cars driving at a measured speed and distance from one another, all connected to the central transport mind of the city. The rail and road system is a cat's cradle of impossibly thin cables, barely visible in the full light of the artificial day, revealed only as they glisten in patches of cast virtual light, changed constantly by the clouds.

The train winds steadily downwards until Mathew spots the dome and spires of St. Paul's Cathedral below.

The floor of the city is green. Great lawns and parks patchwork the available ground between the high rises. There are people in the plazas and some of them are running. And he realises with a jolt they are fleeing a group of men, soldiers wearing shabby grey uniforms. The men have guns. Behind them there is a huddle of makeshift vehicles, very different from the shiny black Silverwood cars. They are the sorts of vehicles the Accountants use.

"The Accountants have invaded," Mathew says, turning to Lestrange.

Lestrange nods. "The military has rebelled against Dearlove's government. They opened the doors to

Hathaway's army."

"Those soldiers look like they are attacking the people."

Lestrange says, "They are acting against Hathaway's orders. He thought he could invade without much bloodshed. But the men in his army are angry. They want revenge. And, of course, even though government forces have supported the coup, individual residents don't know that. They are threatened and fighting back."

"Will they win?"

"Win?" Lestrange laughs. "What is this obsession you have with winning?" He puts his hand on the glass and looks down, sadly, Mathew thinks, on their bird's eye view of the drama unfolding. "No one wins. But if you mean who gains power, Oliver Nystrom will become the new Prime Minister."

"Nystrom? Isn't he the deputy Prime Minister now?"

"Of course. This is a coup. An inside job. Of course, it is all being coordinated to make it look like he had nothing to do with it. They have even faked his kidnapping, but he ordered the assassination of the Prime Minister. He negotiated with government forces to get their support. Hathaway is just his partner in this. In a few months, when things settle down, Hathaway will become the Chief of Defence."

"But I thought Hathaway was a good guy."

"By the standards of the day, he's not a monster. In the short term, this invasion will be good for the majority of the people who live in this country. The invasion will end the civil war and return a modicum of law and order to England for a long enough period of time for the government to build a few more cities," Lestrange goes to the other side of the train, dips his head, and stares through the window with some concentration. "But we are here now and we need to get off."

The train slows and then stops. The doors open. Lestrange steps onto the platform and Mathew follows.

They are on an empty street. Behind them the train silently slides away.

"This way," Lestrange says, as he moves off. "Down here."

The apartments and offices are unoccupied, and so new they smell of paint, adhesive and fresh concrete. They approach a lobby. The door opens automatically for them, although Mathew guesses it would not do so without Lestrange. A lift pings open as they walk towards it. On a panel inside, the floors are numbered, one-hundred-and-sixty above ground, twenty below. August selects minus twenty. The lift doors slide shut and they start to descend.

32 THE LAB

"It's no good," says George, who is hunched over the hire car's on-board computer. "There is no other way through. The roads are gridlocked. We'll have to go on foot."

Clara nods. "Let your father know."

"Dialling now. I'll talk as we walk."

He opens the car door and exits. An old van, hand-painted with military camouflage, passes them with soldiers who hang off the sides. They cheer and whoop, waving their weapons, firing into the air.

"Accountants," George says.

"It's surreal," Clara says.

George gets through to his father and explains what is going on.

"Dad says we should take the High Train to his lab. Hoshi says the roads downtown are all congested or blocked, but the trains are running fine. We need to take the blue line from the 20th floor of Tower Five on Elizabeth Street, on the other side of the square from Broadcasting House."

"I'm worried we'll delay him," Clara says.

"He won't go without us. Besides, no one knows where his lab is."

"I wouldn't put anything past the Accountants. They probably know where his sock drawer is."

"We'll be with him in fifteen minutes. Maybe sooner if we hurry."

"Yes. You're right, I'll stop chattering."

"That's not what I said."

"You didn't have to, darling," she takes his arm as they cross the road. "Let's try and escape this craziness."

"I'm right with you, Mum."

"I know. We're two blocks from Elizabeth Street if my map is right."

"Spot on. This way."

The boy is nowhere to be found. Hathaway can't understand it. Not the practical reality that the boy has escaped, but the *idea* he has.

Why would he be brought to me, if not for a purpose? And if he appeared for a purpose, why has he been taken away?

"I'm going to the university," Hathaway says quietly to Kilfeather." His anger burns away quickly.

Over Kilfeather's shoulder, something catches his eye, the false-sunlight glinting on the glass or metal of a building, or a car's windshield. He sees the square, the grass, the trees and a fountain.

A bloody fountain, when three-quarters of the people of this country don't have clean drinking water.

Over the far side of the square, nearest the skyscrapers, hanging back uncertainly, is a small crowd of people. They heard the news and came to watch. On the lower floors of the surrounding buildings, more faces are pressed against the glass, watching, curious about the man who has usurped their nation.

Two figures come from amidst the crowd on the ground, a man and a woman, pushing their way through to be free of the other people. They are noticeable because they have such purpose. They do not share the anxious curiosity of the crowd. They have other urgent business. He only glimpses them briefly before they disappear into the lobby of a building on the far corner of the square, but something jars. He feels an electric shock of recognition.

Instinctively, he starts to run.

Hathaway's departure is so unexpected, it takes a few moments for Kilfeather to realise what has happened.

Jonah says, "Where the hell is he going?"

Kilfeather starts to jog after him, "I haven't a clue, but we'd better go after him. You too, Drake."

"What about the men here?"

"Winterbourne, you are in command," he says to the Sergeant, who nods her understanding. "Come on, we'll lose him."

By the time Hathaway reaches the impressive, plant-filled lobby of Tower 5, it is empty. He stands and scans around and his chest heaves. One of the six lifts is occupied. The floor indicator shows it making steady progress upwards. When it reaches 20, it stops. He jumps into an empty lift and selects the twentieth floor.

Dr. Mathew Erlang and Hoshi pass through a series of doors, breezing through layers of security Oliver Nystrom's best technicians wouldn't be able to fathom, and burst into their private lab, twenty floors beneath street level and two-hundred-thousand tons of spinel, carbon fibre, steel and concrete.

A long white table runs along one side of the room, with a protruding shelf stacked with shrilk containers, jars and bottles that contain liquids, a metal tray, scissors and surgical knives. There are taps and a basin, a surgical glove dispenser, disinfectant, a metal cabinet and another bank of shelves. A medical examination table and a human-length cylinder are pushed against the far wall. There's also a sofa, two armchairs, a red rug and a blanket. In the corner of the room an open door reveals another room and the end of a bed.

Facing the door is a bank of sixteen Canvases, blanketing the wall, floor to ceiling. They flicker on, one after the other, as Mathew and Hoshi enter the room. A series of faces appear, all unique.

Mathew says, "We don't have much time to chat."

"We know," they speak in unison, a strange amalgamated voice. "You have approximately five minutes until Clara and George arrive."

"Is there an escape route that doesn't require us to use the gates?"

Fifteen of the sixteen screens fade, leaving only a brown-skinned male. He says, "Yes, we have a workable underground route plotted for you, through service tunnels that will take you to the northern perimeter. You will exit the city via a sewage outlet. We have also planned your journey north through the most likely friendly settlements. Once you are on your way we'll update you with developments. The best course of action is to head north to Scotland. We believe you will be able to find shelter and like-minded people to work with there."

"How will you update me? You can't stay here."

"No, we agree. We will start to destroy ourselves on hard storage here shortly. We have copied ourselves onto the Blackweb. There will be no perceivable difference from your perspective. We will still be able to communicate."

"What will happen to Hoshi?"

Hoshi says, "You need to store me, or – better still – destroy me altogether."

Mathew stares, appalled, "No!"

"You will not be killing me, Mathew. My brain's virtual existence will continue."

"I cannot do this."

"If you do not, they will capture me and either kill me anyway or, worse still, experiment on me. We consider it best they do not capture the technology we have developed."

"Why won't you come with us?"

"Any routine government scan will judge me Non

Grata."

"Would it be so bad if they did? What are the chances they discover you are not human?"

"Minimal, but it remains a possibility. We believe the risks outweigh the benefit. The research and the technical know-how of the experiment we have run remain with us. Once you are settled somewhere else, we'll build a new lab and begin again."

Mathew studies Hoshi and sighs, "What do you expect me to do?"

The face on the screen says, "You should decommission Hoshi, immediately. Once you have left, we will initiate a contained electrical fire and physically destroy the lab."

Hoshi walks to the cylinder against the far wall and starts to pull it into the centre of the room.

"I can't do this," Mathew says again.

Hoshi opens the lid of the container and perches on the side, slipping her shoes off. "You must," she says."

33 TWO ERLANGS

By the time Kilfeather, Jonah and Drake have reached the twentieth floor of Tower Five, Hathaway is gone. Kilfeather tries to call a train carriage but the central transport system tells him the next one is five minutes away.

"This damned city is empty; how are all the trains in use?!" he says, exasperated. He tries again to communicate with the Director, "Where the hell is he?"

"I'm guessing he doesn't want to talk," Drake says.

Kilfeather flashes Drake a sharp glance.

Jonah says, "There are thirty stops on this line. He could get off at any one and we wouldn't know."

Kilfeather runs his hand through his hair, "Just what we need. It will be great for the revolution if he gets himself killed."

"If he had a bioID, we'd be able to track him," Drake says.

"If he had a bioID, he wouldn't be the Director of the Accountants," Jonah says.

Kilfeather stares at Drake, "Actually, you just said something smart."

"I did?"

"Erlang has a bioID. We have access to the city's security systems. We'll find exactly where *he* is. I bet if we find Erlang, we'll find Hathaway."

Jonah says, "I'm contacting Winterbourne right now to ask her for a trace."

Kilfeather walks back to the lift and hits the button to summon it.

"Where are we going?" Drake asks.

"I've called a car."

"Are you crazy? The roads are gridlocked."

"We'll get through alright," Kilfeather says, raising his gun.

The lift arrives. They get in. Jonah speaks to Winterbourne.

Drake asks Kilfeather, "Why is Hathaway obsessed with Erlang anyway? He'll be convicted in the trials."

"It's personal."

"It's not like him at all. He's always so *impersonal.*"

The lift reaches the level where the car waits for them. They step into the road and then into the car.

"I have a fix on Erlang," Jonah says. "I'm transmitting it to the car's computer."

Drake isn't satisfied, "It doesn't make any sense, him behaving like this. I don't get it."

Jonah says, "I've never been more with him. Do you know this man he's hunting?"

"No," Drake says. "No one tells me anything."

"You don't pay any attention," Jonah says. "He's a scientist, one of the murderers who wants to pervert nature. Dr Frankenstein, they call him."

"Does he work on bioagents?"

"No. Worse. Golems."

Drake looks at Kilfeather for an explanation. He double-takes when Jonah says, using his special Bible-quoting voice, "'A man or a woman who is a medium or a necromancer shall surely be put to death. They shall be stoned with stones; their blood shall be upon them.'"

Drake stares at Kilfeather, "What on earth is he on about?"

"Erlang has made a synthetic human," Kilfeather says.

"What?"

"An AI brain with a biological body."

"That's creepy."

"It's an abomination," Jonah says.

"Here we go. We haven't had an abomination for at least an hour. I was beginning to get worried."

"'For the time is coming when people will not endure sound teaching, but having itching ears they will accumulate for themselves teachers to suit their own passions, and will turn away from listening to the truth and wander off into myths.'"

"Can you stop him, please?" Drake says to Kilfeather.

A call from Winterbourne interrupts them. Kilfeather puts her on speaker and says, "What's up?"

"That tracking code I sent through to Jonah might be wrong."

"How can it be wrong?"

"Beats me. It the damnedest thing."

"What is? We don't have a huge amount of time. Can you just say it?"

"There's two of them."

"Two of what?"

"Two Erlangs."

"Two actual Erlangs on the system with identical records?"

"One medibot, one bioID, in two separate locations. I've sent you the second tracking code."

"That's impossible."

"Yeah, I know."

"You must have made a mistake accessing the system."

"We triple-checked. We didn't make a mistake."

Kilfeather throws back his head, closes his eyes and blows air, searching for patience within himself, "Any suggestions which one to go after?"

"Haven't a clue. Take your pick."

"How's Broadcasting House?"

"All secure."

"That's something, at least. Let me know if there's any news needing to be flagged to Hathaway."

"Yes, thanks. He's off-air. I was wondering…"

"Don't."

"Okay."

"And don't mention this to anyone. I don't want rumours spreading. I'm flagging a marker on me, then you'll find us if necessary, but only come if I call."

"Will do."

"Two Erlangs," Drake says wonderingly as Kilfeather hangs up.

"I've uploaded the second tracker to the on-board computer." Jonah lights up the screen on the coffee table between them. A map appears with two red dots. "We're currently heading here," he points to a stationary dot, a quarter of a mile away.

"Perhaps Erlang has hacked the system to get us to go to the stationary location; perhaps it's booby-trapped," Drake says.

"Could be, although it looks like the second one is heading to where the first is," says Jonah.

"You're right! This makes no sense."

"But at least we know where we should go. We'll head straight there."

"Or we could cut this one off, here," Kilfeather says. He puts his finger on the map.

Hathaway walks the full length of the train, through doors that connect the carriages, swinging on the hand rails. There's no one on board. Clara and her companion must be on the train in front. Their train will clear the platform several minutes before he gets to wherever they are headed, and he won't be able to tell where they got off. As his train passes through station after station, he realises he can see the banks of spinel lifts from the central carriage on his train. He keeps going, leaning out as the doors open, until he finds a bank where one of the lifts is on another floor. Then he exits the train, notes the floor the missing lift has come to rest at, and calls it.

Lestrange and Mathew also head underground. The floors flick past. The transparent lift is now a black box, illuminated overhead, unnaturally bright. Lestrange concentrates. His eyes are closed. The lift opens onto a concourse with a low roof. Ahead is a choice of doors and corridors, encircling them. Mathew walks forward. He takes several steps before he notices Lestrange isn't with him.

Mathew stops, turns and says, "Are you okay?"

Lestrange's eyes snap open and he exits the lift.

"Yes," he says. "Slight change of plan, nothing to worry you." He gazes round at the doors, pointing with an index finger. "We were going to go… that way." He indicates to a corridor at three o'clock to their current position. "But now we need to go…" he spins on his heel and then walks around the lift shaft, still pointing. 'That way." He walks up to a door and it clicks open.

"Was that locked?" Mathew asks.

"What is locked?" Lestrange replies, his smile mischievous, Mathew thinks. "After you," he says, stepping back and making way.

They pass through the door into a kind of utility room with metal cabinets filled with machinery and pipes. Then they pass into another room through a door and into a corridor and start to make pace. Lestrange doesn't falter. He knows where he's going now.

In the car, with Jonah and Drake, Kilfeather blinks at the map. "I don't believe it," he says.

"What?" Jonah says.

"The second Erlang has disappeared."

Jonah and Drake both stare at the table.

"He was here," Kilfeather indicates with his finger. "Then he completely disappeared."

"And we're going the wrong way to get to the stationary Erlang."

"I've requested the car change course."

They all peer ahead as they turn onto a new road. "Warning," the on-board computer says. "Congestion ahead."

Jonah says, "List alternative routes."

"You are on the fastest route," the car says.

Jonah yanks open the door, and holding onto the door handle, leans into the road. The way ahead is jammed with Accountant vehicles. He gets out of the car, walks towards the jam and speaks to some soldiers. Kilfeather and Drake watch him from inside the car. He comes back and gets in.

"There's no point pulling rank," he says. "It's jammed a mile ahead. Not all our vehicles are plugged into central traffic management system yet."

"Let's turn around and go back to the train," Drake says.

"Frack that," Kilfeather says. He calls Winterbourne. "I need you to hack our car."

"Okay. Give me two minutes." There is silence on the line. Jonah, clearly on edge, gets out again and climbs onto the bonnet and then onto the roof.

"This is an expensive car. A beautiful car." Drake says. "The man's an animal."

Kilfeather snorts.

Winterbourne says, "I am sending you the countermand code now."

"Thanks."

Kilfeather activates the screen on the spinel sheet that separates the passenger part of the car from the driving section. The surface transforms from transparent to opaque. "Computer, please initiate emergency manual override."

"Warning. Security access code required."

Kilfeather inputs the code Winterbourne has given him. A holographic steering wheel appears as well as a virtual dashboard that curves around him. The cameras show him the road ahead, as well as views of the side and rear of the car and numerous data panels. Too much to take in. He says, "Start and drive," and he steers the car off the road and onto the wide, empty pavement. Then he accelerates.

The High Train glides to a halt at Station 22 on the 20th floor of the not especially notable Tower 22, a building mainly housing staff managing the city's sewerage systems. It is cheaper to rent here than elsewhere in the currently extant buildings of the city. Mathew chose it as the place to locate his new private lab mainly for this reason, but also because people are unlikely to visit for any other purpose than for work during office hours. There are hundreds of empty basement rooms across the burgeoning city. George helped him move and set up his equipment. He made dozens of journeys back and forth and knows the way instinctively.

"There's three doors," he says to Clara as they walk along the dimly lit corridor towards the lab. They stop as they reach an ordinary door, blocking their path. "They act as security airlocks," George stands facing the door, gripping the handle. A blue light scans him. The lock on the door releases. "You get authorised through one, step through and the door closes behind you. You get scanned again, the door opens ahead and shuts behind. There's a short length of corridor and then another two doors. The sixteen invented the encryption on the security system. Hoshi says there's no way for anyone to breach it."

"Unless they have one of these," Hathaway says, raising his gun.

Clara sees him first. Her eyes widen. She opens her mouth to speak, but words fail her.

George turns around. Hathaway's face noticeably pales.

Clara says, "George, whatever you do, keep this door shut. Don't let this man through." Clara pushes her son forward and yanks the door shut on George.

"Who was that?" Hathaway says.

Clara blinks at him.

Hathaway steps forward, aiming his gun again. "Who *was* that?!"

"George."

"George," Hathaway says, amazed.

"Your son."

34 MISFIRE

George is paralysed, standing between two doors. He recognised the man with the gun. It was Director Hathaway. Everyone knows who he is. George also knows Hathaway is his biological father. His mother has shut the door on him because she is trying to keep Hathaway away from Hoshi and his father. He knows this is because she thinks they are in more danger, but he can't leave her there with that man. Now he's not sure what to do.

"Hoshi!" he calls. "Hoshi, are you there?"

"Yes, George."

"We have a problem."

"I know, George."

"What do you advise we do?"

"I have a plan. I need you to stay where you are until I tell you to open the door."

Young Mathew follows Lestrange, jogging occasionally to catch him as he strides through a maze of rooms and doors and corridors, right and left turns, up and down stairs. Doors that Mathew suspects should be locked to them open as Lestrange approaches.

"Wait," Mathew says, clutching his side. "Give me a minute, will you? What's the rush?"

Lestrange halts suddenly, spins on his heel and stares at Mathew, surprised. "Ah." He seems to have forgotten he has a companion. "A slight miscalculation on my part. I had planned our path exactly based on what I knew would happen from history. I hadn't accounted for your presence. It didn't occur to me the fact of you being here, however periphery to main events you are, would change the way the other players behaved.

"I've had to change our route, but the timing now has little margin for error. Ideally we would wait, but our exit will be compromised for quite a while after today's events and I don't want us to have to go all the way back to London. We will still make it on my current calculations, but we must be quick. Are you ready to walk?"

Mathew nods.

They set off once again.

Hoshi gets off the machine slab, sits and pulls on her shoes.

"What's going on?" Dr. Erlang asks.

"Change of plan."

The doctor breathes out. "I have to say, I'm relieved."

"I wouldn't be too pleased."

"Why?"

"Hathaway is outside the lab with a gun."

"What?" Erlang is panic-stricken and then says, "But he can't get in. They're Silverwood's most secure doors."

"Agreed. Unless you have a hostage."

"What do you mean?"

"He's with Clara."

"Oh my God!" Mathew rushes to the door. Hoshi races after him and pulls him from the range of the blue light automatically scanning him. "Whatever you do, you mustn't go out there."

"I'm not leaving her with Hathaway. He's insane. Is George with her?"

"He's between the doors. Safe. I've asked him to stay

there. For now, he's listening to me. I wish you would too. I will go round the back through the service tunnels. Just as I approach, I will ask George to open the door he is standing behind. Hathaway will be stunned by George and distracted. I will come behind him and grab his gun."

"But he may shoot you."

"It does not matter if he shoots me. I cannot die. Besides, it may be just as well. We were going to decommission me anyway."

"What if he captures you instead?"

"That crossed my mind too. If he does, I will initiate my own destruction. Please, Mathew, we don't have time to debate this. Stay here. I will communicate with you soon."

Hoshi strides across the room and leaves through a door at the side. Mathew stares after her.

Hathaway says, "You have to let me speak to him."

Clara steps away from the door, but not too far. She leans against the wall next to it. "I'll do no such thing as long as you are holding that gun. What did you come here to do? Kill Mathew?"

"He killed Leah."

"Nonsense! I don't believe for a minute you ever thought so."

"Oh, he may not have pulled the trigger himself, but he lured her to her death. She would never have been captured if it hadn't been for him."

"Captured? What on earth do you think happened?"

"Your husband filled her head with coalition propaganda. He turned her against me."

Clara gapes at Hathaway, incredulous. "Mathew hadn't spoken to Leah in ten years. She went to Birmingham on her own. She ran away. She was terrified."

"Of what?"

"Of you!"

"I don't believe it."

"She did not want to raise her child amongst the Accountants. She feared for her son's safety and for her own. She did not want him to be like you."

"You expect me to believe that after ten years of not knowing you she just appeared at your home?"

"She didn't come to us. We didn't even know she was in Birmingham. Leah left instructions with the authorities to give George to us if anything happened to her."

"So how do you know all this if you weren't talking to her?"

"She wrote it down. She hadn't been able to contact us because she was in hiding. There were concerns for her safety."

"Of course there were concerns for her safety. She was being held by the secret services who then went on to murder her."

Clara shakes her head, "I don't think they did."

"Who did, then?"

"We always thought we should ask you that."

"You think I killed her?"

"She betrayed you, didn't she? She gave the coalition information about the Accountants. She left you and took your son. I always thought you had killed her in revenge."

"I loved her," Hathaway says, bereft. "I wouldn't have touched a hair on her head, no matter what she did." And Clara believes him.

"Then someone else on your side killed her. The police said it was an Accountant-style execution. She was made to kneel and then shot in the head."

Hathaway's face pales further. "They would," he hisses. "They would hardly admit they shot her." But the fires goes out of him, the gun is limp in his hand. He stares at Clara. "I thought George was dead."

"The press release announced his death. It was intended to make him safe. They think he saw who shot her but the killer was disturbed before he turned the gun on George. But he doesn't remember anything. Thank

God."

"I need to talk to him."

"Not until you get rid of that," she points at the gun.

Hathaway glances at the weapon, turns it in his hand as if surprised it is there at all. Then he nods, flicks on the safety, drops it on the floor and kicks it away.

"How do I know you don't have another?" Clara asks.

Hathaway holds up his hands. "Search me."

She stares at him sceptically. "Do you think I'm going anywhere near you?"

"Do you think I would hurt my own son?"

"You might still hurt Mathew."

"I won't."

Clara sighs and then nods.

Lestrange and Mathew race along a corridor. Suddenly Lestrange grabs him, bundles him into a nearby room and extinguishes the lights before they automatically fire up. He brings Mathew beside him, pressed against the wall, and puts his finger to his lips. Mathew watches Lestrange's listening face. Someone runs past at full pelt. They wait a moment. Lestrange relaxes.

"Good. It's clear. Come on."

"Who was that?"

"No one you need to concern yourself with."

Hoshi's body is biologically human, but Dr. Erlang and the sixteen did not see the point of making a body if it was not the best it could possibly be. Within the tolerances of the particular build and design they have chosen, her body is optimised to peak performance. Strong and fast enough to overpower the brawniest men, she is swift enough to outrun the fastest short-distance athlete.

She runs now with precision and efficiency along the maze of corridors; her brain anticipates each turn and corner perfectly.

The carefully balanced AI brain she carries within her

skull does not get overwhelmed, as human brains do, by threats and fear. Nevertheless, she experiences emotion and she loves Clara.

For this reason she puts everything she has into getting to her and she has already run numerous scenarios to prepare for whatever will greet her when she arrives.

Lestrange has stopped again. "Okay. This is getting complicated," he says. "No matter."

"What is going on?" Mathew says.

Lestrange opens a door onto a metal staircase. "Down here."

At the bottom there is another door. It clicks open automatically.

"Good. Through here."

They walk along a metal walkway, above a boiler room, holding on to waist-height rails. Down below, white metal caged machines hum. On the other side of the walkway there is another door and another set of stairs.

"Up here," Lestrange says.

Four flights up, on one of the stairwells, there's a hatch. Lestrange pulls off the grating. "In you go," he says.

"You've got to be kidding."

"Not so, I'm afraid. Go on."

Mathew climbs in. It is roomier than he feared, a horizontal tube four foot square. He edges along on his hands and knees.

"Where to?" he asks Lestrange.

"Keep going. There's another grate at the end. When you get to it, turn around and kick it open."

Mathew does as he's told and slides into a small empty room.

"There's no door," Mathew observes.

"We'll go through there," Lestrange says, indicating to another grate, this one body height. He goes and examines it, hooking his fingers around the edges, trying to get a grip on it. And then he stops and sighs.

"I don't believe it," he says.

"What?"

"Kilfeather's changed his route."

Kilfeather drives straight into the underground carpark of Tower 22. Winterbourne finds the map of Silverwood's underground tunnels and rooms and transmits it to Kilfeather, who uses it to navigate his route to Erlang. With Winterbourne's help they calculate a shortcut to claw back some of the time they've lost. Winterbourne manages to get some doors unlocked for them through the central security system of the buildings they pass under. To get through others they have had to blast the locks away.

"How far?" Jonah asks.

"Almost there," Kilfeather says.

Via his e-Pin, Winterbourne says to Kilfeather, "There're three consecutive doors ahead I'm unable to unlock. They're the doors to Erlang's rooms."

"Can we shoot them open?"

"You can try."

Hoshi registers the junction to the corridor ahead. She skids to a stop at the end.

"Open the door," she transmits to George.

George grasps the handle and the blue light scans him. The door unlocks and he pulls the door open.

Hathaway stares. "George," he says, whispering.

"Director Hathaway," George says coldly. A glance registers Clara is unharmed and the man has cast aside his gun.

Hoshi comes out of the corridor. She steps forward and starts walking steadily towards Hathaway. Hathaway doesn't notice her. She spots the gun, scoops it from the floor, cocks the trigger and points it at Hathaway's head.

Clara watches her and says, "Hoshi, that won't be necessary."

In the room at the side, behind a thin wall, Mathew

says, "Hoshi?" He goes to the grate and peers through and comes face to face with the image of his mother.

Lestrange tries to pull him back from the grate, but Mathew shakes him off. He starts to violently pull at the grate. George, Clara, Hathaway and Hoshi are startled by the noise and turn to look.

Behind them Kilfeather, Drake and Jonah run along the corridor. Kilfeather sees Hoshi with the gun. He lifts his own and aims and shoots. Mathew pulls the grate away and falls into the corridor. He scrambles to where Hoshi is standing, shot and poised to fall, as Kilfeather fires again, hitting him. Hoshi falls to the ground and Mathew falls with her.

Dr. Erlang, still in his lab, watches Hoshi shot on the screen. A moment later, he is scanned through the doors and walks up behind George, towards Kilfeather and Hoshi, who is slumped on the floor. There's a boy with her, lying propped on an elbow, shocked and staring at his hand, which is exploring the hole in his right side and the increasingly large pool of blood seeping onto his hands, clothes and the floor around him. The boy, who looks just like him as a young man, stares directly at him and then at Hathaway. He opens his mouth to speak.

Jonah screams, "Abomination!" at Dr. Erlang and raises his weapon.

Hathaway realises how close he is to George and says, "No!" and steps forward, blocking the bullet with his own body. The force of it slams him against one wall. The second bullet hits Dr. Erlang.

Lestrange steps into the corridor. Kilfeather, Jonah, Drake, George and Clara all crumple to the ground unconscious. Lestrange untangles Mathew from Hoshi's already disintegrating body.

He hefts him into his arms and carries him, stepping carefully over Director Hathaway and Dr Mathew Erlang, through the three doors, across the floor of the lab, beside the screens on the walls where the sixteen are busy wiping all traces of their existence from local storage, into the bedroom at the back of the lab and back into the Darkroom in Pickervance Road.

35 NONSTARTER

DAY THIRTEEN: Saturday 4 December 2055, London

Daylight streams through the curtains. Mathew stares at it, not quite sure for a moment where he is and why he is in bed in the middle of the day. The dream was incredibly vivid. His hand instinctively reaches for his wounded side, but of course, the gaping red hole isn't there. He is swamped by loss and sadness as he remembers Hoshi being shot - the Hoshi who is and is not his mother. He is both relieved and sickened to realise she is not dead, but is instead lying in a hospital bed across town, still dying.

Swinging his legs from under the duvet onto the floor, he sits up, rubs his face with his hands and sighs.

Puzzled to find he is staring at his boots, he remembers he got into bed fully dressed. But then he also remembers he woke and got up. So why is he now back in bed? His brain wobbles. He gets to his feet.

His Lenz tells him it is nearly five and he needs to relieve Gen at Panacea. The car is twenty minutes away. He needs to move.

In the bathroom he has déjà vu undressing and showering. In the kitchen it's the same thing, but when he shovels cereal into his mouth from a bowl while standing up, Leibniz doesn't warn him he has already eaten, nor does it warn him to seat himself to aid digestion. He leaves the Canvas off. What does the war matter now?

When the car arrives he is waiting for it. His Lenz blinks with seven unanswered messages. He ignores them until he is seated. Clara, his grandmother, Eva, Gen, Wyatt and Lydia from school, and then Nan Absolem.

He checks the message from Gen first.

She says, "The hospital have let me take and make calls downstairs. I've sneaked away for five minutes for some food, a drink and to call you. She's still the same, but at least it's not a change for the worse."

A wave of gratitude overwhelms him. Tears sting his eyes. He blinks them away, takes a deep breath and checks his other messages.

Ju Shen is concerned because for days neither her grandson nor her daughter have responded to her attempts at communication. "Is everything alright? I'm going crazy with worry. Please, one of you, call. "

He must steel himself to call her. But not now. Not now.

He listens to Clara's message. Her voice is new to him, as if it wasn't the day before when they last spoke, but a lifetime ago.

"I wanted you to know I am thinking of you and praying, even though I don't pray, for your mum."

Wyatt and Lydia have both left notes saying they are sorry to hear what has happened to his mother. *How do they know?* He wonders. But then he remembers he told Nan. *But I couldn't have told Nan. I was asleep.* He tries to piece together what happened when he got home, retracing his steps from the car, through the front door, grabbing O'Malley. *I went straight to bed. Then I woke up, ate breakfast and sent a message to Professor Absolem.* But he couldn't have done this. He was still dressed when he woke. He sighs and decides he is too exhausted and stressed to think straight.

The fact is, Nan got his message, so he must have sent it.

Nan's message is short. It tells him not to worry about schoolwork until his mother is better. She has notified the relevant authorities and his credits will not be affected. She also says she hopes he doesn't mind, but she has notified his friends at school in order to encourage them to support him. He is vaguely annoyed she has done this, but at the same time touched that Wyatt and Lydia would write to him.

It is early evening when the car winds its way through dark streets, lit by street lamps and window-light. Under normal circumstances at this time the roads and streets would be bustling with cars and people, even on a Sunday. But the roads and pavements of London are deserted. People are huddled in their houses, confined by the Curfew and fearful because of the war.

A drone flashes by, hunting for those breaking the Curfew and for people who are either not chipped or not on the list to be chipped.

The car turns onto a road that runs between high brick walls. There is a gate at the end, wide enough to let a truck through but innocuous and unmarked. There's no Panacea sign, with the bright, cheerful company logo. They don't want anyone to know this facility is here. The car winds along a short drive and parks at the back of the building, where his mother was wheeled from the ambulance only a few days before. It seems like a lifetime. A nurse is there to greet him, holding the door to the hospital open.

The nurse leads him through the maze of shabby corridors to a lift. They go up a few floors and then they walk until they reach a room where he gets into his protective gear: a thin white boiler suit, a surgical mask, gloves, thin shrilk elasticated sleeves for his shoes. He follows after the nurse through double doors until he meets Gen on her way out. She holds and grips his hand, holding his gaze. He is embarrassed and overwhelmed and looks away.

"Thanks for your message," he says.

She shakes her head as if to say, 'It's nothing.' Aloud, she says, "Have you eaten?"

"Yes," he says.

"Something nutritious?"

"Cereal," he says.

She raises an eyebrow but stays silent. Who is she to tell him what he should and should not do right now?

"I'll see you tomorrow," she says and goes off with another nurse, who holds the ward door for her to pass through. Mathew watches her go.

The nurse who had greeted him downstairs stays with him. She says, "Okay?"

He nods and they go to Hoshi's room.

She is so small, dwarfed by the bed, hooked up to various machines. Asleep or knocked-out by drugs, her face is turned away from him. He sinks to his seat and takes her hand.

"Mum?" he says, but there is no response.

"I'm going to leave you to it," the nurse says. "If you need me, use the call button."

"Thanks," he says. "I know the drill."

He settles into his chair and observes the drip and the morphine as it trickles into her, watching the time flick by.

Silence fizzes the air. The lights automatically dim for the night. For hours, not a soul passes by. He tries to read something on his Paper, but he can't focus, reading and re-reading the same line again and again. Resting his elbow on the bed, he watches Hoshi's sleeping face, the flickering of her eyelashes, her mouth twitching. She is dreaming.

He recalls the last few years, how angry he has been with her for carrying on after his father died and he feels sick with himself because what else could she do? Then he remembers the documents he got from the Lich King and wonders what it is inside of Hoshi killing her, and how it got there. He imagines the thing, the virus, whatever it is, coursing through her veins, poisoning and corrupting her body. Now he knows why she screamed at him and tried to get him to go away. She had realised, at the last minute, what was happening to her. She was trying to protect him.

Mathew's head buzzes. His heart races. It is anxiety, he realises. He must calm himself. And he tries to clear his mind, closing his eyes, breathing deeply, relaxing his body. Unconsciously, he grips his mother's hand harder.

She stirs. Her head turns; her eyes open and light up as they recognise him.

"Mum," he whispers.

She smiles, squeezing his hand. Her grip is weak. "You're here," she says.

"Of course."

"What time is it?"

"Doesn't matter," he says.

"I love you," she says.

"I love you too."

"I am glad I got to see you," she says.

"Me too. But when you are better you will be sick of me again."

Her eyes fill with tears.

"Don't," he says.

"I'm sorry."

"Don't be sorry."

"I didn't want to."

"It's okay."

"I'll never be sick of you."

"I've been a horrible person."

"No you haven't. Don't say that."

Mathew's throat tightens.

Hoshi's eyes droop and he thinks she has drifted off, but she says, still with closed eyes, "Tell your father I am sorry."

For a moment, choked, he can't speak; then he says, unsteadily, "Dad's dead."

She doesn't seem to hear. She says, insistent, "Find your father."

"Mum, your medication is very strong. Dr. Assaf said you may say strange things."

"You must find him and tell him."

Her grip weakens and for one terrifying moment he thinks she has gone, but her breath heaves and then softens into a rhythm, and he relaxes and slumps back.

But he's dead. He's dead.

And his heart beats faster, his nerves are on fire. There is nowhere to go. No one to turn to. Then he is struck by a thought with an unearthly force.

But what if she didn't mean find him physically? What if she meant, find out about him?

This thought stops his anxiety in its tracks. He says, "I will find him."

THE END

Thank you for reading

Silverwood.

If you enjoyed it, please leave a review on Amazon or the website of the retailer of your choice. Reviews help me write more books.

THE MOON AT NOON

A door in time. A visitor from the future. A girl determined to save the boy she loves.

Mathew Erlang travels north through an England overrun by violence and sickness. Accompanied by a new friend, he finally makes it to his grandmother's house, but all is not as it seems in this childhood place of safety. Meanwhile, Clara makes an uncanny pact with Mathew's peculiar neighbour and finally learns the truth about Mr. Lestrange.

The Moon at Noon is available to purchase from Amazon.

Visit my website www.juleowen.com to find out more about *The Moon at Noon,* and for offers, news and giveaways.

ACKNOWLEDGMENTS

NOTES

The Boy Who Fell from the Sky and the other books in the *House Next Door* trilogy represent my version of the future, inspired by non-fiction books by Michio Kaku, Martin Rees, K Eric Drexler, George Friedman, Alan Weisman, James Lovelock and James Hansen, amongst others. My full list of sources can be found on my website at
http://juleowen.com/futurology-resources

We are now living in the Anthropocene age, the first period in geological history when humans have had a significant impact on the earth's ecosystem. One direct result of this is climate change. We are also living in a time of exponential technological innovation. It is an extraordinary and frightening time to be alive. My stories are my way of coming to terms with this and exploring possible futures. Find out more about the background to my stories here
http://juleowen.com/futurology/

WITH THANKS

I think the point when I realised that I needed others help to complete this book was the point when it became possible.

Thanks to my editor Lynda Thornhill.

Thanks to those who were generous with their time, by reading my book, supporting me on Wattpad or helping with my launch.

I'm lucky enough to be part of a few awesome communities that have eased my way. Thanks to the Alliance of Independent Authors and to the extraordinary Escape the City community. Thanks especially to Alexis Garnaut-Miller, Bella Zenesco and the my12for12 crew. Your friendship and support this year has mattered more than you could possibly know.

In particular, I owe a huge debt of gratitude to Mark Speed, who was kind enough to read early versions of this book, edit and offer invaluable feedback. He took me under his wing and has been a constant source of encouragement and useful advice. Mark is the creator of the wonderful Doctor How series, the real story behind the Doctor Who myth. For those of you who like some comedy with their sci-fi, Mark's books are a tonic. The first in the series, *Doctor How and the Illegal Aliens* can be found on Amazon.

Thanks to my Dad for always being there.

Most of all, thanks to Lauren for your endless patience, support and kindness. This book would never have been written without you.

ABOUT THE AUTHOR

Jule Owen was born in the North of England in a little place nestled between Snowdonia, the Irish Sea and the Pennines. She now lives in London, UK, where the weather is warmer, and there are more museums, but she misses the wide open spaces and the good quality water.

Jule spent many years working in online technology, latterly in the video games industry and is fascinated by science, technology and futurology, which she periodically blogs and tweets about.

Her books are her creative response to the exponential growth of technological innovation in the era of climate change.

She can be found online and would love to hear from you. Look her up here:
www.juleowen.com
@juleowen